THE WRECK OF THE TITAN
OR, FUTILITY

THE WRECK OF THE TITAN OR, FUTILITY

BY

Morgan Robertson

ISBN: 978-93-5128-501-4

First Published in 1898
Indian Reprint in 2017

Published by

Kalpaz Publications
C-30, Satyawati Nagar,
Delhi – 110052
E-mail: kalpaz@hotmail.com
Website: kalpazpublications.com
Ph.: +91-9212142040

Cataloging in Publication Data—DK
Courtesy: D.K. Agencies (P) Ltd. <docinfo@dkagencies.com>

Robertson, Morgan, 1861-1915, **author.**
The wreck of the titan or, futility / by Morgan Robertson.
pages cm
Short stories.
"First published in 1898"—Title page verso.
Contents: The wreck of the Titan — The pirates — Beyond the spectrum — In the valley of the shadow.
ISBN 9789351285014

1. Sea stories, American. 2. Shipwrecks—Fiction. I. Title.

PS2719.R38W74 2017 DDC 813.52 23

CONTENTS

THE WRECK OF THE TITAN

CHAPTER I

She was the largest craft afloat and the greatest of the works of men. In her construction and maintenance were involved every science, profession, and trade known to civilization. On her bridge were officers, who, besides being the pick of the Royal Navy, had passed rigid examinations in all studies that pertained to the winds, tides, currents, and geography of the sea; they were not only seamen, but scientists. The same professional standard applied to the personnel of the engine-room, and the steward's department was equal to that of a first-class hotel.

Two brass bands, two orchestras, and a theatrical company entertained the passengers during waking hours; a corps of physicians attended to the temporal, and a corps of chaplains to the spiritual, welfare of all on board, while a well-drilled fire-company soothed the fears of nervous ones and added to the general entertainment by daily practice with their apparatus.

From her lofty bridge ran hidden telegraph lines to the bow, stern engine-room, crow's-nest on the foremast, and to all parts of the ship where work was done, each wire terminating in a marked dial with a movable indicator, containing in its scope every order and answer required in handling the massive hulk, either at the dock or at sea—which eliminated, to a great extent, the hoarse, nerve-racking shouts of officers and sailors.

From the bridge, engine-room, and a dozen places on her deck the ninety-two doors of nineteen water-tight compartments could be closed in half a minute by turning a lever. These doors would also close automatically in the presence of water. With nine compartments flooded the ship would still float, and as no known accident of the sea could possibly fill this many, the steamship *Titan* was considered practically unsinkable.

Built of steel throughout, and for passenger traffic only, she carried no combustible cargo to threaten her destruction by fire; and the immunity from the demand for cargo space had enabled her designers to discard the flat, kettle-bottom of cargo boats and give her the sharp dead-rise—or slant from the keel—of a steam yacht, and this improved her behavior in a seaway. She was eight hundred feet long, of seventy thousand tons' displacement, seventy-five thousand horse-power, and on her trial trip had steamed at a rate of twenty-five knots an hour over the bottom, in the face of unconsidered winds, tides, and currents. In short, she was a floating city—containing within her steel walls all that tends to minimize the dangers and discomforts of the Atlantic voyage—all that makes life enjoyable.

Unsinkable—indestructible, she carried as few boats as would satisfy the laws. These, twenty-four in number, were securely covered and lashed down to their chocks on the upper deck, and if launched would hold five hundred people. She carried no useless, cumbersome life-rafts; but—because the law required it—each of the three thousand berths in the passengers', officers', and crew's quarters contained a cork jacket, while about twenty circular life-buoys were strewn along the rails.

In view of her absolute superiority to other craft, a rule of navigation thoroughly believed in by some captains, but not yet openly followed, was announced by the steamship company to apply to the *Titan*: She would steam at full speed in fog, storm, and sunshine, and on the Northern Lane Route, winter and summer, for the following good and substantial reasons: First, that if another craft should strike her, the force of the impact would be distributed over a larger area if the *Titan* had full headway, and the brunt of the damage would be borne by the other. Second, that if the *Titan* was the aggressor she would certainly destroy the other craft, even at half-speed, and perhaps damage her own bows; while at full speed, she would cut her in two with no more damage to herself than a paintbrush could remedy. In either case, as the lesser of two evils, it was best that the smaller hull should suffer. A third reason was that, at full speed, she could be more easily steered out of danger, and a fourth, that in case of an end-on collision with an iceberg—the only thing afloat that she could not conquer—her bows would be crushed in but a few feet further at full than at half speed, and at the most three compartments would be flooded—which would not matter with six more to spare.

So, it was confidently expected that when her engines had limbered themselves, the steamship *Titan* would land her passengers three thousand miles away with the promptitude and regularity of a railway train. She had beaten all records on her maiden voyage, but, up to the third return trip, had not lowered the time between Sandy Hook and Daunt's Rock to the five-day limit; and it was unofficially rumored among the two thousand passengers who had embarked at New York that an effort would now be made to do so.

CHAPTER II

Eight tugs dragged the great mass to midstream and pointed her nose down the river; then the pilot on the bridge spoke a word or two; the first officer blew a short blast on the whistle and turned a lever; the tugs gathered in their lines and drew off; down in the bowels of the ship three small engines were started, opening the throttles of three large ones; three propellers began to revolve; and the mammoth, with a vibratory tremble running through her great frame, moved slowly to sea.

East of Sandy Hook the pilot was dropped and the real voyage begun. Fifty feet below her deck, in an inferno of noise, and heat, and light, and shadow, coal-passers wheeled the picked fuel from the bunkers to the fire-hold, where half-naked stokers, with faces like those of tortured fiends, tossed it into the eighty white-hot mouths of the furnaces. In the engine-room, oilers passed to and fro, in and out of the plunging, twisting, glistening steel, with oil-cans and waste, overseen by the watchful staff on duty, who listened with strained hearing for a false note in the confused jumble of sound—a clicking of steel out of tune, which would indicate a loosened key or nut. On deck, sailors set the triangular sails on the two masts, to add their propulsion to the momentum of the record-breaker, and the passengers dispersed themselves as suited their several tastes. Some were seated in steamer chairs, well wrapped—for, though it was April, the salt air was chilly—some paced the deck, acquiring their sea legs; others listened to the orchestra in the music-room, or read or wrote in the library, and a few took to their berths—seasick from the slight heave of the ship on the ground-swell.

The decks were cleared, watches set at noon, and then began the never-ending cleaning-up at which steamship sailors put in so much of their time. Headed by a six-foot boatswain, a gang came aft on the starboard side, with paint-buckets and brushes, and distributed themselves along the rail.

"Davits an' stanchions, men—never mind the rail," said the boatswain. "Ladies, better move your chairs back a little. Rowland, climb down out o' that—you'll be overboard. Take a ventilator—no, you'll spill paint—put your bucket away an' get some sandpaper from the yeoman. Work inboard till you get it out o' you."

The sailor addressed—a slight-built man of about thirty, black-bearded and bronzed to the semblance of healthy vigor, but watery-eyed and unsteady of movement—came down from the rail and shambled forward with his bucket. As he reached the group of ladies to whom the boatswain had spoken, his gaze rested on one—a sunny-haired young woman with the blue of the sea in her eyes—who had arisen at his approach. He started, turned aside as if to avoid her, and raising his hand in an embarrassed half-salute, passed on. Out of the boatswain's sight he leaned against the deck-house and panted, while he held his hand to his breast.

"What is it?" he muttered, wearily; "whisky nerves, or the dying flutter of a starved love. Five years, now—and a look from her eyes can stop the blood in my veins—can bring back all the heart-hunger and helplessness, that leads a man to insanity—or this." He looked at his trembling hand, all scarred and tar-stained, passed on forward, and returned with the sandpaper.

The young woman had been equally affected by the meeting. An expression of mingled surprise and terror had come to her pretty, but rather weak face; and without acknowledging his half-salute, she had caught up a little child from the deck behind her, and turning into the saloon door, hurried to the library, where she sank into a chair beside a military-looking gentleman, who glanced up from a book and remarked: "Seen the sea-serpent, Myra, or the Flying Dutchman? What's up?"

"Oh, George—no," she answered in agitated tones. "John Rowland is here—Lieutenant Rowland. I've just seen him—he is so changed—he tried to speak to me."

"Who—that troublesome flame of yours? I never met him, you know, and you haven't told me much about him. What is he—first cabin?" "No, he seems to be a common sailor; he is working, and is dressed in old clothes—all dirty. And such a dissipated face, too. He seems to have fallen—so low. And it is all since—"

"Since you soured on him? Well, it is no fault of yours, dear. If a man has it in him he'll go to the dogs anyhow. How is his sense of injury? Has he a grievance or a grudge? You're badly upset. What did he say?"

"I don't know—he said nothing—I've always been afraid of him. I've met him three times since then, and he puts such a frightful look in his eyes—and he was so violent, and headstrong, and so terribly angry,—that time. He accused me of leading him on, and playing with him; and he said something about an immutable law of chance, and a governing balance of events—that I couldn't understand, only where he said that for all the suffering we inflict on others, we receive an equal amount ourselves. Then he went away—in such a passion. I've imagined ever since that he would take some revenge—he might steal our Myra—our baby." She strained the smiling child to her breast and went on. "I liked him at first, until I found out that he was an atheist—why, George, he actually denied the existence of God—and to me, a professing Christian."

"He had a wonderful nerve," said the husband, with a smile; "didn't know you very well, I should say."

"He never seemed the same to me after that," she resumed; "I felt as though in the presence of something unclean. Yet I thought how glorious it would be if I could save him to God, and tried to convince him of the loving care of Jesus; but he only ridiculed all I hold sacred, and said, that much as he valued my good opinion, he would not be a hypocrite to gain it, and that he would be honest with himself and others, and express his honest unbelief—the idea; as though one could be honest without God's help—and then, one day, I smelled liquor on his breath—he always smelled of tobacco—and I gave him up. It was then that he—that he broke out."

"Come out and show me this reprobate," said the husband, rising. They went to the door and the young woman peered out. "He is the last man down there—close to the cabin," she said as she drew in. The husband stepped out.

"What! that hang-dog ruffian, scouring the ventilator? So, that's Rowland, of the navy, is it! Well, this is a tumble. Wasn't he broken for conduct unbecoming an officer? Got roaring drunk at the President's levee, didn't he? I think I read of it."

"I know he lost his position and was terribly disgraced," answered the wife.

"Well, Myra, the poor devil is harmless now. We'll be across in a few days, and you needn't meet him on this broad deck. If he hasn't lost all sensibility, he's as embarrassed as you. Better stay in now—it's getting foggy."

CHAPTER III

When the watch turned out at midnight, they found a vicious half-gale blowing from the northeast, which, added to the speed of the steamship, made, so far as effects on her deck went, a fairly uncomfortable whole gale of chilly wind. The head sea, choppy as compared with her great length, dealt the *Titan* successive blows, each one attended by supplementary tremors to the continuous vibrations of the engines—each one sending a cloud of thick spray aloft that reached the crow's-nest on the foremast and battered the pilot-house windows on the bridge in a liquid bombardment that would have broken ordinary glass. A fog-bank, into which the ship had plunged in the afternoon, still enveloped her—damp and impenetrable; and into the gray, ever-receding wall ahead, with two deck officers and three lookouts straining sight and hearing to the utmost, the great racer was charging with undiminished speed.

At a quarter past twelve, two men crawled in from the darkness at the ends of the eighty-foot bridge and shouted to the first officer, who had just taken the deck, the names of the men who had relieved them. Backing up to the pilot-house, the officer repeated the names to a quartermaster within, who entered them in the log-book. Then the men vanished—to their coffee and "watch-below." In a few moments another dripping shape appeared on the bridge and reported the crow's-nest relief.

"Rowland, you say?" bawled the officer above the howling of the wind. "Is he the man who was lifted aboard, drunk, yesterday?"

"Yes, sir."

"Is he still drunk?"

"Yes, sir."

"All right—that'll do. Enter Rowland in the crow's-nest, quartermaster," said the officer; then, making a funnel of his hands, he roared out: "Crow's-nest, there."

"Sir," came the answer, shrill and clear on the gale.

"Keep your eyes open—keep a sharp lookout."

"Very good, sir."

"Been a man-o'-war's-man, I judge, by his answer. They're no good," muttered the officer. He resumed his position at the forward side of the bridge where the wooden railing afforded some shelter from the raw wind, and began the long vigil which would only end when the second officer relieved him, four hours later. Conversation—except in the line of duty—was forbidden among the bridge officers of the *Titan*, and his watchmate, the third officer, stood on the other side of the large bridge binnacle, only leaving this position occasionally to glance in at the compass—which seemed to be his sole duty at sea. Sheltered by one of the deck-houses below, the boatswain and the watch paced back and forth, enjoying the only two hours respite which steamship rules afforded, for the day's work had ended with the going down of the other watch, and at two o'clock the washing of the 'tween-deck would begin, as an opening task in the next day's labor.

By the time one bell had sounded, with its repetition from the crow's-nest, followed by a long-drawn cry—"all's well"—from the lookouts, the last of the two thousand passengers had retired, leaving the spacious cabins and steerage in possession of the watchmen; while, sound asleep in his cabin abaft the chart-room was the captain, the commander who never commanded—unless the ship was in danger; for the pilot had charge, making and leaving port, and the officers, at sea.

Two bells were struck and answered; then three, and the boatswain and his men were lighting up for a final smoke, when there rang out overhead a startling cry from the crow's-nest:

"Something ahead, sir—can't make it out."

The first officer sprang to the engine-room telegraph and grasped the lever. "Sing out what you see," he roared.

"Hard aport, sir—ship on the starboard tack—dead ahead," came the cry.

"Port your wheel—hard over," repeated the first officer to the quartermaster at the helm—who answered and obeyed. Nothing as yet could be seen from the bridge. The powerful steering-engine in the stern ground the rudder over; but before three degrees on the compass card were traversed by the lubber's-point, a seeming thickening of the darkness and fog ahead resolved itself into the square sails of a deep-laden ship, crossing the *Titan's* bow, not half her length away.

"H—l and d—" growled the first officer. "Steady on your course, quartermaster," he shouted. "Stand from under on deck." He turned a lever which closed compartments, pushed a button marked—"Captain's Room," and crouched down, awaiting the crash.

There was hardly a crash. A slight jar shook the forward end of the *Titan* and sliding down her fore-topmast-stay and rattling on deck came a shower of small spars, sails, blocks, and wire rope. Then, in the darkness to starboard and port, two darker shapes shot by—the two halves of the ship she had cut through; and from one of these shapes, where still burned a binnacle light, was heard, high above the confused murmur of shouts and shrieks, a sailorly voice:

"May the curse of God light on you and your cheese-knife, you brass-bound murderers."

The shapes were swallowed in the blackness astern; the cries were hushed by the clamor of the gale, and the steamship *Titan* swung back to her course. The first officer had not turned the lever of the engine-room telegraph.

The boatswain bounded up the steps of the bridge for instructions.

"Put men at the hatches and doors. Send every one who comes on deck to the chart-room. Tell the watchman to notice what the passengers have learned, and clear away that wreck forward as soon as possible." The voice of the officer was hoarse and strained as he gave these directions, and the "aye, aye, sir" of the boatswain was uttered in a gasp.

CHAPTER IV

The crow's-nest "lookout," sixty feet above the deck, had seen every detail of the horror, from the moment when the upper sails of the doomed ship had appeared to him above the fog to the time when the last tangle of wreckage was cut away by his watchmates below. When relieved at four bells, he descended with as little strength in his limbs as was compatible with safety in the rigging. At the rail, the boatswain met him.

"Report your relief, Rowland," he said, "and go into the chart-room!"

On the bridge, as he gave the name of his successor, the first officer seized his hand, pressed it, and repeated the boatswain's order. In the chart-room, he found the captain of the *Titan*, pale-faced and intense in manner, seated at a table, and, grouped around him, the whole of the watch on deck except the officers, lookouts, and quartermasters. The cabin watchmen were there, and some of the watch below, among whom were stokers and coal-passers, and also, a few of the idlers—lampmen, yeomen, and butchers, who, sleeping forward, had been awakened by the terrific blow of the great hollow knife within which they lived.

Three carpenters' mates stood by the door, with sounding-rods in their hands, which they had just shown the captain—dry. Every face, from the captain's down, wore a look of horror and expectancy. A quartermaster followed Rowland in and said:

"Engineer felt no jar in the engine-room, sir; and there's no excitement in the stokehold."

"And you watchmen report no alarm in the cabins. How about the steerage? Is that man back?" asked the captain. Another watchman appeared as he spoke.

"All asleep in the steerage, sir," he said. Then a quartermaster entered with the same report of the forecastles.

"Very well," said the captain, rising; "one by one come into my office—watchmen first, then petty officers, then the men. Quartermasters will watch the door—that no man goes out until I have seen him." He passed into another room, followed by a watchman, who presently emerged and went on deck with a more pleasant expression of face. Another entered and came out; then another, and another, until every man but Rowland had been within the sacred precincts, all to wear the same pleased, or satisfied, look on reappearing. When Rowland entered, the captain, seated at a desk, motioned him to a chair, and asked his name.

"John Rowland," he answered. The captain wrote it down.

"I understand," he said, "that you were in the crow's-nest when this unfortunate collision occurred."

"Yes, sir; and I reported the ship as soon as I saw her."

"You are not here to be censured. You are aware, of course, that nothing could be done, either to avert this terrible calamity, or to save life afterward."

"Nothing at a speed of twenty-five knots an hour in a thick fog, sir." The captain glanced sharply at Rowland and frowned.

"We will not discuss the speed of the ship, my good man," he said, "or the rules of the company. You will find, when you are paid at Liverpool, a package addressed to you at the company's office containing one hundred pounds in banknotes. This, you will receive for your silence in regard to this collision—the reporting of which would embarrass the company and help no one."

"On the contrary, captain, I shall not receive it. On the contrary, sir, I shall speak of this wholesale murder at the first opportunity!"

The captain leaned back and stared at the debauched face, the trembling figure of the sailor, with which this defiant speech so little accorded. Under ordinary circumstances, he would have sent him on deck to be dealt with by the officers. But this was not an ordinary circumstance. In the watery eyes was a look of shock, and horror, and honest indignation; the accents were those of an educated man; and the consequences hanging over himself and the company for which he worked—already complicated by and involved in his efforts to avoid them—which this man might precipitate, were so extreme, that such questions as insolence and difference in rank were not to be thought of. He must meet and subdue this Tartar on common ground—as man to man.

"Are you aware, Rowland," he asked, quietly, "that you will stand alone—that you will be discredited, lose your berth, and make enemies?"

"I am aware of more than that," answered Rowland, excitedly. "I know of the power vested in you as captain. I know that you can order me into irons from this room for any offense you wish to imagine. And I know that an unwitnessed, uncorroborated entry in your official log concerning me would be evidence enough to bring me life imprisonment. But I also know something of admiralty law; that from my prison cell I can send you and your first officer to the gallows."

"You are mistaken in your conceptions of evidence. I could not cause your conviction by a log-book entry; nor could you, from a prison, injure me. What are you, may I ask—an ex-lawyer?"

"A graduate of Annapolis. Your equal in professional technic."

"And you have interest at Washington?"

"None whatever."

"And what is your object in taking this stand—which can do you no possible good, though certainly not the harm you speak of?"

"That I may do one good, strong act in my useless life—that I may help to arouse such a sentiment of anger in the two countries as will forever end this wanton destruction of life and property for the sake of speed—that will save the hundreds of fishing-craft, and others, run down yearly, to their owners, and the crews to their families."

Both men had risen and the captain was pacing the floor as Rowland, with flashing eyes and clinched fists, delivered this declaration.

"A result to be hoped for, Rowland," said the former, pausing before him, "but beyond your power or mine to accomplish. Is the amount I named large enough? Could you fill a position on my bridge?"

"I can fill a higher; and your company is not rich enough to buy me."

"You seem to be a man without ambition; but you must have wants."

"Food, clothing, shelter—and whisky," said Rowland with a bitter, self-contemptuous laugh. The captain reached down a decanter and two glasses from a swinging tray and said as he placed them before him:

"Here is one of your wants; fill up." Rowland's eyes glistened as he poured out a glassful, and the captain followed.

"I will drink with you, Rowland," he said; "here is to our better understanding." He tossed off the liquor; then Rowland, who had waited, said: "I prefer drinking alone, captain," and drank the whisky at a gulp. The captain's face flushed at the affront, but he controlled himself.

"Go on deck, now, Rowland," he said; "I will talk with you again before we reach soundings. Meanwhile, I request—not require, but request—that you hold no useless conversation with your shipmates in regard to this matter."

To the first officer, when relieved at eight bells, the captain said: "He is a broken-down wreck with a temporarily active conscience; but is not the man to buy or intimidate: he knows too much. However, we've found his weak point. If he gets snakes before we dock, his testimony is worthless. Fill him up and I'll see the surgeon, and study up on drugs."

When Rowland turned out to breakfast at seven bells that morning, he found a pint flask in the pocket of his pea-jacket, which he felt of but did not pull out in sight of his watchmates.

"Well, captain," he thought, "you are, in truth, about as puerile, insipid a scoundrel as ever escaped the law. I'll save you your drugged Dutch courage for evidence." But it was not drugged, as he learned later. It was good whisky—a leader—to warm his stomach while the captain was studying.

CHAPTER V

An incident occurred that morning which drew Rowland's thoughts far from the happenings of the night. A few hours of bright sunshine had brought the passengers on deck like bees from a hive, and the two broad promenades resembled, in color and life, the streets of a city. The watch was busy at the inevitable scrubbing, and Rowland, with a swab and bucket, was cleaning the white paint on the starboard taffrail, screened from view by the after deck-house, which shut off a narrow space at the stern. A little girl ran into the inclosure, laughing and screaming, and clung to his legs, while she jumped up and down in an overflow of spirits.

"I wunned 'way," she said; "I wunned 'way from mamma."

Drying his wet hands on his trousers, Rowland lifted the tot and said, tenderly: "Well, little one, you must run back to mamma. You're in bad company." The innocent eyes smiled into his own, and then—a foolish proceeding, which only bachelors are guilty of—he held her above the rail in jesting menace. "Shall I drop you over to the fishes, baby?" he asked, while his features softened to an unwonted smile. The child gave a little scream of fright, and at that instant a young woman appeared around the corner. She sprang toward Rowland like a tigress, snatched the child, stared at him for a moment with dilated eyes, and then disappeared, leaving him limp and nerveless, breathing hard.

"It is her child," he groaned. "That was the mother-look. She is married—married." He resumed his work, with a face as near the color of the paint he was scrubbing as the tanned skin of a sailor may become.

Ten minutes later, the captain, in his office, was listening to a complaint from a very excited man and woman.

"And you say, colonel," said the captain, "that this man Rowland is an old enemy?"

"He is—or was once—a rejected admirer of Mrs. Selfridge. That is all I know of him—except that he has hinted at revenge. My wife is certain of what she saw, and I think the man should be confined."

"Why, captain," said the woman, vehemently, as she hugged her child, "you should have seen him; he was just about to drop Myra over as I seized her—and he had such a frightful leer on his face, too. Oh, it was hideous. I shall not sleep another wink in this ship—I know."

"I beg you will give yourself no uneasiness, madam," said the captain, gravely. "I have already learned something of his antecedents—that he is a disgraced and broken-down naval officer; but, as he has sailed three voyages with us, I had credited his willingness to work before-the-mast to his craving for liquor, which he could not satisfy without money. However—as you think—he may be following you. Was he able to learn of your movements—that you were to take passage in this ship?"

"Why not?" exclaimed the husband; "he must know some of Mrs. Selfridge's friends."

"Yes, yes," she said, eagerly; "I have heard him spoken of, several times."

"Then it is clear," said the captain. "If you will agree, madam, to testify against him in the English courts, I will immediately put him in irons for attempted murder."

"Oh, do, captain," she exclaimed. "I cannot feel safe while he is at liberty. Of course I will testify."

"Whatever you do, captain," said the husband, savagely, "rest assured that I shall put a bullet through his head if he meddles with me or mine again. Then you can put me in irons."

"I will see that he is attended to, colonel," replied the captain as he bowed them out of his office.

But, as a murder charge is not always the best way to discredit a man; and as the captain did not believe that the man who had defied him would murder a child; and as the charge would be difficult to prove in any case, and would cause him much trouble and annoyance, he did not order the arrest of John Rowland, but merely directed that, for the time, he should be kept at work by day in the 'tween-deck, out of sight of the passengers.

Rowland, surprised at his sudden transfer from the disagreeable scrubbing to a "soldier's job" of painting life-buoys in the warm 'tween-deck, was shrewd enough to know that he was being closely watched by the boatswain that morning, but not shrewd enough to affect any symptoms of intoxication or drugging, which might have satisfied his anxious superiors and brought him more whisky. As a result of his brighter eyes and steadier voice—due to the curative sea air—when he turned out for the first dog-watch on deck at four o'clock, the captain and boatswain held an interview in the chart-room, in which the former said: "Do not be alarmed. It is not poison. He is half-way into the horrors now, and this will merely bring them on. He will see snakes, ghosts, goblins, shipwrecks, fire, and all sorts of things. It works in two or three hours. Just drop it into his drinking pot while the port forecastle is empty."

There was a fight in the port forecastle—to which Rowland belonged—at supper-time, which need not be described beyond mention of the fact that Rowland, who was not a participant, had his pot of tea dashed from his hand before he had taken three swallows. He procured a fresh supply and finished his supper; then, taking no part in his watchmates' open discussion of the fight, and guarded discussion of collisions, rolled into his bunk and smoked until eight bells, when he turned out with the rest.

CHAPTER VI

"Rowland," said the big boatswain, as the watch mustered on deck; "take the starboard bridge lookout."

"It is not my trick, boats'n," said Rowland, in surprise.

"Orders from the bridge. Get up there."

Rowland grumbled, as sailors may when aggrieved, and obeyed. The man he relieved reported his name, and disappeared; the first officer sauntered down the bridge, uttered the official, "keep a good lookout," and returned to his post; then the silence and loneliness of a night-watch at sea, intensified by the never-ceasing hum of the engines, and relieved only by the sounds of distant music and laughter from the theater, descended on the forward part of the ship. For the fresh westerly wind, coming with the *Titan*, made nearly a calm on her deck; and the dense fog, though overshone by a bright star-specked sky, was so chilly that the last talkative passenger had fled to the light and life within.

When three bells—half-past nine—had sounded, and Rowland had given in his turn the required call—"all's well"—the first officer left his post and approached him.

"Rowland," he said as he drew near; "I hear you've walked the quarter-deck."

"I cannot imagine how you learned it, sir," replied Rowland; "I am not in the habit of referring to it."

"You told the captain. I suppose the curriculum is as complete at Annapolis as at the Royal Naval College. What do you think of Maury's theories of currents?"

"They seem plausible," said Rowland, unconsciously dropping the "sir"; "but I think that in most particulars he has been proven wrong."

"Yes, I think so myself. Did you ever follow up another idea of his—that of locating the position of ice in a fog by the rate of decrease in temperature as approached?"

"Not to any definite result. But it seems to be only a matter of calculation, and time to calculate. Cold is negative heat, and can be treated like radiant energy, decreasing as the square of the distance."

The officer stood a moment, looking ahead and humming a tune to himself; then, saying: "Yes, that's so," returned to his place.

"Must have a cast-iron stomach," he muttered, as he peered into the binnacle; "or else the boats'n dosed the wrong man's pot."

Rowland glanced after the retreating officer with a cynical smile. "I wonder," he said to himself, "why he comes down here talking navigation to a foremast hand. Why am I up here—out of my turn? Is this something in line with that bottle?" He resumed the short pacing back and forth on the end of the bridge, and the rather gloomy train of thought which the officer had interrupted.

"How long," he mused, "would his ambition and love of profession last him after he had met, and won, and lost, the only woman on earth to him? Why is it—that failure to hold the affections of one among the millions of women who live, and love, can outweigh every blessing in life, and turn a man's nature into a hell, to consume him? Who did she marry? Some one, probably a stranger long after my banishment, who came to her possessed of a few qualities of mind or physique that pleased her,—who did not need to love her—his chances were better without that—and he steps coolly and easily into my heaven. And they tell us, that 'God doeth all things well,' and that there is a heaven where all our unsatisfied wants are attended to—provided we have the necessary faith in it. That means, if it means anything, that after a lifetime of unrecognized allegiance, during which I win nothing but her fear and contempt, I may be rewarded by the love and companionship of her soul. Do I love her soul? Has her soul beauty of face and the figure and carriage of a Venus? Has her soul deep, blue eyes and a sweet, musical voice? Has it wit, and grace, and charm? Has it a wealth of pity for suffering? These are the things I loved. I do not love her soul, if she has one. I do not want it. I want her—I need her." He stopped in his walk and leaned against the bridge railing, with eyes fixed on the fog ahead. He was speaking his thoughts aloud now, and the first officer drew within hearing, listened a moment, and went back. "Working on him," he whispered to the third officer. Then he pushed the button which called the captain, blew a short blast of the steam whistle as a call to the boatswain, and resumed his watch on the drugged lookout, while the third officer conned the ship.

The steam call to the boatswain is so common a sound on a steamship as to generally pass unnoticed. This call affected another besides the boatswain. A little night-gowned figure arose from an under berth in a saloon stateroom, and, with wide-open, staring eyes, groped its way to the deck, unobserved by the watchman. The white, bare little feet felt no cold as they pattered the planks of the deserted promenade, and the little figure had reached the steerage entrance by the time the captain and boatswain had reached the bridge.

"And they talk," went on Rowland, as the three watched and listened; "of the wonderful love and care of a merciful God, who controls all things—who has given me my defects, and my capacity for loving, and then placed Myra Gaunt in my way. Is there mercy to me in this? As part of a great evolutionary principle, which develops the race life at the expense of the individual, it might be consistent with the idea of a God—a first cause. But does the individual who perishes, because unfitted to survive, owe any love, or gratitude to this God? He does not! On the supposition that He exists, I deny it! And on the complete lack of evidence that He does exist, I affirm to myself the integrity of cause and effect—which is enough to explain the Universe, and me. A merciful God—a kind, loving, just, and merciful God—" he burst into a fit of incongruous laughter, which stopped short as he clapped his hands to his stomach and then to his head. "What ails me?" he gasped; "I feel as though I had swallowed hot coals—and my head—and my eyes—I can't see." The pain left him in a moment and the laughter returned. "What's wrong with the starboard anchor? It's moving. It's changing. It's a—what? What on earth is it? On end—and the windlass—and the spare anchors—and the davits—all alive—all moving."

The sight he saw would have been horrid to a healthy mind, but it only moved this man to increased and uncontrollable merriment. The two rails below leading to the stem had arisen before him in a shadowy triangle; and within it were the deck-fittings he had mentioned. The windlass had become a thing of horror, black and forbidding. The two end barrels were the bulging, lightless eyes of a non-descript monster, for which the cable chains had multiplied themselves into innumerable legs and tentacles. And this thing was crawling around within the triangle. The anchor-davits were many-headed serpents which danced on their tails, and the anchors themselves writhed and squirmed in the shape of immense hairy caterpillars, while faces appeared on the two white lantern-towers—grinning and leering at him. With his hands on the bridge rail, and tears streaming down his face, he laughed at the strange sight, but did not speak; and the three, who had quietly approached, drew back to await, while below on the promenade deck, the little white figure, as though attracted by his laughter, turned into the stairway leading to the upper deck.

The phantasmagoria faded to a blank wall of gray fog, and Rowland found sanity to mutter, "They've drugged me"; but in an instant he stood in the darkness of a garden—one that he had known. In the distance were the lights of a house, and close to him was a young girl, who turned from him and fled, even as he called to her.

By a supreme effort of will, he brought himself back to the present, to the bridge he stood upon, and to his duty. "Why must it haunt me through the years?" he groaned; "drunk then—drunk since. She could have saved me, but she chose to damn me." He strove to pace up and down, but staggered, and clung to the rail; while the three watchers approached again, and the little white figure below climbed the upper bridge steps.

"The survival of the fittest," he rambled, as he stared into the fog; "cause and effect. It explains the Universe—and me." He lifted his hand and spoke loudly, as though to some unseen familiar of the deep. "What will be the last effect? Where in the scheme of ultimate balance—under the law of the correlation of energy, will my wasted wealth of love be gathered, and weighed, and credited? What will balance it, and where will I be? Myra,—Myra," he called; "do you know what you have lost? Do you know, in your goodness, and purity, and truth, of what you have done? Do you know—"

The fabric on which he stood was gone, and he seemed to be poised on nothing in a worldless universe of gray—alone. And in the vast, limitless emptiness there was no sound, or life, or change; and in his heart neither fear, nor wonder, nor emotion of any kind, save one—the unspeakable hunger of a love that had failed. Yet it seemed that he was not John Rowland, but some one, or something else; for presently he saw himself, far away—millions of billions of miles; as though on the outermost fringes of the void—and heard his own voice, calling. Faintly, yet distinctly, filled with the concentrated despair of his life, came the call: "Myra,—Myra."

There was an answering call, and looking for the second voice, he beheld her—the woman of his love—on the opposite edge of space; and her eyes held the tenderness, and her voice held the pleading that he had known but in dreams. "Come back," she called; "come back to me." But it seemed that the two could not understand; for again he heard the despairing cry: "Myra, Myra, where are you?" and again the answer: "Come back. Come."

Then in the far distance to the right appeared a faint point of flame, which grew larger. It was approaching, and he dispassionately viewed it; and when he looked again for the two, they were gone, and in their places were two clouds of nebula, which resolved into myriad points of sparkling light and color—whirling, encroaching, until they filled all space. And through them the larger light was coming—and growing larger—straight for him.

He heard a rushing sound, and looking for it, saw in the opposite direction a formless object, as much darker than the gray of the void as the flame was brighter, and it too was growing larger, and coming. And it seemed to him that this light and darkness were the good and evil of his life, and he watched, to see which would reach him first, but felt no surprise or regret when he saw that the darkness was nearest. It came, closer and closer, until it brushed him on the side.

"What have we here, Rowland?" said a voice. Instantly, the whirling points were blotted out; the universe of gray changed to the fog; the flame of light to the moon rising above it, and the shapeless darkness to the form of the first officer. The little white figure, which had just darted past the three watchers, stood at his feet. As though warned by an inner subconsciousness of danger, it had come in its sleep, for safety and care, to its mother's old lover—the strong and the weak—the degraded and disgraced, but exalted—the persecuted, drugged, and all but helpless John Rowland.

With the readiness with which a man who dozes while standing will answer the question that wakens him, he said—though he stammered from the now waning effect of the drug: "Myra's child, sir; it's asleep." He picked up the night-gowned little girl, who screamed as she wakened, and folded his pea-jacket around the cold little body.

"Who is Myra?" asked the officer in a bullying tone, in which were also chagrin and disappointment. "You've been asleep yourself."

Before Rowland could reply a shout from the crow's-nest split the air.

"Ice," yelled the lookout; "ice ahead. Iceberg. Right under the bows." The first officer ran amidships, and the captain, who had remained there, sprang to the engine-room telegraph, and this time the lever was turned. But in five seconds the bow of the *Titan* began to lift, and ahead, and on either hand, could be seen, through the fog, a field of ice, which arose in an incline to a hundred feet high in her track. The music in the theater ceased, and among the babel of shouts and cries, and the deafening noise of steel, scraping and crashing over ice, Rowland heard the agonized voice of a woman crying from the bridge steps: "Myra—Myra, where are you? Come back."

CHAPTER VII

Seventy-five thousand tons—dead-weight—rushing through the fog at the rate of fifty feet a second, had hurled itself at an iceberg. Had the impact been received by a perpendicular wall, the elastic resistance of bending plates and frames would have overcome the momentum with no more damage to the passengers than a severe shaking up, and to the ship than the crushing in of her bows and the killing, to a man, of the watch below. She would have backed off, and, slightly down by the head, finished the voyage at reduced speed, to rebuild on insurance money, and benefit, largely, in the end, by the consequent advertising of her indestructibility. But a low beach, possibly formed by the recent overturning of the berg, received the *Titan*, and with her keel cutting the ice like the steel runner of an ice-boat, and her great weight resting on the starboard bilge, she rose out of the sea, higher and higher—until the propellers in the stern were half exposed—then, meeting an easy, spiral rise in the ice under her port bow, she heeled, overbalanced, and crashed down on her side, to starboard.

The holding-down bolts of twelve boilers and three triple-expansion engines, unintended to hold such weights from a perpendicular flooring, snapped, and down through a maze of ladders, gratings, and fore-and-aft bulkheads came these giant masses of steel and iron, puncturing the sides of the ship, even where backed by solid, resisting ice; and filling the engine- and boiler-rooms with scalding steam, which brought a quick, though tortured death, to each of the hundred men on duty in the engineer's department.

Amid the roar of escaping steam, and the bee-like buzzing of nearly three thousand human voices, raised in agonized screams and callings from within the inclosing walls, and the whistling of air through hundreds of open deadlights as the water, entering the holes of the crushed and riven starboard side, expelled it, the *Titan* moved slowly backward and launched herself into the sea, where she floated low on her side—a dying monster, groaning with her death-wound.

A solid, pyramid-like hummock of ice, left to starboard as the steamer ascended, and which projected close alongside the upper, or boat-deck, as she fell over, had caught, in succession, every pair of davits to starboard, bending and wrenching them, smashing boats, and snapping tackles and gripes, until, as the ship cleared herself, it capped the pile of wreckage strewing the ice in front of, and around it, with the end and broken stanchions of the bridge. And in this shattered, box-like structure, dazed by the sweeping fall through an arc of seventy-foot radius, crouched Rowland, bleeding from a cut in his head, and still holding to his breast the little girl—now too frightened to cry.

By an effort of will, he aroused himself and looked. To his eyesight, twisted and fixed to a shorter focus by the drug he had taken, the steamship was little more than a blotch on the moon-whitened fog; yet he thought he could see men clambering and working on the upper davits, and the nearest boat—No. 24—seemed to be swinging by the tackles. Then the fog shut her out, though her position was still indicated by the roaring of steam from her iron lungs. This ceased in time, leaving behind it the horrid humming sound and whistling of air; and when this too was suddenly hushed, and the ensuing silence broken by dull, booming reports—as from bursting compartments—Rowland knew that the holocaust was complete; that the invincible *Titan*, with nearly all of her people, unable to climb vertical floors and ceilings, was beneath the surface of the sea.

Mechanically, his benumbed faculties had received and recorded the impressions of the last few moments; he could not comprehend, to the full, the horror of it all. Yet his mind was keenly alive to the peril of the woman whose appealing voice he had heard and recognized—the woman of his dream, and the mother of the child in his arms. He hastily examined the wreckage. Not a boat was intact. Creeping down to the water's edge, he hailed, with all the power of his weak voice, to possible, but invisible boats beyond the fog—calling on them to come and save the child—to look out for a woman who had been on deck, under the bridge. He shouted this woman's name—the one that he knew—encouraging her to swim, to tread water, to float on wreckage, and to answer him, until he came to her. There was no response, and when his voice had grown hoarse and futile, and his feet numb from the cold of the thawing ice, he returned to the wreckage, weighed down and all but crushed by the blackest desolation that had, so far, come into his unhappy life. The little girl was crying and he tried to soothe her.

"I want mamma," she wailed.

"Hush, baby, hush," he answered, wearily and bitterly; "so do I—more than Heaven, but I think our chances are about even now. Are you cold, little one? We'll go inside, and I'll make a house for us."

He removed his coat, tenderly wrapped the little figure in it, and with the injunction: "Don't be afraid, now," placed her in the corner of the bridge, which rested on its forward side. As he did so, the bottle of whisky fell out of the pocket. It seemed an age since he had found it there, and it required a strong effort of reasoning before he remembered its full significance. Then he raised it, to hurl it down the incline of ice, but stopped himself.

"I'll keep it," he muttered; "it may be safe in small quantities, and we'll need it on this ice." He placed it in a corner; then, removing the canvas cover from one of the wrecked boats, he hung it over the open side and end of the bridge, crawled within, and donned his coat—a ready-made, slop-chest garment, designed for a larger man—and buttoning it around himself and the little girl, lay down on the hard woodwork. She was still crying, but soon, under the influence of the warmth of his body, ceased and went to sleep.

Huddled in a corner, he gave himself up to the torment of his thoughts. Two pictures alternately crowded his mind; one, that of the woman of his dream, entreating him to come back—which his memory clung to as an oracle; the other, of this woman, cold and lifeless, fathoms deep in the sea. He pondered on her chances. She was close to, or on the bridge steps; and boat No. 24, which he was almost sure was being cleared away as he looked, would swing close to her as it descended. She could climb in and be saved—unless the swimmers from doors and hatches should swamp the boat. And, in his agony of mind, he cursed these swimmers, preferring to see her, mentally, the only passenger in the boat, with the watch-on-deck to pull her to safety.

The potent drug he had taken was still at work, and this, with the musical wash of the sea on the icy beach, and the muffled creaking and crackling beneath and around him—the voice of the iceberg—overcame him finally, and he slept, to waken at daylight with limbs stiffened and numb—almost frozen.

And all night, as he slept, a boat with the number twenty-four on her bow, pulled by sturdy sailors and steered by brass-buttoned officers, was making for the Southern Lane—the highway of spring traffic. And, crouched in the stern-sheets of this boat was a moaning, praying woman, who cried and screamed at intervals, for husband and baby, and would not be comforted, even when one of the brass-buttoned officers assured her that her child was safe in the care of John Rowland, a brave and trusty sailor, who was certainly in the other boat with it. He did not tell her, of course, that Rowland had hailed from the berg as she lay unconscious, and that if he still had the child, it was with him there—deserted.

CHAPTER VIII

Rowland, with some misgivings, drank a small quantity of the liquor, and wrapping the still sleeping child in the coat, stepped out on the ice. The fog was gone and a blue, sailless sea stretched out to the horizon. Behind him was ice—a mountain of it. He climbed the elevation and looked at another stretch of vacant view from a precipice a hundred feet high. To his left the ice sloped to a steeper beach than the one behind him, and to the right, a pile of hummocks and taller peaks, interspersed with numerous cañons and caves, and glistening with waterfalls, shut out the horizon in this direction. Nowhere was there a sail or steamer's smoke to cheer him, and he retraced his steps. When but half-way to the wreckage, he saw a moving white object approaching from the direction of the peaks.

His eyes were not yet in good condition, and after an uncertain scrutiny he started at a run; for he saw that the mysterious white object was nearer the bridge than himself, and rapidly lessening the distance. A hundred yards away, his heart bounded and the blood in his veins felt cold as the ice under foot, for the white object proved to be a traveler from the frozen North, lean and famished—a polar bear, who had scented food and was seeking it—coming on at a lumbering run, with great red jaws half open and yellow fangs exposed. Rowland had no weapon but a strong jackknife, but this he pulled from his pocket and opened as he ran. Not for an instant did he hesitate at a conflict that promised almost certain death; for the presence of this bear involved the safety of a child whose life had become of more importance to him than his own. To his horror, he saw it creep out of the opening in its white covering, just as the bear turned the corner of the bridge.

"Go back, baby, go back," he shouted, as he bounded down the slope. The bear reached the child first, and with seemingly no effort, dashed it, with a blow of its massive paw, a dozen feet away, where it lay quiet. Turning to follow, the brute was met by Rowland.

The bear rose to his haunches, sank down, and charged; and Rowland felt the bones of his left arm crushing under the bite of the big, yellow-fanged jaws. But, falling, he buried the knife-blade in the shaggy hide, and the bear, with an angry snarl, spat out the mangled member and dealt him a sweeping blow which sent him farther along the ice than the child had gone. He arose, with broken ribs, and—scarcely feeling the pain—awaited the second charge. Again was the crushed and useless arm gripped in the yellow vise, and again was he pressed backward; but this time he used the knife with method. The great snout was pressing his breast; the hot, fetid breath was in his nostrils; and at his shoulder the hungry eyes were glaring into his own. He struck for the left eye of the brute and struck true. The five-inch blade went in to the handle, piercing the brain, and the animal, with a convulsive spring which carried him half-way to his feet by the wounded arm, reared up, with paws outstretched, to full eight feet of length, then sagged down, and with a few spasmodic kicks, lay still. Rowland had done what no Innuit hunter will attempt—he had fought and killed the Tiger-of-the-North with a knife.

It had all happened in a minute, but in that minute he was crippled for life; for in the quiet of a hospital, the best of surgical skill could hardly avail to reset the fractured particles of bone in the limp arm, and bring to place the crushed ribs. And he was adrift on a floating island of ice, with the temperature near the freezing point, and without even the rude appliances of the savage.

He painfully made his way to the little pile of red and white, and lifted it with his uninjured arm, though the stooping caused him excruciating torture. The child was bleeding from four deep, cruel scratches, extending diagonally from the right shoulder down the back; but he found upon examination that the soft, yielding bones were unbroken, and that her unconsciousness came from the rough contact of the little forehead with the ice; for a large lump had raised.

Of pure necessity, his first efforts must be made in his own behalf; so wrapping the baby in his coat he placed it in his shelter, and cut and made from the canvas a sling for his dangling arm. Then, with knife, fingers, and teeth, he partly skinned the bear—often compelled to pause to save himself from fainting with pain—and cut from the warm but not very thick layer of fat a broad slab, which, after bathing the wounds at a near-by pool, he bound firmly to the little one's back, using the torn night-gown for a bandage.

He cut the flannel lining from his coat, and from that of the sleeves made nether garments for the little limbs, doubling the surplus length over the ankles and tying in place with rope-yarns from a boat-lacing. The body lining he wrapped around her waist, inclosing the arms, and around the whole he passed turn upon turn of canvas in strips, marling the mummy-like bundle with yarns, much as a sailor secures chafing-gear to the doubled parts of a hawser—a process when complete, that would have aroused the indignation of any mother who saw it. But he was only a man, and suffering mental and physical anguish.

By the time he had finished, the child had recovered consciousness, and was protesting its misery in a feeble, wailing cry. But he dared not stop—to become stiffened with cold and pain. There was plenty of fresh water from melting ice, scattered in pools. The bear would furnish food; but they needed fire, to cook this food, keep them warm, and the dangerous inflammation from their hurts, and to raise a smoke to be seen by passing craft.

He recklessly drank from the bottle, needing the stimulant, and reasoning, perhaps rightly, that no ordinary drug could affect him in his present condition; then he examined the wreckage—most of it good kindling wood. Partly above, partly below the pile, was a steel lifeboat, decked over air-tight ends, now doubled to more than a right angle and resting on its side. With canvas hung over one half, and a small fire in the other, it promised, by its conducting property, a warmer and better shelter than the bridge. A sailor without matches is an anomaly. He whittled shavings, kindled the fire, hung the canvas and brought the child, who begged piteously for a drink of water.

He found a tin can—possibly left in a leaky boat before its final hoist to the davits—and gave her a drink, to which he had added a few drops of the whisky. Then he thought of breakfast. Cutting a steak from the hindquarters of the bear, he toasted it on the end of a splinter and found it sweet and satisfying; but when he attempted to feed the child, he understood the necessity of freeing its arms—which he did, sacrificing his left shirtsleeve to cover them. The change and the food stopped its crying for a while, and Rowland lay down with it in the warm boat. Before the day had passed the whisky was gone and he was delirious with fever, while the child was but little better.

CHAPTER IX

With lucid intervals, during which he replenished or rebuilt the fire, cooked the bear-meat, and fed and dressed the wounds of the child, this delirium lasted three days. His suffering was intense. His arm, the seat of throbbing pain, had swollen to twice the natural size, while his side prevented him taking a full breath, voluntarily. He had paid no attention to his own hurts, and it was either the vigor of a constitution that years of dissipation had not impaired, or some anti-febrile property of bear-meat, or the absence of the exciting whisky that won the battle. He rekindled the fire with his last match on the evening of the third day and looked around the darkening horizon, sane, but feeble in body and mind.

If a sail had appeared in the interim, he had not seen it; nor was there one in sight now. Too weak to climb the slope, he returned to the boat, where the child, exhausted from fruitless crying, was now sleeping. His unskillful and rather heroic manner of wrapping it up to protect it from cold had, no doubt, contributed largely to the closing of its wounds by forcibly keeping it still, though it must have added to its present sufferings. He looked for a moment on the wan, tear-stained little face, with its fringe of tangled curls peeping above the wrappings of canvas, and stooping painfully down, kissed it softly; but the kiss awakened it and it cried for its mother. He could not soothe it, nor could he try; and with a formless, wordless curse against destiny welling up from his heart, he left it and sat down on the wreckage at some distance away.

"We'll very likely get well," he mused, gloomily, "unless I let the fire go out. What then? We can't last longer than the berg, and not much longer than the bear. We must be out of the tracks—we were about nine hundred miles out when we struck; and the current sticks to the fog-belt here—about west-sou'west—but that's the surface water. These deep fellows have currents of their own. There's no fog; we must be to the southward of the belt—between the Lanes. They'll run their boats in the other Lane after this, I think—the money-grabbing wretches. Curse them—if they've drowned her. Curse them, with their water-tight compartments, and their logging of the lookouts. Twenty-four boats for three thousand people—lashed down with tarred gripe-lashings—thirty men to clear them away, and not an axe on the boat-deck or a sheath-knife on a man. Could she have got away? If they got that boat down, they might have taken her in from the steps; and the mate knew I had her child—he would tell her. Her name must be Myra, too; it was her voice I heard in that dream. That was hasheesh. What did they drug me for? But the whisky was all right. It's all done with now, unless I get ashore—but will I?"

The moon rose above the castellated structure to the left, flooding the icy beach with ashen-gray light, sparkling in a thousand points from the cascades, streams, and rippling pools, throwing into blackest shadow the gullies and hollows, and bringing to his mind, in spite of the weird beauty of the scene, a crushing sense of loneliness—of littleness—as though the vast pile of inorganic desolation which held him was of far greater importance than himself, and all the hopes, plans, and fears of his lifetime. The child had cried itself to sleep again, and he paced up and down the ice.

"Up there," he said, moodily, looking into the sky, where a few stars shone faintly in the flood from the moon; "Up there—somewhere—they don't know just where—but somewhere up above, is the Christians' Heaven. Up there is their good God—who has placed Myra's child here—their good God whom they borrowed from the savage, bloodthirsty race that invented him. And down below us—somewhere again—is their hell and their bad god, whom they invented themselves. And they give us our choice—Heaven or hell. It is not so—not so. The great mystery is not solved—the human heart is not helped in this way. No good, merciful God created this world or its conditions. Whatever may be the nature of the causes at work beyond our mental vision, one fact is indubitably proven—that the qualities of mercy, goodness, justice, play no part in the governing scheme.

And yet, they say the core of all religions on earth is the belief in this. Is it? Or is it the cowardly, human fear of the unknown—that impels the savage mother to throw her babe to a crocodile—that impels the civilized man to endow churches—that has kept in existence from the beginning a class of soothsayers, medicine-men, priests, and clergymen, all living on the hopes and fears excited by themselves?

"And people pray—millions of them—and claim they are answered. Are they? Was ever supplication sent into that sky by troubled humanity answered, or even heard? Who knows? They pray for rain and sunshine, and both come in time. They pray for health and success and both are but natural in the marching of events. This is not evidence. But they say that they know, by spiritual uplifting, that they are heard, and comforted, and answered at the moment. Is not this a physiological experiment? Would they not feel equally tranquil if they repeated the multiplication table, or boxed the compass?

"Millions have believed this—that prayers are answered—and these millions have prayed to different gods. Were they all wrong or all right? Would a tentative prayer be listened to? Admitting that the Bibles, and Korans, and Vedas, are misleading and unreliable, may there not be an unseen, unknown Being, who knows my heart—who is watching me now? If so, this Being gave me my reason, which doubts Him, and on Him is the responsibility. And would this being, if he exists, overlook a defect for which I am not to blame, and listen to a prayer from me, based on the mere chance that I might be mistaken? Can an unbeliever, in the full strength of his reasoning powers, come to such trouble that he can no longer stand alone, but must cry for help to an imagined power? Can such time come to a sane man—to me?" He looked at the dark line of vacant horizon. It was seven miles away; New York was nine hundred; the moon in the east over two hundred thousand, and the stars above, any number of billions. He was alone, with a sleeping child, a dead bear, and the Unknown. He walked softly to the boat and looked at the little one for a moment; then, raising his head, he whispered: "For you, Myra."

Sinking to his knees the atheist lifted his eyes to the heavens, and with his feeble voice and the fervor born of helplessness, prayed to the God that he denied. He begged for the life of the waif in his care—for the safety of the mother, so needful to the little one—and for courage and strength to do his part and bring them together. But beyond the appeal for help in the service of others, not one word or expressed thought of his prayer included himself as a beneficiary. So much for pride. As he rose to his feet, the flying-jib of a bark appeared around the corner of ice to the right of the beach, and a moment later the whole moon-lit fabric came into view, wafted along by the faint westerly air, not half a mile away.

He sprang to the fire, forgetting his pain, and throwing on wood, made a blaze. He hailed, in a frenzy of excitement: "Bark ahoy! Bark ahoy! Take us off," and a deep-toned answer came across the water.

"Wake up, Myra," he cried, as he lifted the child; "wake up. We're going away."

"We goin' to mamma?" she asked, with no symptoms of crying.

"Yes, we're going to mamma, now—that is," he added to himself; "if that clause in the prayer is considered."

Fifteen minutes later as he watched the approach of a white quarter-boat, he muttered: "That bark was there—half a mile back in this wind—before I thought of praying. Is that prayer answered? Is she safe?"

CHAPTER X

On the first floor of the London Royal Exchange is a large apartment studded with desks, around and between which surges a hurrying, shouting crowd of brokers, clerks, and messengers. Fringing this apartment are doors and hallways leading to adjacent rooms and offices, and scattered through it are bulletin-boards, on which are daily written in duplicate the marine casualties of the world. At one end is a raised platform, sacred to the presence of an important functionary. In the technical language of the "City," the apartment is known as the "Room," and the functionary, as the "Caller," whose business it is to call out in a mighty sing-song voice the names of members wanted at the door, and the bare particulars of bulletin news prior to its being chalked out for reading.

It is the headquarters of Lloyds—the immense association of underwriters, brokers, and shipping-men, which, beginning with the customers at Edward

Lloyd's coffee-house in the latter part of the seventeenth century, has, retaining his name for a title, developed into a corporation so well equipped, so splendidly organized and powerful, that kings and ministers of state appeal to it at times for foreign news.

Not a master or mate sails under the English flag but whose record, even to forecastle fights, is tabulated at Lloyds for the inspection of prospective employers. Not a ship is cast away on any inhabitable coast of the world, during underwriters' business hours, but what that mighty sing-song cry announces the event at Lloyds within thirty minutes.

One of the adjoining rooms is known as the Chart-room. Here can be found in perfect order and sequence, each on its roller, the newest charts of all nations, with a library of nautical literature describing to the last detail the harbors, lights, rocks, shoals, and sailing directions of every coast-line shown on the charts; the tracks of latest storms; the changes of ocean currents, and the whereabouts of derelicts and icebergs. A member at Lloyds acquires in time a theoretical knowledge of the sea seldom exceeded by the men who navigate it.

Another apartment—the Captain's room—is given over to joy and refreshment, and still another, the antithesis of the last, is the Intelligence office, where anxious ones inquire for and are told the latest news of this or that overdue ship.

On the day when the assembled throng of underwriters and brokers had been thrown into an uproarious panic by the Crier's announcement that the great *Titan* was destroyed, and the papers of Europe and America were issuing extras giving the meager details of the arrival at New York of one boat-load of her people, this office had been crowded with weeping women and worrying men, who would ask, and remain to ask again, for more news. And when it came—a later cablegram,—giving the story of the wreck and the names of the captain, first officer, boatswain, seven sailors, and one lady passenger as those of the saved, a feeble old gentleman had raised his voice in a quavering scream, high above the sobbing of women, and said:

"My daughter-in-law is safe; but where is my son,—where is my son, and my grandchild?" Then he had hurried away, but was back again the next day, and the next. And when, on the tenth day of waiting and watching, he learned of another boat-load of sailors and children arrived at Gibraltar, he shook his head, slowly, muttering: "George, George," and left the room. That night, after telegraphing the consul at Gibraltar of his coming, he crossed the channel.

In the first tumultuous riot of inquiry, when underwriters had climbed over desks and each other to hear again of the wreck of the *Titan*, one—the noisiest of all, a corpulent, hook-nosed man with flashing black eyes—had broken away from the crowd and made his way to the Captain's room, where, after a draught of brandy, he had seated himself heavily, with a groan that came from his soul.

"Father Abraham," he muttered; "this will ruin me."

Others came in, some to drink, some to condole—all, to talk.

"Hard hit, Meyer?" asked one.

"Ten thousand," he answered, gloomily.

"Serve you right," said another, unkindly; "have more baskets for your eggs. Knew you'd bring up."

Though Mr. Meyer's eyes sparkled at this, he said nothing, but drank himself stupid and was assisted home by one of his clerks. From this on, neglecting his business—excepting to occasionally visit the bulletins—he spent his time in the Captain's room drinking heavily, and bemoaning his luck. On the tenth day he read with watery eyes, posted on the bulletin below the news of the arrival at Gibraltar of the second boat-load of people, the following:

> "Life-buoy of *Royal Age*, London, picked up among wreckage in Lat. 45-20, N. Lon. 54-31, W. Ship *Arctic*, Boston, Capt. Brandt."

"Oh, mine good God," he howled, as he rushed toward the Captain's room.

"Poor devil—poor damn fool of an Israelite," said one observer to another. "He covered the whole of the *Royal Age*, and the biggest chunk of the *Titan*. It'll take his wife's diamonds to settle."

Three weeks later, Mr. Meyer was aroused from a brooding lethargy, by a crowd of shouting underwriters, who rushed into the Captain's room, seized him by the shoulders, and hurried him out and up to a bulletin.

"Read it, Meyer—read it. What d'you think of it?" With some difficulty he read aloud, while they watched his face:

> "John Rowland, sailor of the *Titan*, with child passenger, name unknown, on board *Peerless*, Bath, at Christiansand, Norway. Both dangerously ill. Rowland speaks of ship cut in half night before loss of *Titan*."

"What do you make of it, Meyer—*Royal Age*, isn't it?" asked one.

"Yes," vociferated another, "I've figured back. Only ship not reported lately. Overdue two months. Was spoken same day fifty miles east of that iceberg."

"Sure thing," said others. "Nothing said about it in the captain's statement—looks queer."

"Vell, vwhat of it," said Mr. Meyer, painfully and stupidly: "dere is a collision clause in der *Titan's* policy; I merely bay the money to der steamship company instead of to der *Royal Age* beeple."

"But why did the captain conceal it?" they shouted at him. "What's his object—assured against collision suits?"

"Der looks of it, berhaps—looks pad."

"Nonsense, Meyer, what's the matter with you? Which one of the lost tribes did you spring from—you're like none of your race—drinking yourself stupid like a good Christian. I've got a thousand on the *Titan*, and if I'm to pay it I want to know why. You've got the heaviest risk and the brain to fight for it—you've got to do it. Go home, straighten up, and attend to this. We'll watch Rowland till you take hold. We're all caught."

They put him into a cab, took him to a Turkish bath, and then home.

The next morning he was at his desk, clear-eyed and clear-headed, and for a few weeks was a busy, scheming man of business.

CHAPTER XI

On a certain morning, about two months after the announcement of the loss of the *Titan*, Mr. Meyer sat at his desk in the Rooms, busily writing, when the old gentleman who had bewailed the death of his son in the Intelligence office tottered in and took a chair beside him.

"Good morning, Mr. Selfridge," he said, scarcely looking up; "I suppose you have come to see der insurance paid over. Der sixty days are up."

"Yes, yes, Mr. Meyer," said the old gentleman, wearily; "of course, as merely a stockholder, I can take no active part; but I am a member here, and naturally a little anxious. All I had in the world—even to my son and grandchild—was in the *Titan*."

"It is very sad, Mr. Selfridge; you have my deepest sympathy. I pelieve you are der largest holder of *Titan* stock—about one hundred thousand, is it not?"

"About that."

"I am der heaviest insurer; so Mr. Selfridge, this battle will be largely petween you and myself."

"Battle—is there to be any difficulty?" asked Mr. Selfridge, anxiously.

"Berhaps—I do not know. Der underwriters and outside companies have blaced matters in my hands and will not bay until I take der initiative. We must hear from one John Rowland, who, with a little child, was rescued from der berg and taken to Christiansand. He has been too sick to leave der ship which found him and is coming up der Thames in her this morning. I have a carriage at der dock and expect him at my office py noon. Dere is where we will dransact this little pizness—not here."

"A child—saved," queried the old gentleman; "dear me, it may be little Myra. She was not at Gibraltar with the others. I would not care—I would not care much about the money, if she was safe. But my son—my only son—is gone; and, Mr. Meyer, I am a ruined man if this insurance is not paid."

"And I am a ruined man if it is," said Mr. Meyer, rising. "Will you come around to der office, Mr. Selfridge? I expect der attorney and Captain Bryce are dere now." Mr. Selfridge arose and accompanied him to the street.

A rather meagerly-furnished private office in Threadneedle Street, partitioned off from a larger one bearing Mr. Meyer's name in the window, received the two men, one of whom, in the interests of good business, was soon to be impoverished. They had not waited a minute before Captain Bryce and Mr. Austen were announced and ushered in. Sleek, well-fed, and gentlemanly in manner, perfect types of the British naval officer, they bowed politely to Mr. Selfridge when Mr. Meyer introduced them as the captain and first officer of the *Titan*, and seated themselves. A few moments later brought a shrewd-looking person whom Mr. Meyer addressed as the attorney for the steamship company, but did not introduce; for such are the amenities of the English system of caste.

"Now then, gentlemen," said Mr. Meyer, "I pelieve we can broceed to pizness up to a certain point—berhaps further. Mr. Thompson, you have the affidavit of Captain Bryce?"

"I have," said the attorney, producing a document which Mr. Meyer glanced at and handed back.

"And in this statement, captain," he said, "you have sworn that der voyage was uneventful up to der moment of der wreck—that is," he added, with an oily smile, as he noticed the paling of the captain's face—"that nothing occurred to make der *Titan* less seaworthy or manageable?"

"That is what I swore to," said the captain, with a little sigh.

"You are part owner, are you not, Captain Bryce?"

"I own five shares of the company's stock."

"I have examined der charter and der company lists," said Mr. Meyer; "each boat of der company is, so far as assessments and dividends are concerned, a separate company. I find you are listed as owning two sixty-seconds of der *Titan* stock. This makes you, under der law, part owner of der *Titan*, and responsible as such."

"What do you mean, sir, by that word responsible?" said Captain Bryce, quickly.

For answer, Mr. Meyer elevated his black eyebrows, assumed an attitude of listening, looked at his watch and went to the door, which, as he opened, admitted the sound of carriage wheels.

"In here," he called to his clerks, then faced the captain.

"What do I mean, Captain Bryce?" he thundered. "I mean that you have concealed in your sworn statement all reference to der fact that you collided with and sunk the ship *Royal Age* on der night before the wreck of your own ship."

"Who says so—how do you know it?" blustered the captain. "You have only that bulletin statement of the man Rowland—an irresponsible drunkard."

"The man was lifted aboard drunk at New York," broke in the first officer, "and remained in a condition of delirium tremens up to the shipwreck. We did not meet the *Royal Age* and are in no way responsible for her loss."

"Yes," added Captain Bryce, "and a man in that condition is liable to see anything. We listened to his ravings on the night of the wreck. He was on lookout—on the bridge. Mr. Austen, the boats'n, and myself were close to him."

Before Mr. Meyer's oily smile had indicated to the flustered captain that he had said too much, the door opened and admitted Rowland, pale, and weak, with empty left sleeve, leaning on the arm of a bronze-bearded and manly-looking giant who carried little Myra on the other shoulder, and who said, in the breezy tone of the quarter-deck:

"Well, I've brought him, half dead; but why couldn't you give me time to dock my ship? A mate can't do everything."

"And this is Captain Barry, of der *Peerless*," said Mr. Meyer, taking his hand. "It is all right, my friend; you will not lose. And this is Mr. Rowland—and this is der little child. Sit down, my friend. I congratulate you on your escape."

"Thank you," said Rowland, weakly, as he seated himself; "they cut my arm off at Christiansand, and I still live. That is my escape."

Captain Bryce and Mr. Austen, pale and motionless, stared hard at this man, in whose emaciated face, refined by suffering to the almost spiritual softness of age, they hardly recognized the features of the troublesome sailor of the *Titan*. His clothing, though clean, was ragged and patched.

Mr. Selfridge had arisen and was also staring, not at Rowland, but at the child, who, seated in the lap of the big Captain Barry, was looking around with wondering eyes. Her costume was unique. A dress of bagging-stuff, put together—as were her canvas shoes and hat—with sail-twine in sail-makers' stitches, three to the inch, covered skirts and underclothing made from old flannel shirts. It represented many an hour's work of the watch-below, lovingly bestowed by the crew of the *Peerless*; for the crippled Rowland could not sew. Mr. Selfridge approached, scanned the pretty features closely, and asked:

"What is her name?"

"Her first name is Myra," answered Rowland. "She remembers that; but I have not learned her last name, though I knew her mother years ago—before her marriage."

"Myra, Myra," repeated the old gentleman; "do you know me? Don't you know me?" He trembled visibly as he stooped and kissed her. The little forehead puckered and wrinkled as the child struggled with memory; then it cleared and the whole face sweetened to a smile.

"Gwampa," she said.

"Oh, God, I thank thee," murmured Mr. Selfridge, taking her in his arms. "I have lost my son, but I have found his child—my granddaughter."

"But, sir," asked Rowland, eagerly; "you—this child's grandfather? Your son is lost, you say? Was he on board the *Titan*? And the mother—was she saved, or is she, too—" he stopped unable to continue.

"The mother is safe—in New York; but the father, my son, has not yet been heard from," said the old man, mournfully.

Rowland's head sank and he hid his face for a moment in his arm, on the table at which he sat. It had been a face as old, and worn, and weary as that of the white-haired man confronting him. On it, when it raised—flushed, bright-eyed and smiling—was the glory of youth.

"I trust, sir," he said, "that you will telegraph her. I am penniless at present, and, besides, do not know her name."

"Selfridge—which, of course, is my own name. Mrs. Colonel, or Mrs. George Selfridge. Our New York address is well known. But I shall cable her at once; and, believe me, sir, although I can understand that our debt to you cannot be named in terms of money, you need not be penniless long. You are evidently a capable man, and I have wealth and influence."

Rowland merely bowed, slightly, but Mr. Meyer muttered to himself: "Vealth and influence. Berhaps not. Now, gentlemen," he added, in a louder tone, "to pizness. Mr. Rowland, will you tell us about der running down of der *Royal Age*?"

"Was it the *Royal Age*?" asked Rowland. "I sailed in her one voyage. Yes, certainly."

Mr. Selfridge, more interested in Myra than in the coming account, carried her over to a chair in the corner and sat down, where he fondled and talked to her after the manner of grandfathers the world over, and Rowland, first looking steadily into the faces of the two men he had come to expose, and whose presence he had thus far ignored, told, while they held their teeth tight together and often buried their finger-nails in their palms, the terrible story of the cutting in half of the ship on the first night out from New York, finishing with the attempted bribery and his refusal.

"Vell, gentlemen, vwhat do you think of that?" asked Mr. Meyer, looking around.

"A lie, from beginning to end," stormed Captain Bryce.

Rowland rose to his feet, but was pressed back by the big man who had accompanied him—who then faced Captain Bryce and said, quietly:

"I saw a polar bear that this man killed in open fight. I saw his arm afterward, and while nursing him away from death I heard no whines or complaints. He can fight his own battles when well, and when sick I'll do it for him. If you insult him again in my presence I'll knock your teeth down your throat."

CHAPTER XII

There was a moment's silence while the two captains eyed one another, broken by the attorney, who said:

"Whether this story is true or false, it certainly has no bearing on the validity of the policy. If this happened, it was after the policy attached and before the wreck of the *Titan*."

"But der concealment—der concealment," shouted Mr. Meyer, excitedly.

"Has no bearing, either. If he concealed anything it was done after the wreck, and after your liability was confirmed. It was not even barratry. You must pay this insurance."

"I will not bay it. I will not. I will fight you in der courts." Mr. Meyer stamped up and down the floor in his excitement, then stopped with a triumphant smile, and shook his finger into the face of the attorney.

"And even if der concealment will not vitiate der policy, der fact that he had a drunken man on lookout when der *Titan* struck der iceberg will be enough. Go ahead and sue. I will not pay. He was part owner."

"You have no witnesses to that admission," said the attorney. Mr. Meyer looked around the group and the smile left his face.

"Captain Bryce was mistaken," said Mr. Austen. "This man was drunk at New York, like others of the crew. But he was sober and competent when on lookout. I discussed theories of navigation with him during his trick on the bridge that night and he spoke intelligently."

"But you yourself said, not ten minutes ago, that this man was in a state of delirium tremens up to der collision," said Mr. Meyer.

"What I said and what I will admit under oath are two different things," said the officer, desperately. "I may have said anything under the excitement of the moment—when we were accused of such an infamous crime. I say now, that John Rowland, whatever may have been his condition on the preceding night, was a sober and competent lookout at the time of the wreck of the *Titan*."

"Thank you," said Rowland, dryly, to the first officer; then, looking into the appealing face of Mr. Meyer, he said:

"I do not think it will be necessary to brand me before the world as an inebriate in order to punish the company and these men. Barratry, as I understand it, is the unlawful act of a captain or crew at sea, causing damage or loss; and it only applies when the parties are purely employees. Did I understand rightly—that Captain Bryce was part owner of the *Titan*?"

"Yes," said Mr. Meyer, "he owns stock; and we insure against barratry; but this man, as part owner, could not fall back on it."

"And an unlawful act," went on Rowland, "perpetrated by a captain who is part owner, which might cause shipwreck, and, during the perpetration of which shipwreck really occurs, will be sufficient to void the policy."

"Certainly," said Mr. Meyer, eagerly. "You were drunk on der lookout—you were raving drunk, as he said himself. You will swear to this, will you not, my friend? It is bad faith with der underwriters. It annuls der insurance. You admit this, Mr. Thompson, do you not?"

"That is law," said the attorney, coldly.

"Was Mr. Austen a part owner, also?" asked Rowland, ignoring Mr. Meyer's view of the case.

"One share, is it not, Mr. Austen?" asked Mr. Meyer, while he rubbed his hands and smiled. Mr. Austen made no sign of denial and Rowland continued:

"Then, for drugging a sailor into a stupor, and having him on lookout out of his turn while in that condition, and at the moment when the *Titan* struck the iceberg, Captain Bryce and Mr. Austen have, as part owners, committed an act which nullifies the insurance on that ship."

"You infernal, lying scoundrel!" roared Captain Bryce. He strode toward Rowland with threatening face. Half-way, he was stopped by the impact of a huge brown fist which sent him reeling and staggering across the room toward Mr. Selfridge and the child, over whom he floundered to the floor—a disheveled heap,—while the big Captain Barry examined teeth-marks on his knuckles, and every one else sprang to their feet.

"I told you to look out," said Captain Barry. "Treat my friend respectfully." He glared steadily at the first officer, as though inviting him to duplicate the offense; but that gentleman backed away from him and assisted the dazed Captain Bryce to a chair, where he felt of his loosened teeth, spat blood upon

Mr. Meyer's floor, and gradually awakened to a realization of the fact that he had been knocked down—and by an American.

Little Myra, unhurt but badly frightened, began to cry and call for Rowland in her own way, to the wonder, and somewhat to the scandal of the gentle old man who was endeavoring to soothe her.

"Dammy," she cried, as she struggled to go to him; "I want Dammy—Dammy—Da-a-may."

"Oh, what a pad little girl," said the jocular Mr. Meyer, looking down on her. "Where did you learn such language?"

"It is my nickname," said Rowland, smiling in spite of himself. "She has coined the word," he explained to the agitated Mr. Selfridge, who had not yet comprehended what had happened; "and I have not yet been able to persuade her to drop it—and I could not be harsh with her. Let me take her, sir." He seated himself, with the child, who nestled up to him contentedly and soon was tranquil.

"Now, my friend," said Mr. Meyer, "you must tell us about this drugging." Then while Captain Bryce, under the memory of the blow he had received, nursed himself into an insane fury; and Mr. Austen, with his hand resting lightly on the captain's shoulder ready to restrain him, listened to the story; and the attorney drew up a chair and took notes of the story; and Mr. Selfridge drew his chair close to Myra and paid no attention to the story at all, Rowland recited the events prior to and succeeding the shipwreck. Beginning with the finding of the whisky in his pocket, he told of his being called to the starboard bridge lookout in place of the rightful incumbent; of the sudden and strange interest Mr. Austen displayed as to his knowledge of navigation; of the pain in his stomach, the frightful shapes he had seen on the deck beneath and the sensations of his dream—leaving out only the part which bore on the woman he loved; he told of the sleep-walking child which awakened him, of the crash of ice and instant wreck, and the fixed condition of his eyes which prevented their focusing only at a certain distance, finishing his story—to explain his empty sleeve—with a graphic account of the fight with the bear.

"And I have studied it all out," he said, in conclusion. "I was drugged—I believe, with hasheesh, which makes a man see strange things—and brought up on the bridge lookout where I could be watched and my ravings listened to and recorded, for the sole purpose of discrediting my threatened testimony in regard to the collision of the night before. But I was only half-drugged, as I spilled part of my tea at supper. In that tea, I am positive, was the hasheesh."

"You know all about it, don't you," snarled Captain Bryce, from his chair, "'twas not hasheesh; 'twas an infusion of Indian hemp; you don't know—" Mr. Austen's hand closed over his mouth and he subsided.

"Self-convicted," said Rowland, with a quiet laugh. "Hasheesh is made from Indian hemp."

"You hear this, gentlemen," exclaimed Mr. Meyer, springing to his feet and facing everybody in turn. He pounced on Captain Barry. "You hear this confession, captain; you hear him say Indian hemp? I have a witness now, Mr. Thompson. Go right on with your suit. You hear him, Captain Barry. You are disinterested. You are a witness. You hear?"

"Yes, I heard it—the murdering scoundrel," said the captain.

Mr. Meyer danced up and down in his joy, while the attorney, pocketing his notes, remarked to the discomfited Captain Bryce: "You are the poorest fool I know," and left the office.

Then Mr. Meyer calmed himself, and facing the two steamship officers, said, slowly and impressively, while he poked his forefinger almost into their faces:

"England is a fine country, my friends—a fine country to leave pehind sometimes. Dere is Canada, and der United States, and Australia, and South Africa—all fine countries, too—fine countries to go to with new names. My friends, you will be bulletined and listed at Lloyds in less than half an hour, and you will never again sail under der English flag as officers. And, my friends, let me say, that in half an hour after you are bulletined, all Scotland Yard will be looking for you. But my door is not locked."

Silently they arose, pale, shamefaced, and crushed, and went out the door, through the outer office, and into the street.

CHAPTER XIII

Mr. Selfridge had begun to take an interest in the proceedings. As the two men passed out he arose and asked:

"Have you reached a settlement, Mr. Meyer? Will the insurance be paid?"

"No," roared the underwriter, in the ear of the puzzled old gentleman; while he slapped him vigorously on the back; "it will not be paid. You or I must have been ruined, Mr. Selfridge, and it has settled on you. I do not pay der *Titan's* insurance—nor will der other insurers. On der contrary, as der collision clause in der policy is void with der rest, your company must reimburse me for der insurance which I must pay to der *Royal Age* owners—that is, unless our good friend here, Mr. Rowland, who was on der lookout at der time, will swear that her lights were out."

"Not at all," said Rowland. "Her lights were burning—look to the old gentleman," he exclaimed. "Look out for him. Catch him!"

Mr. Selfridge was stumbling toward a chair. He grasped it, loosened his hold, and before anyone could reach him, fell to the floor, where he lay, with ashen lips and rolling eyes, gasping convulsively.

"Heart failure," said Rowland, as he knelt by his side. "Send for a doctor."

"Send for a doctor," repeated Mr. Meyer through the door to his clerks; "and send for a carriage, quick. I don't want him to die in der office."

Captain Barry lifted the helpless figure to a couch, and they watched, while the convulsions grew easier, the breath shorter, and the lips from ashen gray to blue. Before a doctor or carriage had come, he had passed away.

"Sudden emotion of some kind," said the doctor when he did arrive. "Violent emotion, too. Hear bad news?"

"Bad and good," answered the underwriter. "Good, in learning that this dear little girl was his granddaughter—bad, in learning that he was a ruined man. He was der heaviest stockholder in der *Titan*. One hundred thousand pounds, he owned, of der stock, all of which this poor, dear little child will not get." Mr. Meyer looked sorrowful, as he patted Myra on the head.

Captain Barry beckoned to Rowland, who, slightly flushed, was standing by the still figure on the couch and watching the face of Mr. Meyer, on which annoyance, jubilation, and simulated shock could be seen in turn.

"Wait," he said, as he turned to watch the doctor leave the room. "Is this so, Mr. Meyer," he added to the underwriter, "that Mr. Selfridge owned *Titan* stock, and would have been ruined, had he lived, by the loss of the insurance money?"

"Yes, he would have been a poor man. He had invested his last farthing—one hundred thousand pounds. And if he had left any more it would be assessed to make good his share of what der company must bay for der *Royal Age*, which I also insured."

"Was there a collision clause in the *Titan's* policy?"

"Dere was."

"And you took the risk, knowing that she was to run the Northern Lane at full speed through fog and snow?"

"I did—so did others."

"Then, Mr. Meyer, it remains for me to tell you that the insurance on the *Titan* will be paid, as well as any liabilities included in and specified by the collision clause in the policy. In short, I, the one man who can prevent it, refuse to testify."

"Vwhat-a-t?"

Mr. Meyer grasped the back of a chair and, leaning over it, stared at Rowland.

"You will not testify? Vwhat you mean?"

"What I said; and I do not feel called upon to give you my reasons, Mr. Meyer."

"My good friend," said the underwriter, advancing with outstretched hands to Rowland, who backed away, and taking Myra by the hand, moved toward the door. Mr. Meyer sprang ahead, locked it and removed the key, and faced them.

"Oh, mine goot Gott," he shouted, relapsing in his excitement into the more pronounced dialect of his race; "vwhat I do to you, hey? Vwhy you go pack on me, hey? Haf I not bay der doctor's bill? Haf I not bay for der carriage? Haf I not treat you like one shentleman? Haf I not, hey? I sit you down in mine office and call you Mr. Rowland. Haf I not been one shentleman?"

"Open that door," said Rowland, quietly.

"Yes, open it," repeated Captain Barry, his puzzled face clearing at the prospect of action on his part. "Open it or I'll kick it down."

"But you, mine friend—heard der admission of der captain—of der drugging. One goot witness will do: two is petter. But you will swear, mine friend, you will not ruin me."

"I stand by Rowland," said the captain, grimly. "I don't remember what was said, anyhow; got a blamed bad memory. Get away from that door."

Grievous lamentation—weepings and wailings, and the most genuine gnashing of teeth—interspersed with the feebler cries of the frightened Myra and punctuated by terse commands in regard to the door, filled that private office, to the wonder of the clerks without, and ended, at last, with the crashing of the door from its hinges.

Captain Barry, Rowland, and Myra, followed by a parting, heart-borne malediction from the agitated underwriter, left the office and reached the street. The carriage that had brought them was still waiting.

"Settle inside," called the captain to the driver. "We'll take another, Rowland."

Around the first corner they found a cab, which they entered, Captain Barry giving the driver the direction—"Bark *Peerless*, East India Dock."

"I think I understand the game, Rowland," he said, as they started; "you don't want to break this child."

"That's it," answered Rowland, weakly, as he leaned back on the cushion, faint from the excitement of the last few moments. "And as for the right or wrong of the position I am in—why, we must go farther back for it than the question of lookouts. The cause of the wreck was full speed in a fog. All hands on lookout could not have seen that berg. The underwriters knew the speed and took the risk. Let them pay."

"Right—and I'm with you on it. But you must get out of the country. I don't know the law on the matter, but they may compel you to testify. You can't ship 'fore the mast again—that's settled. But you can have a berth mate with me as long as I sail a ship—if you'll take it; and you're to make my cabin your home as long as you like; remember that. Still, I know you want to get across with the kid, and if you stay around until I sail it may be months before you get to New York, with the chance of losing her by getting foul of English law. But just leave it to me. There are powerful interests at stake in regard to this matter."

What Captain Barry had in mind, Rowland was too weak to inquire. On their arrival at the bark he was assisted by his friend to a couch in the cabin, where he spent the rest of the day, unable to leave it. Meanwhile, Captain Barry had gone ashore again.

Returning toward evening, he said to the man on the couch: "I've got your pay, Rowland, and signed a receipt for it to that attorney. He paid it out of his own pocket. You could have worked that company for fifty thousand, or more; but I knew you wouldn't touch their money, and so, only struck him for your wages. You're entitled to a month's pay. Here it is—American money—about seventeen." He gave Rowland a roll of bills.

"Now here's something else, Rowland," he continued, producing an envelope. "In consideration of the fact that you lost all your clothes and later, your arm, through the carelessness of the company's officers, Mr. Thompson offers you this." Rowland opened the envelope. In it were two first cabin tickets from Liverpool to New York. Flushing hotly, he said, bitterly:

"It seems that I'm not to escape it, after all."

"Take 'em, old man, take 'em; in fact, I took 'em for you, and you and the kid are booked. And I made Thompson agree to settle your doctor's bill and expenses with that Sheeny. 'Tisn't bribery. I'd heel you myself for the run over, but, hang it, you'll take nothing from me. You've got to get the young un over. You're the only one to do it. The old gentleman was an American, alone here—hadn't even a lawyer, that I could find. The boat sails in the morning and the night train leaves in two hours. Think of that mother, Rowland. Why, man, I'd travel round the world to stand in your shoes when you hand Myra over. I've got a child of my own." The captain's eyes were winking hard and fast, and Rowland's were shining.

"Yes, I'll take the passage," he said, with a smile. "I accept the bribe."

"That's right. You'll be strong and healthy when you land, and when that mother's through thanking you, and you have to think of yourself, remember—I want a mate and will be here a month before sailing. Write to me, care o'

Lloyds, if you want the berth, and I'll send you advance money to get back with."

"Thank you, captain," said Rowland, as he took the other's hand and then glanced at his empty sleeve; "but my going to sea is ended. Even a mate needs two hands."

"Well, suit yourself, Rowland; I'll take you mate without any hands at all while you had your brains. It's done me good to meet a man like you; and—say, old man, you won't take it wrong from me, will you? It's none o' my business, but you're too all-fired good a man to drink. You haven't had a nip for two months. Are you going to begin?"

"Never again," said Rowland, rising. "I've a future now, as well as a past."

CHAPTER XIV

It was near noon of the next day that Rowland, seated in a steamer-chair with Myra and looking out on a sail-spangled stretch of blue from the saloon-deck of a west-bound liner, remembered that he had made no provisions to have Mrs. Selfridge notified by cable of the safety of her child; and unless Mr. Meyer or his associates gave the story to the press it would not be known.

"Well," he mused, "joy will not kill, and I shall witness it in its fullness if I take her by surprise. But the chances are that it will get into the papers before I reach her. It is too good for Mr. Meyer to keep."

But the story was not given out immediately. Mr. Meyer called a conference of the underwriters concerned with him in the insurance of the *Titan* at which it was decided to remain silent concerning the card they hoped to play, and to spend a little time and money in hunting for other witnesses among the *Titan's* crew, and in interviewing Captain Barry, to the end of improving his memory. A few stormy meetings with this huge obstructionist convinced them of the futility of further effort in his direction, and, after finding at the end of a week that every surviving member of the *Titan's* port watch, as well as a few of the other, had been induced to sign for Cape voyages, or had otherwise disappeared, they decided to give the story told by Rowland to the press in the hope that publicity would avail to bring to light corroboratory evidence.

And this story, improved upon in the repeating by Mr. Meyer to reporters, and embellished still further by the reporters as they wrote it up, particularly in the part pertaining to the polar bear,—blazoned out in the great dailies of England and the Continent, and was cabled to New York, with the name of the steamer in which John Rowland had sailed (for his movements had been traced in the search for evidence), where it arrived, too late for publication, the morning of the day on which, with Myra on his shoulder, he stepped down the gang-plank at a North River dock. As a consequence, he was surrounded on the dock by enthusiastic reporters, who spoke of the story and asked for details. He refused to talk, escaped them, and gaining the side streets, soon found himself in crowded Broadway, where he entered the office of the steamship company in whose employ he had been wrecked, and secured from the *Titan's* passenger-list the address of Mrs. Selfridge—the only woman saved. Then he took a car up Broadway and alighted abreast of a large department store.

"We're going to see mamma, soon, Myra," he whispered in the pink ear; "and you must go dressed up. It don't matter about me; but you're a Fifth Avenue baby—a little aristocrat. These old clothes won't do, now." But she had forgotten the word "mamma," and was more interested in the exciting noise and life of the street than in the clothing she wore. In the store, Rowland asked for, and was directed to the children's department, where a young woman waited on him.

"This child has been shipwrecked," he said. "I have sixteen dollars and a half to spend on it. Give it a bath, dress its hair, and use up the money on a dress, shoes, and stockings, underclothing, and a hat." The young woman stooped and kissed the little girl from sheer sympathy, but protested that not much could be done.

"Do your best," said Rowland; "it is all I have. I will wait here."

An hour later, penniless again, he emerged from the store with Myra, bravely dressed in her new finery, and was stopped at the corner by a policeman who had seen him come out, and who marveled, doubtless, at such juxtaposition of rags and ribbons.

"Whose kid ye got?" he demanded.

"I believe it is the daughter of Mrs. Colonel Selfridge," answered Rowland, haughtily—too haughtily, by far.

"Ye believe—but ye don't know. Come back into the shtore, me tourist, and we'll see who ye shtole it from."

"Very well, officer; I can prove possession." They started back, the officer with his hand on Rowland's collar, and were met at the door by a party of three or four people coming out. One of this party, a young woman in black, uttered a piercing shriek and sprang toward them.

"Myra!" she screamed. "Give me my baby—give her to me."

She snatched the child from Rowland's shoulder, hugged it, kissed it, cried, and screamed over it; then, oblivious to the crowd that collected, incontinently fainted in the arms of an indignant old gentleman.

"You scoundrel!" he exclaimed, as he flourished his cane over Rowland's head with his free arm. "We've caught you. Officer, take that man to the station-house. I will follow and make a charge in the name of my daughter."

"Then he shtole the kid, did he?" asked the policeman.

"Most certainly," answered the old gentleman, as, with the assistance of the others, he supported the unconscious young mother to a carriage. They all entered, little Myra screaming for Rowland from the arms of a female member of the party, and were driven off.

"C'm an wi' me," uttered the officer, rapping his prisoner on the head with his club and jerking him off his feet.

Then, while an approving crowd applauded, the man who had fought and conquered a hungry polar bear was dragged through the streets like a sick animal by a New York policeman. For such is the stultifying effect of a civilized environment.

CHAPTER XV

In New York City there are homes permeated by a moral atmosphere so pure, so elevated, so sensitive to the vibrations of human woe and misdoing, that their occupants are removed completely from all consideration of any but the spiritual welfare of poor humanity. In these homes the news-gathering, sensation-mongering daily paper does not enter.

In the same city are dignified magistrates—members of clubs and societies—who spend late hours, and often fail to arise in the morning in time to read the papers before the opening of court.

Also in New York are city editors, bilious of stomach, testy of speech, and inconsiderate of reporters' feelings and professional pride. Such editors, when a reporter has failed, through no fault of his own, in successfully interviewing a celebrity, will sometimes send him news-gathering in the police courts, where printable news is scarce.

On the morning following the arrest of John Rowland, three reporters, sent by three such editors, attended a hall of justice presided over by one of the late-rising magistrates mentioned above. In the anteroom of this court, ragged, disfigured by his clubbing, and disheveled by his night in a cell, stood Rowland, with other unfortunates more or less guilty of offense against society. When his name was called, he was hustled through a door, along a line of policemen—each of whom added to his own usefulness by giving him a shove—and into the dock, where the stern-faced and tired-looking magistrate glared at him. Seated in a corner of the court-room were the old gentleman of the day before, the young mother with little Myra in her lap, and a number of other ladies—all excited in demeanor; and all but the young mother directing venomous glances at Rowland. Mrs. Selfridge, pale and hollow-eyed, but happy-faced, withal, allowed no wandering glance to rest on him.

The officer who had arrested Rowland was sworn, and testified that he had stopped the prisoner on Broadway while making off with the child, whose rich clothing had attracted his attention. Disdainful sniffs were heard in the corner with muttered remarks: "Rich indeed—the idea—the flimsiest prints." Mr. Gaunt, the prosecuting witness, was called to testify.

"This man, your Honor," he began, excitedly, "was once a gentleman and a frequent guest at my house. He asked for the hand of my daughter, and as his request was not granted, threatened revenge. Yes, sir. And out on the broad Atlantic, where he had followed my daughter in the guise of a sailor, he attempted to murder that child—my grandchild; but was discovered—"

"Wait," interrupted the magistrate. "Confine your testimony to the present offense."

"Yes, your Honor. Failing in this, he stole, or enticed the little one from its bed, and in less than five minutes the ship was wrecked, and he must have escaped with the child in—"

"Were you a witness of this?"

"I was not there, your Honor; but we have it on the word of the first officer, a gentleman—"

"Step down, sir. That will do. Officer, was this offense committed in New York?"

"Yes, your Honor; I caught him meself."

"Who did he steal the child from?"

"That leddy over yonder."

"Madam, will you take the stand?"

With her child in her arms, Mrs. Selfridge was sworn and in a low, quavering voice repeated what her father had said. Being a woman, she was allowed by the woman-wise magistrate to tell her story in her own way. When she spoke of the attempted murder at the taffrail, her manner became excited. Then she told of the captain's promise to put the man in irons on her agreeing to testify against him—of the consequent decrease in her watchfulness, and her missing the child just before the shipwreck—of her rescue by the gallant first officer, and his assertion that he had seen her child in the arms of this man—the only man on earth who would harm it—of the later news that a boat containing sailors and children had been picked up by a Mediterranean steamer—of the detectives sent over, and their report that a sailor answering this man's description had refused to surrender a child to the consul at Gibraltar and had disappeared with it—of her joy at the news that Myra was alive, and despair of ever seeing her again until she had met her in this man's arms on Broadway the day before. At this point, outraged maternity overcame her. With cheeks flushed, and eyes blazing scorn and anger, she pointed at Rowland

and all but screamed: "And he has mutilated—tortured my baby. There are deep wounds in her little back, and the doctor said, only last night, that they were made by a sharp instrument. And he must have tried to warp and twist the mind of my child, or put her through frightful experiences; for he has taught her to swear—horribly—and last night at bedtime, when I told her the story of Elisha and the bears and the children, she burst out into the most uncontrollable screaming and sobbing."

Here her testimony ended in a breakdown of hysterics, between sobs of which were frequent admonitions to the child not to say that bad word; for Myra had caught sight of Rowland and was calling his nickname.

"What shipwreck was this—where was it?" asked the puzzled magistrate of nobody in particular.

"The *Titan*," called out half a dozen newspaper men across the room.

"The *Titan*," repeated the magistrate. "Then this offense was committed on the high seas under the English flag. I cannot imagine why it is brought into this court. Prisoner, have you anything to say?"

"Nothing, your Honor." The answer came in a kind of dry sob.

The magistrate scanned the ashen-faced man in rags, and said to the clerk of the court: "Change this charge to vagrancy—eh—"

The clerk, instigated by the newspaper men, was at his elbow. He laid a morning paper before him, pointed to certain big letters and retired. Then the business of the court suspended while the court read the news. After a moment or two the magistrate looked up.

"Prisoner," he said, sharply, "take your left sleeve out of your breast!" Rowland obeyed mechanically, and it dangled at his side. The magistrate noticed, and read on. Then he folded the paper and said:

"You are the man who was rescued from an iceberg, are you not?" The prisoner bowed his head.

"Discharged!" The word came forth in an unjudicial roar. "Madam," added the magistrate, with a kindling light in his eye, "this man has merely saved your child's life. If you will read of his defending it from a polar bear when you go home, I doubt that you will tell it any more bear stories. Sharp instrument—umph!" Which was equally unjudicial on the part of the court.

Mrs. Selfridge, with a mystified and rather aggrieved expression of face, left the court-room with her indignant father and friends, while Myra shouted profanely for Rowland, who had fallen into the hands of the reporters. They would have entertained him after the manner of the craft, but he would not be entertained—neither would he talk. He escaped and was swallowed up in the world without; and when the evening papers appeared that day, the events of the trial were all that could be added to the story of the morning.

CHAPTER XVI

On the morning of the next day, a one-armed dock lounger found an old fish-hook and some pieces of string which he knotted together; then he dug some bait and caught a fish. Being hungry and without fire, he traded with a coaster's cook for a meal, and before night caught two more, one of which he traded, the other, sold. He slept under the docks—paying no rent—fished, traded, and sold for a month, then paid for a second-hand suit of clothes and the services of a barber. His changed appearance induced a boss stevedore to hire him tallying cargo, which was more lucrative than fishing, and furnished, in time, a hat, pair of shoes, and an overcoat. He then rented a room and slept in a bed. Before long he found employment addressing envelopes for a mailing firm, at which his fine and rapid penmanship secured him steady work; and in a few months he asked his employers to indorse his application for a Civil Service examination. The favor was granted, the examination easily passed, and he addressed envelopes while he waited. Meanwhile he bought new and better clothing and seemed to have no difficulty in impressing those whom he met with the fact that he was a gentleman. Two years from the time of his examination he was appointed to a lucrative position under the Government, and as he seated himself at the desk in his office, could have been heard to remark: "Now John Rowland, your future is your own. You have merely suffered in the past from a mistaken estimate of the importance of women and whisky."

But he was wrong, for in six months he received a letter which, in part, read as follows:

> "Do not think me indifferent or ungrateful. I have watched from a distance while you made your wonderful fight for your old standards. You have won, and I am glad and I congratulate you. But Myra will not let me rest. She asks for you continually and cries at times. I can bear it no longer. Will you not come and see Myra?"

And the man went to see—Myra.

THE PIRATES

PROLOGUE

Two young men met in front of the post-office of a small country town. They were of about the same age—eighteen—each was well dressed, comely, and apparently of good family; and each had an expression of face that would commend him to strangers, save that one of them, the larger of the two, had what is called a "bad eye"—that is, an eye showing just a little too much white above the iris. In the other's eye white predominated below the iris. The former is usually the index of violent though restrained temper; the latter of an intuitive, psychic disposition, with very little self-control. The difference in character so indicated may lead one person to the Presidency, another to the gallows. And—though no such results are promised—with similar divergence of path, of pain and pleasure, of punishment and reward, is this story concerned.

The two boys were schoolmates and friends, with never a quarrel since they had known each other; they had graduated together from the high school, but neither had been valedictorian. They later had sought the competitive examination given by the congressman of the district for an appointment to the Naval Academy, and had won out over all, but so close together that the congressman had decreed another test.

They had taken it, and since then had waited for the letter that named the winner; hence the daily visits to the post-office, ending in this one, when the larger boy, about to go up the steps, met the smaller coming down with an opened letter, and smiling.

"I've got it, Jack," said the smaller boy, joyously. "Here it is. I win, but, of course, you're the alternate. Read it."

He handed the letter to Jack, but it was declined.

"What's the use?" was the somewhat sulky response. "I've lost, sure enough. All I've got to do is to forget it."

"Then let me read it to you," said the winner, eagerly. "I want you to feel glad about it—same as I would if you had passed first. Listen:

"'MR. WILLIAM DENMAN.

"'DEAR SIR: I am glad to inform you that you have successfully passed the second examination for an appointment to the Naval Academy, winning by three points in history over the other contestant, Mr. John Forsythe, who, of course, is the alternate in case you do not pass the entrance examination at Annapolis.

"'Be ready at any time for instructions from the Secretary of the Navy to report at Annapolis. Sincerely yours,

JACOB BLAND.'"

"What do I care for that?" said Forsythe. "I suppose I've got a letter in there, too. Let's see."

While Denman waited, Forsythe entered the post-office, and soon emerged, reading a letter.

"Same thing," he said. "I failed by three points in my special study. How is it, Bill?" he demanded, fiercely, as his disappointment grew upon him. "I've beaten not only you, but the whole class from the primary up, in history, ancient, modern, and local, until now. There's something crooked here." His voice sank to a mutter.

"Crooked, Jack! What are you talking about?" replied Denman, hotly.

"Oh, I don't know, Bill. Never mind. Come on, if you're going home."

They walked side by side in the direction of their homes—near together and on the outskirts of the town—each busy with his thoughts. Denman, though proud and joyous over the prize he had won, was yet hurt by the speech and manner of Forsythe, and hurt still further by the darkening cloud on his face as they walked on.

Forsythe's thoughts were best indicated by his suddenly turning toward Denman and blurting out:

"Yes, I say; there's something crooked in this. I can beat you in history any day in the week, but your dad and old Bland are close friends. I see it now."

Denman turned white as he answered:

"Do you want me to report your opinion to my father and Mr. Bland?"

"Oh, you would, would you? And take from me the alternate, too! Well, you're a cur, Bill Denman. Go ahead and report."

They were now on a block bounded by vacant lots, and no one was within sight. Denman stopped, threw off his coat, and said:

"No, I'll not report your opinion, but—you square yourself, Jack Forsythe, and I'll show you the kind of cur I am."

Forsythe turned, saw the anger in Denman's eyes, and promptly shed his coat.

It was a short fight, of one round only. Each fought courageously, and with such fistic skill as schoolboys acquire, and each was equal to the other in strength; but one possessed about an inch longer reach than the other, which decided the battle.

Denman, with nose bleeding and both eyes closing, went down at last, and could not arise, nor even see the necessity of rising. But soon his brain cleared, and he staggered to his feet, his head throbbing viciously and his face and clothing smeared with blood from his nose, to see between puffed eyelids the erect figure of Forsythe swaggering around a distant corner. He stanched the blood with his handkerchief, but as there was not a brook, a ditch, or a puddle in the neighborhood, he could only go home as he was, trusting that he would meet no one.

"Licked!" he muttered. "For the first time in my life, too! What'll the old gentleman and mother say?"

What the father and mother might say, or what they did say, has no part in this story; but what another person said may have a place and value, and will be given here. This person was the only one he met before reaching home—a very small person, about thirteen years old, with big gray eyes and long dark ringlets, who ran across the street to look at him.

"Why, Billie Denman!" she cried, shocked and anxious. "What has happened to you? Run over?"

"No, Florrie," he answered, painfully. "I've been licked. I had a fight."

"But don't you know it's wrong to fight, Billie?"

"Maybe," answered Denman, trying to get more blood from his face to the already saturated handkerchief. "But we all do wrong—sometimes."

The child planted herself directly before him, and looked chidingly into his discolored and disfigured face.

"Billie Denman," she said, shaking a small finger at him, "of course I'm sorry, but, if you have been fighting when you know it is wrong, why—why, it served you right."

Had he not been aching in every joint, his nose, his lips, and his eyes, this unjust speech might have amused him. As it was he answered testily:

"Florence Fleming, you're only a kid yet, though the best one I know; and if I should tell you the name I was called and which brought on the fight, you would not understand. But you'll grow up some day, and then you will understand. Now, remember this fight, and when some woman, or possibly some man, calls you a—a cat, you'll feel like fighting, too."

"But I wouldn't mind," she answered, firm in her position. "Papa called me a kitten to-day, and I didn't get mad."

"Well, Florrie," he said, wearily, "I won't try to explain. I'm going away before long, and perhaps I won't come back again. But if I do, there'll be another fight."

"Going away, Billie!" she cried in alarm. "Where to?"

"To Annapolis. I may stay, or I may come back. I don't know."

"And you are going away, and you don't know that you'll come back! Oh, Billie, I'm sorry. I'm sorry you got licked, too. Who did it? I hate him. Who licked you, Billie?"

"Never mind, Florrie. He'll tell the news, and you'll soon know who he is."

He walked on, but the child headed him and faced him. There were tears in the gray eyes.

"And you're going away, Billie!" she exclaimed again. "When are you going?"

"I don't know," he answered. "Whenever I am sent for. If I don't see you again, good-by, Florrie girl." He stooped to kiss her, but straightened up, remembering the condition of his face.

"But I will see you again," she declared. "I will, I will. I'll come to your house. And, Billie—I'm sorry I scolded you, really I am."

He smiled ruefully. "Never mind that, Florrie; you always scolded me, you know, and I'm used to it."

"But only when you did wrong, Billie," she answered, gravely, "and somehow I feel that this time you have not done wrong. But I won't scold the next time you *really* do wrong. I promise."

"Oh, yes, you will, little girl. It's the privilege and prerogative of your sex."

He patted her on the head and went on, leaving her staring, open-eyed and tearful. She was the child of a neighbor; he had mended her dolls, soothed her griefs, and protected her since infancy, but she was only as a small sister to him.

While waiting for orders to Annapolis, he saw her many times, but she did not change to him. She changed, however; she had learned the name of his assailant, and through her expressed hatred for him, and through her sympathy for Billie as the disfigurements left his face, she passed the border between childhood and womanhood.

When orders came, he stopped at her home, kissed her good-by, and went to Annapolis, leaving her sad-eyed and with quivering lips.

And he did not come back.

CHAPTER I

She was the largest, fastest, and latest thing in seagoing destroyers, and though the specifications called for but thirty-six knots' speed, she had made thirty-eight on her trial trip, and later, under careful nursing by her engineers, she had increased this to forty knots an hour—five knots faster than any craft afloat—and, with a clean bottom, this speed could be depended upon at any time it was needed.

She derived this speed from six water-tube boilers, feeding at a pressure of three hundred pounds live steam to five turbine engines working three screws, one high-pressure turbine on the center shaft, and four low-pressure on the wing shafts. Besides these she possessed two "astern" turbines and two cruising turbines—all four on the wing shafts.

She made steam with oil fuel, there being no coal on board except for heating and cooking, and could carry a hundred and thirty tons of it, which gave her a cruising radius of about two thousand miles; also, with "peace tanks" filled, she could steam three thousand miles without replenishing. This would carry her across the Atlantic at thirteen knots' speed, but if she was in a hurry, using all turbines, she would exhaust her oil in two days.

When in a hurry, she was a spectacle to remember. Built on conventional lines, she showed at a mile's distance nothing but a high bow and four short funnels over a mighty bow wave that hid the rest of her long, dark-hued hull, and a black, horizontal cloud of smoke that stretched astern half a mile before the wind could catch and rend it.

She carried four twenty-one-inch torpedo tubes and a battery of six twelve-pounder, rapid-fire guns; also, she carried two large searchlights and a wireless equipment of seventy miles reach, the aërials of which stretched from the truck of her short signal mast aft to a short pole at the taffrail.

Packed with machinery, she was a "hot box," even when at rest, and when in action a veritable bake oven. She had hygienic air space below decks for about a dozen men, and this number could handle her; but she carried berths and accommodations for sixty.

Her crew was not on board, however. Newly scraped and painted in the dry dock, she had been hauled out, stored, and fueled by a navy-yard gang, and now lay at the dock, ready for sea—ready for her draft of men in the morning, and with no one on board for the night but the executive officer, who, with something on his mind, had elected to remain, while the captain and other commissioned officers went ashore for the night.

Four years at the Naval Academy, a two years' sea cruise, and a year of actual service had made many changes in Denman. He was now twenty-five, an ensign, but, because of his position as executive, bearing the complimentary title of lieutenant.

He was a little taller and much straighter and squarer of shoulder than when he had gone to the academy. He had grown a trim mustache, and the sun and winds of many seas had tanned his face to the color of his eyes; which were of a clear brown, and only in repose did they now show the old-time preponderance of white beneath the brown.

In action these eyes looked out through two slits formed by nearly parallel eyelids, and with the tightly closed lips and high arching eyebrows—sure sign of the highest and best form of physical and moral courage—they gave his face a sort of "take care" look, which most men heeded.

Some women would have thought him handsome, some would not; it all depended upon the impression they made on him, and the consequent look in his eyes.

At Annapolis he had done well; he was the most popular man of his class, had won honors from his studies and fist fights from his fellows, while at sea he had shown a reckless disregard for his life, in such matters as bursting flues, men overboard, and other casualties of seafaring, that brought him many type-written letters from Washington, a few numbers of advancement, and the respect and admiration of all that knew or had heard of him.

His courage, like Mrs. Cæsar's morals, was above suspicion. Yet there was one man in the world who was firmly convinced that Lieutenant Denman had a yellow streak in him, and that man was Denman himself.

He had never been home since his departure for Annapolis. He had promised a small girl that if he came back there would be another fight, in which, as he mentally vowed, he would redeem himself. In this he had been sincere, but as the months at the academy went on, with the unsettled fight still in the future, his keen resentment died away, leaving in its place a sense of humiliation and chagrin.

He still meant to go back, however, and would have done so when vacation came; but a classmate invited him to his home, and there he went, glad of the reprieve from an embarrassing, and, as it seemed to him now, an undignified conflict with a civilian. But the surrender brought its sting, and his self-respect lessened.

At the next vacation he surrendered again, and the sting began eating into his soul. He thought of the overdue redemption he had promised himself at all times and upon all occasions, but oftenest just before going to sleep, when the mental picture of Jack Forsythe swaggering around the corner, while *he* lay conquered and helpless on the ground, would accompany him through his dreams, and be with him when he wakened in the morning.

It became an obsession, and very soon the sudden thought of his coming fight with Forsythe brought the uplift of the heart and the slight choking sensation that betokened nothing but fear.

He would not admit it at first, but finally was compelled to. Honest with himself as he was with others, he finally yielded in the mental struggle, and accepted the dictum of his mind. He was afraid to fight Jack Forsythe, with no reference to, or regard for, his standing as an officer and a gentleman.

But now, it seemed, all this was to leave him. A month before, he had thought strongly of his child friend Florrie, and, with nothing to do one afternoon, he had written her a letter—a jolly, rollicking letter, filled with masculine colloquialisms and friendly endearments, such as he had bestowed upon her at home; and it was the dignity of her reply—received that day—with the contents of the letter, which was the "something on his mind" that kept him aboard.

His cheeks burned as he realized that she was now about twenty years old, a young lady, and that his letter to her had been sadly conceived and much out of place. But the news in the letter, which began with "Dear Sir," and ended with "Sincerely yours," affected him most. It read:

> "I presume you know that your enemy, Jack Forsythe, took his disappointment so keenly that he never amounted to much at home, and about two years ago enlisted in the navy. This relieves you, as father tells me, from the necessity of thrashing him—as you declared you would. Officers and enlisted men cannot fight, he said, as the officer has the advantage, and can always order the man to jail. I thank you very much for remembering me after all these years—in fact, I shall never forget your kindness."

His cheeks and ears had burned all day, and when his fellow officers had gone, and he was alone, he reread the letter.

"Sarcasm and contempt between every line," he muttered. "She expected me—the whole town expected me—to come back and lick that fellow. Well"—his eyelids became rigidly parallel—"I'll do it. When I find him, I'll get shore leave for both of us, take him home, and square the account."

This resolution did him good; the heat left his cheek, and the sudden jump of the heart did not come with the occasional thought of the task. Gradually the project took form; he would learn what ship Forsythe was in, get transferred to her, and when in port arrange the shore leave. He could not fight him in the navy, but as man to man, in civilian's clothing in the town park, he would fight him and thrash him before the populace.

It was late when he had finished the planning. He lighted a last cigar, and sauntered around the deck until the cigar was consumed. Then he went to his room and turned in, thinking of the caustic words of Miss Florrie, forgiving her the while, and wondering how she looked—grown up.

They were pleasant thoughts to go to sleep on, but sleep did not come. It was an intensely hot, muggy night, and the mosquitoes were thick. He tried another room, then another, and at last, driven out of the wardroom by the pests, he took refuge in the steward's pantry, and spreading his blanket on the floor, went to sleep on it.

CHAPTER II

He slept soundly, and as he slept the wind blew up from the east, driving the mosquitoes to cover and bringing with it a damp, impenetrable fog that sank down over the navy yard and hid sentry from sentry, compelling them to count their steps as they paced.

They were scattered through the yard, at various important points, one at the gangway of each ship at the docks, others at corners and entrances to the different walks that traversed the green lawn, and others under the walls of the huge naval prison.

One of these, whose walk extended from corner to corner, heard something, and paused often to listen intently, his eyes peering around into the fog. But the sound was not repeated while he listened—only as his footfalls sounded soggily on the damp path were they punctuated by this still, small sound, that he could not localize or remember.

If asked, he might have likened it to the rustling of paper, or the sound of a cat's claws digging into a carpet.

But at last it ceased, and he went back and forth many times without hearing it; then, when about half-way from corner to corner, a heavy body came down from above, landing on his head and shoulders and bearing him to earth, while his rifle was knocked from his hand and big fingers clutched his throat.

He struggled and endeavored to call out. But the grip on his throat was too strong, and finally he quieted, his last flicker of consciousness cognizing other dropping bodies and the muttered and whispered words of men.

So much for this sentry.

"I know the way," whispered the garroter, and a few gathered around him. "We'll make a bee line for the dock and avoid 'em. Then, if we can't find a boat, we'll swim for it. It's the only way."

"Right," whispered another; "fall in here, behind Jenkins—all of you."

The whispered word was passed along, and in single file the dark-brown bodies, each marked on knee and elbow with a white number, followed the leader, Jenkins. He led them across the green, around corners where sentries were not, and down to the dock where lay the destroyer.

Here was a sentry, pacing up and down; but so still was their approach that he did not see them until they were right upon him.

"Who goes—" he started, but the challenge was caught in his throat. He, too, was choked until consciousness almost left him; then the stricture was relaxed while they questioned him.

"Got a boat around here?" hissed Jenkins in his ear. "Whisper—don't speak."

"No," gasped the sentry, unable to speak louder had he dared.

"How many men are aboard the destroyer?" was asked.

"None now. Crew joins in the morning."

"Nobody on board, you say? Lie quiet. If you raise a row, I'll drop you overboard. Come here, you fellows."

They closed about him, thirteen in all, and listened to his project. He was a pilot of the bay. How many machinists were there in the party? Four claimed the rating.

"Right enough," said Jenkins. "We'll run her out. She's oil fuel, as I understand. You can fire up in ten minutes, can't you? Good. Come on. Wait, though."

Jenkins, with his grip of steel, was equal to the task of tearing a strip from his brown prison jacket, and with this he securely gagged the poor sentry. Another strip from another jacket bound his hands behind him, and still another secured him to a mooring cleat, face upward. This done, they silently filed aboard, and spread about through the interior. The sentry had spoken truly, they agreed, when they mustered together. There was no one on board, and the machinists reported plenty of oil fuel.

Soon the fires were lighted, and the indicator began to move, as the boilers made steam. They did not wait for full pressure. Jenkins had spread out a chart in the pilot-house, and when the engines could turn over he gave the word. Lines were taken in except a spring to back on; then this was cast off, and the long, slim hull moved almost silently away from the dock.

Jenkins steered by the light of a match held over the compass until there was steam enough to turn the dynamos, then the electrics were turned on in the pilot-house, engine room, and side-light boxes—by which time the dock was out of sight in the fog, and they dared speak in articulate words. Their language was profane but joyous, and their congratulations hearty and sincere.

A table knife is an innocent and innocuous weapon, but two table knives are not, for one can be used against the other so skillfully as to form a fairly good hack saw, with which prison bars may be sawed. The sawing of steel bars was the sound that the sentry had heard mingling with his footfalls.

Jenkins, at the wheel, called to the crowd. "Take the wheel, one of you," he ordered. "I've just rounded the corner. Keep her sou'east, half south for a mile. I'll be here, then. I want to rig the log over the stern."

The man answered, and Jenkins departed with the boat's patent log. Down in the engine and boiler rooms were the four machinists—engineers, they would be called in merchant steamers—and under their efforts the engines turned faster, while a growing bow wave spread from each side of the sharp stem.

The fog was still thick, so thick that the fan-shaped beams from the side lights could not pierce it as far as the bow, and the forward funnel was barely visible—a magnified black stump.

Jenkins was back among them soon, remarking that she was making twenty knots already. Then he slowed down, ordered the lead hove, each side, and ringing full speed, quietly took the wheel, changing the course again to east, quarter north, and ordering a man aloft to keep a lookout in the thinner fog for lights ahead.

In a few minutes the man reported—a fixed white light four points off the starboard bow, and a little later a fixed white-and-red flashlight two points off the port bow.

"Good," grunted Jenkins. "I know just where I am. Come down from aloft," he called, "and watch out for buoys. I'm going out the South and Hypocrite Channels."

Then a dull boom rang out from astern, followed by another and another, and Jenkins laughed.

"They've found that sentry," he said, "and have telephoned Fort Independence; but it's no good. They've only got salute guns. We passed that fort twenty minutes ago."

"Any others?" they asked.

"Fort Warren, down on the Narrows. That's why I'm going out through the Hypocrite. Keep your eyes peeled for buoys, you ginks, and keep those leads going."

Calm and imperturbable, a huge, square-faced giant of a man, Jenkins naturally assumed the leadership of this band of jail-breakers. The light from the binnacle illuminated a countenance of rugged yet symmetrical features, stamped with prison pallor, but also stamped with a stronger imprint of refinement. A man palpably out of place, no doubt. A square peg in a round hole; a man with every natural attribute of a master of men. Some act of rage or passion, perhaps, some non-adjustment to an unjust environment, had sent him to the naval prison, to escape and become a pirate; for that was the legal status of all.

Soon the wind shifted and the fog cleared to seaward, but still held its impenetrable wall between them and the town. Then they turned on both searchlights, and saw buoys ahead, to starboard and port.

Jenkins boasted a little. "I've run these channels for years," he said, "and I know them as I know the old backyard at home. Hello, what's up?"

A man had run to the pilot-house door in great excitement.

"An officer aboard," he whispered. "I was down looking for grub, and saw him. He's been asleep."

"Take the wheel," said Jenkins, calmly. "Keep her as she goes, and leave that black buoy to starboard." Then he stepped out on deck.

CHAPTER III

Seamen, officers as well as men, accustomed to "watch and watch," of four hours' alternate duty and sleep, usually waken at eight bells, even when sure of an all night's sleep. It was long after midnight when Denman had gone to sleep on the pantry floor, and the slight noise of getting under way did not arouse him; but when eight bells came around again, he sat up, confused, not conscious that he had been called, but dimly realizing that the boat was at sea, and that he was culpable in not being on deck.

The crew had come, no doubt, and he had over-slept. He did not immediately realize that it was still dark, and that if the crew had come the steward would have found him.

He dressed hurriedly in his room, and went on deck, spying a fleeing man in brown mounting the steps ahead of him, and looked around. Astern was a fog bank, and ahead the open sea, toward which the boat was charging at full speed. As he looked, a man came aft and faced him. Denman expected that he would step aside while he passed, but he did not; instead he blocked his way.

"Are you an officer of this boat, sir?" asked the man, respectfully.

"I am. What do you want?"

"Only to tell you, sir, that she is not now under the control of the Navy Department. My name is Jenkins, and with twelve others I escaped from the prison to-night, and took charge of this boat for a while. We did not know you were on board."

Denman started back and felt for his pocket pistol, but it was in his room. However, Jenkins had noticed the movement, and immediately sprang upon him, bearing him against the nearest ventilator, and pinioning his arms to his side.

"None o' that, sir," said the giant, sternly. "Are there any others on board besides yourself?"

"Not that I know of," answered Denman, with forced calmness. "The crew had not joined when I went to sleep. What do you intend to do with me?"

He had seen man after man approach from forward, and now a listening group surrounded him.

"That's for you to decide, sir. If you will renounce your official position, we will put you on parole; if you will not, you will be confined below decks until we are ready to leave this craft. All we want is our liberty."

"How do you intend to get it? Every warship in the world will chase this boat."

"There is not a craft in the world that can catch her," rejoined Jenkins; "but that is beside the point. Will you go on parole, sir, or in irons?"

"How many are there in this party?"

"Thirteen—all told; and that, too, is beside the point. Answer quickly, sir. I am needed at the wheel."

"I accept your offer," said Denman, "because I want fresh air, and nothing will be gained in honor and integrity in my resisting you. However, I shall not assist you in any way. Even if I see you going to destruction, I shall not warn you."

"That is enough, sir," answered Jenkins. "You give your word of honor, do you, as an American naval officer, not to interfere with the working of this boat or the movements of her crew until after we have left her?"

"I give you my word," said the young officer, not without some misgivings. "You seem to be in command. What shall I call you?"

"Herbert Jenkins, seaman gunner."

"Captain Jenkins," growled a man, and others repeated it.

"Captain Jenkins," responded Denman, "I greet you cordially. My name is William Denman, ensign in the United States Navy, and formally executive officer of this boat."

A suppressed exclamation came from the group; a man stepped forward, peered closely into Denman's face, and stepped back.

"None o' that, Forsythe," said Jenkins, sternly. "We're all to treat Mr. Denman with respect. Now, you fellows, step forward, and introduce yourselves. I know only a few of you by name."

Jenkins went to the wheel, picked up the buoys played upon by the searchlights, and sent the man to join the others, as one after another faced Denman and gave his name.

"Guess you know me, Mr. Denman," said Forsythe, the first to respond.

"I know you, Forsythe," answered Denman, hot and ashamed; for at the sight and sound of him the old heart jump and throat ache had returned. He fought it down, however, and listened to the names as the men gave them:

William Hawkes, seaman; George Davis, seaman; John Kelly, gunner's mate; Percy Daniels, ship's cook, and Thomas Billings, wardroom steward.

John Casey and Frank Munson, they explained, were at the searchlights forward; and down below were the four machinists, Riley, Sampson, King, and Dwyer.

Denman politely bowed his acknowledgments, and asked the ratings of the searchlight men.

"Wireless operators," they answered.

"You seem well-equipped and well-chosen men," he said, "to run this boat, and to lead the government a lively dance for a while. But until the end comes, I hope we will get on together without friction."

In the absence of the masterful Jenkins, they made embarrassed replies—all but Forsythe, who remained silent. For no sudden upheaval and reversing of relations will eliminate the enlisted man's respect for an officer.

Daylight had come, and Jenkins, having cleared the last of the buoys, called down the men at the searchlights.

"You're wireless sharps, aren't you?" he asked. "Go down to the apparatus, and see if you can pick up any messages. The whole coast must be aroused."

The two obeyed him, and went in search of the wireless room. Soon one returned. "The air's full o' talk," he said. "Casey's at the receiver, still listening, but I made out only a few words like 'Charleston,' 'Brooklyn,' 'jail,' 'pirates,' 'Pensacola,' and one phrasing 'Send in pursuit.'"

"The open sea for us," said Jenkins, grimly, "until we can think out a plan. Send one of those sogers to the wheel."

A "soger"—one who, so far, had done no work—relieved him, and he mustered his men, all but two in the engine room, to a council amidships. Briefly he stated the situation, as hinted at by Denman and verified by the wireless messages. Every nation in the world would send its cruisers after them, and no civilized country would receive them.

There was but one thing to do under the circumstances—make for the wild coast of Africa, destroy the boat, and land, each man to work out his future as he could.

After a little parley they assented, taking no thought of fuel or food, and trusting to Jenkins' power to navigate. Then, it being broad daylight, they raided the boat's stores for clothing, and discarded their prison suits of brown for the blue of the navy—Jenkins, the logical commander, donning the uniform of the captain, as large a man as himself.

Next they chose their bunks in the forecastle, and, as they left it for the deck, Jenkins picked up a bright object from the floor, and absently put it in his trousers pocket.

CHAPTER IV

The boat was now charging due east at full speed, out into the broad Atlantic, and, as the full light of the day spread over the sea, a few specks and trails of smoke astern showed themselves; but whether or not they were pursuing craft that had crept close in the darkness while they were making steam could not be determined; for they soon sank beneath the horizon.

Assured of immediate safety, Jenkins now stationed his crew. Forsythe was a seaman; he and Hawkes, Davis, and Kelly, the gunner's mate, would comprise the deck force. Riley, Sampson, King, and Dwyer, all machinists, would attend to the engine and boilers. Casey and Munson, the two wireless operators, would attend to their department, while Daniels and Billings, the cook and steward, would cook and serve the meals.

There would be no officers, Jenkins declared. All were to stand watch, and work faithfully and amicably for the common good; and all disputes were to be referred to him. To this they agreed, for, though many there were of higher comparative rating in the navy, Jenkins had a strong voice, a dominating personality, and a heavy fist.

But Jenkins had his limitations, as came out during the confab. He could not navigate; he had been an expert pilot of Boston Bay before joining the navy, but in the open sea he was as helpless as any.

"However," he said, in extenuation, "we only need to sail about southeast to reach the African coast, and when we hit it we'll know it." So the course was changed, and soon they sat down to their breakfast; such a meal as they had not tasted in years—wardroom "grub," every mouthful.

Denman was invited, and, as he was a prisoner on parole, was not too dignified to accept, though he took no part in the hilarious conversation. But neither did Forsythe.

Denman went to his room, locked up his private papers, and surrendered his revolver to Jenkins, who declined it; he then put it with his papers and returned to the deck, seating himself in a deck chair on the quarter. The watch below had gone down, and those on deck, under Jenkins, who stood no watch, busied themselves in the necessary cleaning up of decks and stowing below of the fenders the boat had worn at the dock.

Forsythe had gone below, and Denman was somewhat glad in his heart to be free of him until he had settled his mind in regard to his attitude toward him.

Manifestly he, a prisoner on parole, could not seek a conflict with him. On the contrary, should Forsythe seek it, by word or deed, he could not meet him without breaking his parole, which would bring him close confinement.

Then, too, that prospective fight and vindication before Miss Florrie and his townsmen seemed of very small importance compared with the exigency at hand—the stealing by jail-breakers of the navy's best destroyer and one of its officers.

His duty was to circumvent those fellows, and return the boat to the government. To accomplish this he must be tactful and diplomatic, deferring action until the time should come when he could safely ask to be released from parole; and with regard to this he was glad that Forsythe, though as evil-eyed as before, and with an additional truculent expression of the face, had thus far shown him no incivility. He was glad, too, because in his heart there were no revengeful thoughts about Forsythe—nothing but thoughts of a duty to himself that had been sadly neglected.

Thus tranquilized, he lit a cigar and looked around the horizon.

A speck to the north caught his eye, and as he watched, it became a spot, then a tangible silhouette—a battle-ship, though of what country he could not determine.

It was heading on a course that would intercept their own, and in a short time, at the speed they were making, the destroyer would be within range of her heavy guns, one shell from which could break the frail craft in two.

Jenkins and his crowd were busy, the man at the wheel was steering by compass and looking ahead, and it was the wireless operator on watch—Casey—who rushed on deck, looked at the battle-ship, and shouted to Jenkins.

"Don't you see that fellow?" he yelled, excitedly. "I heard him before I saw him. He asked: 'What ship is that?'"

Jenkins looked to the north, just in time to see a tongue of red dart from a casemate port; then, as the bark of the gun came down the wind, a spurt of water lifted from the sea about a hundred yards ahead.

"Port your wheel—hard over," yelled Jenkins, running forward. The destroyer swung to the southward, showing her stern to the battle-ship, and increasing her speed as the engine-room staff nursed the oil feed and the turbines. Black smoke—unconsumed carbon that even the blowers could not ignite—belched up from the four short funnels, and partly hid her from the battle-ship's view.

But, obscure though she was, she could not quite hide herself in her smoke nor could her speed carry her faster than the twelve-inch shells that now came plowing through the air. They fell close, to starboard and to port, and a few came perilously near to the stern; but none hit or exploded, and soon they were out of range and the firing ceased, the battle-ship heading to the west.

Jenkins came aft, and looked sternly at Denman, still smoking his cigar.

"Did you see that fellow before we did?" he asked.

"I did," answered Denman, returning his stare.

"Why didn't you sing out? If we're sunk, you drown, too, don't you?"

"You forget, Captain Jenkins, that I accepted my parole on condition that I should neither interfere with you nor assist you."

"But your life—don't you value that?"

"Not under some conditions. If I cannot emerge from this adventure with credit and honor intact, I prefer death. Do you understand?"

Jenkins' face worked visibly, as anger left it and wondering doubt appeared. Then his countenance cleared, and he smiled.

"You're right, sir. I understand now. But you know what we mean to do, don't you? Make the African coast and scatter. You can stand for that, can't you?"

"Not unless I have to. But you will not reach the coast. You will be hunted down and caught before then."

Jenkins' face clouded again. "And what part will you play if that comes?" he asked.

"No part, active or resistant, unless first released from parole. But if I ask for that release, it will be at a time when I am in greater danger than now, I promise you that."

"Very well, sir. Ask for it when you like." And Jenkins went forward.

The course to the southeast was resumed, but in half an hour two other specks on the southern horizon resolved into scout cruisers heading their way, and they turned to the east, still rushing at full speed.

They soon dropped the scouts, however, but were again driven to the north by a second battle-ship that shelled their vicinity for an hour before they got out of range.

It was somewhat discouraging; but, as darkness closed down, they once more headed their course, and all night they charged along at forty knots, with lights extinguished, but with every man's eyes searching the darkened horizon for other lights. They dodged a few, but daylight brought to view three cruisers ahead and to port that showed unmistakable hostility in the shape of screaming shells and solid shot.

Again they charged to the north, and it was mid-day before the cruisers were dropped. They were French, as all knew by their build.

Though there was no one navigating the boat, Denman, in view of future need of it, took upon himself the winding of the chronometers; and the days went on, Casey and Munson reporting messages sent from shore to ship; battle-ships, cruisers, scouts, and destroyers appearing and disappearing, and their craft racing around the Atlantic like a hunted fox.

Jenkins did his best to keep track of the various courses; but, not skilled at "traverse," grew bewildered at last, and frankly intimated that he did not know where they were.

CHAPTER V

One morning there was a council of war amidships to which Denman was not invited until it had adjourned as a council to become a committee of ways and means. Then they came aft in a body, and asked him to navigate.

"No," said Denman, firmly, rising to his feet and facing them. "I will not navigate unless you surrender this craft to me, and work her back to Boston, where you will return to the prison."

"Well, we won't do that," shouted several, angrily.

"Wait, you fellows," said Jenkins, firmly, "and speak respectfully to an officer, while he acts like one. Mr. Denman, your position need not be changed for the worse. You can command this boat and all hands if you will take us to the African coast."

"My *position* would be changed," answered Denman. "If I command this boat, I take her back to Boston, not to the African coast."

"Very well, sir," said Jenkins, a shade of disappointment on his face. "We cannot force you to join us, or help us; so—well, come forward, you fellows."

"Say, Jenkins!" broke in Forsythe. "You're doing a lot of dictating here, and I've wondered why! Who gave you the right to decide? You admit your incompetency; you can't navigate, can you?"

"No, I cannot," retorted Jenkins, flushing. "Neither can I learn, at my age. Neither can you."

"I can't?" stormed Forsythe, his eyes glaring white as he glanced from Jenkins to Denman and back. "Well, I'll tell you I can. I tell you I haven't forgotten all I learned at school, and that I can pick up navigation without currying favor from this milk-fed thief. You know well"—he advanced and held his fist under Denman's face—"that I won the appointment you robbed me of, and that the uniform you wear belongs to me."

At the first word Denman's heart gave the old, familiar thump and jump into his throat. Then came a quick reaction—a tingling at the hair roots, an opening of the eyes, followed by their closing to narrow slits, and, with the full weight of his body behind, he crashed his fist into Forsythe's face, sending him reeling and whirling to the deck.

He would have followed, to repeat the punishment, but the others stopped him. In an intoxication of ecstasy at the unexpected adjustment of his mental poise, he struck out again and again, and floored three or four of them before Jenkins backed him against the companion.

"He's broken his parole—put him in irons—chuck him overboard," they chorused, and closed around him threateningly, though Forsythe, his hand to his face, remained in the background.

"That's right, sir," said Jenkins, holding Denman at the end of one long arm. "You have violated your agreement with us, and we must consider you a prisoner under confinement."

"All right," panted Denman. "Iron me, if you like, but first form a ring and let me thrash that dog. He thrashed me at school when I was the smaller and weaker. I've promised him a licking. Let me give it to him."

"No, sir, we will not," answered Jenkins. "Things are too serious for fighting. You must hand me that pistol and any arms you may have, and be confined to the wardroom. And you, Forsythe," he said, looking at the victim, "if you can master navigation, get busy and make good. And you other ginks get out of here. Talk it over among yourselves, and if you agree with Forsythe that I'm not in command here, get busy, too, and I'll overrule you."

He released Denman, moved around among them, looking each man steadily in the face, and they straggled forward.

"Now, sir," he said to Denman, "come below."

Denman followed him down the companion and into the wardroom. Knowing the etiquette as well as Jenkins, he led him to his room, opened his desk and all receptacles, and Jenkins secured the revolver.

"Is this all you have, sir?" asked Jenkins.

"Why do you ask that?" answered Denman, hotly. "As a prisoner, why may I not lie to you?"

"Because, Mr. Denman, I think you wouldn't. However, I won't ask; I'll search this room and the whole boat, confiscating every weapon. You will have the run of your stateroom and the wardroom, but will not be allowed on deck. And you will not be annoyed, except perhaps to lend Forsythe any books he may want. He's the only educated man in the crowd."

"Better send him down under escort," responded Denman, "if you want him back."

"Yes, yes, that'll be attended to. I've no part in your private affairs, sir; but you gave him one good one, and that ought to be enough for a while. If you tackle him again, you'll have the whole bunch at you. Better let well enough alone."

Denman sat down in his room, and Jenkins departed. Soon he came back with three others—the steadiest men of the crew—and they made a systematic search for weapons in the wardroom and all staterooms opening from it. Then they locked the doors leading to the captain's quarters and the doors leading forward, and went on deck, leaving Denman a prisoner, free to concoct any antagonistic plans that came to his mind.

But he made none, as yet; he was too well-contented and happy, not so much in being released from a somewhat false position as a prisoner under parole as in the lifting of the burden of the years, the shame, humiliation, chagrin, and anger dating from the school-day thrashing. He smiled as he recalled the picture of Forsythe staggering along the deck. The smile became a grin, then a soft chuckle, ending in joyous laughter; then he applied the masculine leveler of all emotion—he smoked.

The staterooms—robbed of all weapons—were left open, and, as each room contained a deadlight, or circular window, he had a view of the sea on each beam, but nothing ahead or astern; nor could he hear voices on deck unless pitched in a high key, for the men, their training strong upon them, remained forward.

There was nothing on either horizon at present. The boat was storming along to the southward, as he knew by a glance at the "telltale" overhead, and all seemed well with the runaways until a sudden stopping of the engines roused him up, to peer out the deadlights, and speculate as to what was ahead.

But he saw nothing, from either side, and strained his ears for sounds from the deck. There was excitement above. Voices from forward came to him, muffled, but angry and argumentative. They grew louder as the men came aft, and soon he could distinguish Jenkins' loud profanity, drowning the protests of the others.

"She's afire and her boats are burned. There's a woman aboard. I tell you we're not going to let 'em drown. Over with that boat, or I'll stretch some o' you out on deck— Oh, you will, Forsythe?"

Then came a thud, as of the swift contact of two hard objects, and a sound as of a bag of potatoes falling to the deck, which told Denman that some one had been knocked down.

"Go ahead with the machine, Sampson," said Jenkins again, "and forward, there. Port your wheel, and steer for the yacht."

Denman sprang to a starboard deadlight and looked. He could now see, slantwise through the thick glass, a large steam yacht, afire from her mainmast to her bow, and on the still intact quarter-deck a woman frantically beckoning. Men, nearer the fire, seemed to be fighting it.

The picture disappeared from view as the boat, under the impulse of her engines and wheel, straightened to a course for the wreck. Soon the engines stopped again, and Denman heard the sounds of a boat being lowered. He saw this boat leave the side, manned by Hawkes, Davis, Forsythe, and Kelly, but it soon left his field of vision, and he waited.

Then came a dull, coughing, prolonged report, and the voices on deck broke out.

"Blown up!" yelled Jenkins. "She's sinking forward! She's cut in two! Where are they? Where's the woman? That wasn't powder, Riley. What was it?"

"Steam," answered the machinist, coolly. "They didn't rake the fires until too late, I suppose, and left the engine under one bell possibly, while they steered 'fore the wind with the preventer tiller."

"They've got somebody. Can you see? It's the woman! Blown overboard. See any one else? I don't."

Riley did not answer, and soon Jenkins spoke again.

"They're coming back. Only the woman—only the woman out o' the whole crowd."

"They'd better hurry up," responded Riley. "What's that over to the nor'ard?"

"Nothing but a tramp," said Jenkins, at length. "But we don't want to be interviewed. Bear a hand, you fellows," he shouted. "Is the woman dead?"

"No—guess not," came the answer, through the small deadlight. "Fainted away since we picked her up. Burned or scalded, somewhat."

CHAPTER VI

Denman saw the boat for a moment or two as it came alongside, and noticed the still form of the woman in the stern sheets, her face hidden by a black silk neckerchief. Then he could only know by the voices that they were lifting her aboard and aft to the captain's quarters. But he was somewhat surprised to see the door that led to these quarters opened by Jenkins, who beckoned him.

"We've picked up a poor woman, sir," he said, "and put her in here. Now, we're too busy on deck to 'tend to her, Mr. Denman, and then—we don't know how; but—well, you're an educated man, and a gentleman. Would you mind? I've chased the bunch out, and I won't let 'em bother you. It's just an extension of your cruising radius."

"Certainly," said Denman. "I'll do what I can for her."

"All right, sir. I'll leave this door open, but I must lock the after companion."

He went on deck by the wardroom stairs, while Denman passed through to the woman. She lay on a transom, dripping water from her clothing to the carpet, and with the black cloth still over her face; but, on hearing his footsteps, she removed it, showing a countenance puffed and crimson from the scalding of the live steam that had blown her overboard. Then, groaning pitifully, she sat up, and looked at him through swollen eyelids.

"What is it?" she exclaimed, weakly. "What has happened? Where is father?"

"Madam," said Denman, gently, "you have been picked up from a steam yacht which exploded her boilers. Are you in pain? What can I do for you?"

"I don't know. Yes, I am in pain. My face."

"Wait, and I will get you what I can from the medicine-chest."

Denman explored the surgeon's quarters, and returned with bandages and a mixture of linseed oil and lime water. He gently laved and bound the poor woman's face, and then led her to the captain's berth.

"Go in," he said. "Take off your wet clothes, and put on his pajamas. Here they are"—he produced them from a locker—"and then turn in. I will be here, and will take care of you."

He departed, and when he saw the wet garments flung out, he gathered them and hung them up to dry. It was all he could do, except to look through the surgeon's quarters for stimulants, which he found. He poured out a strong dose of brandy, which he gave to the woman, and had the satisfaction of seeing her sink into profound slumber; then, returning to the wardroom, he found Jenkins waiting for him.

"I am after a sextant, Mr. Denman," he said, "an almanac—a nautical almanac. Forsythe wants them."

"You must find them yourself, then," answered Denman. "Neither under parole nor confinement will I aid you in any way unless you surrender."

"Nonsense," said Jenkins, impatiently, as he stepped past Denman, and approached a bookcase. "When we're through with the boat you can have her."

He had incautiously turned his back. Denman saw the protruding butt of his pistol in Jenkins' pocket, and, without any formulated plan for the future, only seeing a momentary advantage in the possession of the weapon, pounced on his shoulders, and endeavored to secure it.

But he was not able to; he could only hold on, his arms around Jenkins' neck, while the big sailor hove his huge body from side to side, and, gripping his legs, endeavored to shake him off.

No word was spoken—only their deep breathing attested to their earnestness, and they thrashed around the wardroom like a dog and a cat, Denman, in the latter similitude, in the air most of the time. But he was getting the worst of it, and at last essayed a trick he knew of, taught him in Japan, and to be used as a last resort.

Gripping his legs tightly around the body of Jenkins, he sagged down and pressed the tips of his forefingers into two vulnerable parts of the thick neck, where certain important nerves approach the surface—parts as vulnerable as the heel of Achilles. Still clinging, he mercilessly continued the pressure, while Jenkins swayed back and forth, and finally fell backward to the floor.

Denman immediately secured the pistol; then, panting hard, he examined his victim. Jenkins was breathing with the greatest difficulty, but could not speak or move, and his big eyes glared piteously up at his conqueror. The latter would have ironed him at once, but the irons were forward in the armroom, so he temporarily bound him hand and foot with neckties replevined from his fellow officers' staterooms.

Then, relieving Jenkins of his keys, he went through the forward door to the armroom, from which he removed, not only wrist and leg arms, but every cutlass and service revolver that the boat was stocked with, and a plentiful supply of ammunition.

First properly securing the still inert and helpless Jenkins, he dragged him to a corner, and then stowed the paraphernalia of war in his room, loading as many as a dozen of the heavy revolvers.

He was still without a plan, working under intense excitement, and could only follow impulses, the next of which was to lock the wardroom companion down which Jenkins had come, and to see that the forward door and the after companion were secured. This done, he sat down abreast of his prisoner to watch him, and think it out. There was no change in Jenkins; he still breathed hard, and endeavored unsuccessfully to speak, while his eyes—the angry glare gone from them—looked up inquiringly.

"Oh, you're all right, Captain Jenkins," said Denman. "You'll breathe easier to-morrow, and in a week, perhaps, you may speak in a whisper; but you are practically deprived from command. So make the best of it."

Jenkins seemed willing to, but this did not solve the problem; there were twelve other recalcitrants on deck who might not be so easily jujutsued into weakness and dumbness.

As the situation cleared, he saw two ways of solving it, one, to remain below, and from the shelter of his room to pot them one by one as they came down; the other, to take the initiative, assert himself on deck behind the menace of cocked revolvers, and overawe them into submission.

The first plan involved hunger, for he could eat nothing not provided by them; the other, a quick and certain ending of the false position he was in—a plan very appealing to his temperament.

He rose to his feet with a final inspection of Jenkins' bonds, and, going to his room, belted and armed himself with three heavy revolvers, then opened the wardroom companion door, and stepped to the deck. No one was in sight, except the man at the wheel, not now steering in the close, armored conning tower, but at the upper wheel on the bridge.

He looked aft, and, spying Denman, gave a shout of warning.

But no one responded, and Denman, with a clear field, advanced forward, looking to the right and left, until he reached the engine-room hatch, down which he peered. Riley's anxious face looked up at him, and farther down was the cringing form of King, his mate of the starboard watch. Denman did not know their names, but he sternly commanded them to come up.

"We can't leave the engines, sir," said Riley, shrinking under the cold argument of two cold, blue tubes pointed at them.

"Shut off your gas, and never mind your engines," commanded Denman. "Come up on deck quietly, or I'll put holes in you."

King shut off the gas, Riley turned a valve that eased off the making steam, and the two appeared before Denman.

"Lie down on deck, the two of you," said Denman, sharply. "Take off your neckerchiefs, and give them to me."

They obeyed him. He took the two squares of black silk—similar to that which had covered the face of the rescued woman, and with them he bound their hands tightly behind their backs.

"Lie still, now," he said, "until I settle matters."

They could rise and move, but could not thwart him immediately. He went forward, and mounted to the bridge.

"How are you heading?" he demanded, with a pistol pointed toward the helmsman.

"South—due south, sir," answered the man—it was Davis, of the starboard watch.

"Leave the wheel. The engine is stopped. Down on deck with you, and take off your neckerchief."

Davis descended meekly, gave him his neckerchief, and was bound as were the others. Then Denman looked for the rest.

So far—good. He had three prisoners on deck and one in the wardroom; the rest were below, on duty or asleep. They were in the forecastle—the crew's quarters—in the wireless room below the bridge, in the galley just forward of the wardroom. Denman had his choice, and decided on the forecastle as the place containing the greatest number. Down the fore-hatch he went, and entered the apartment. A man rolled out of a bunk, and faced him.

"Up with your hands," said Denman, softly. "Up, quickly."

The man's hands went up. "All right, sir," he answered, sleepily and somewhat weakly. "My name's Hawkes, and I haven't yet disobeyed an order from an officer."

"Don't," warned Denman, sharply. "Take off your neckerchief."

Off came the black silk square.

"Wake up the man nearest you. Tie his hands behind his back, and take off his necktie."

It was a machinist named Sampson who was wakened and bound, with the cold, blue tube of Denman's pistol looking at him; and then it was Dwyer, his watch mate, and Munson, the wireless man off duty, ending with old Kelly, the gunner's mate—each tied with the neckerchief of the last man wakened, and Hawkes, the first to surrender, with the neckerchief of Kelly.

"On deck with you all," commanded Denman, and he drove them up the steps to the deck, where they lay down beside Riley, King, and Davis. None spoke or protested. Each felt the inhibition of the presence of a commissioned officer, and Denman might have won—might have secured the rest and brought them under control—had not a bullet sped from the after companion, which, besides knocking his cap from his head, inflicted a glancing wound on his scalp and sent him headlong to the deck.

CHAPTER VII

After the rescue of the woman, all but those on duty had mustered forward near the bridge, Jenkins with a pair of binoculars to his eyes inspecting a receding steamer on the horizon, the others passing comments. All had agreed that she was a merchant craft—the first they had met at close quarters—but not all were agreed that she carried no wireless equipment. Jenkins, even with the glasses, could not be sure, but he *was* sure of one thing, he asserted. Even though the steamer had recognized and reported their position, it made little difference.

"Well," said Forsythe, "if she can report us, why can't we? Why can't we fake a report—send out a message that we've been seen a thousand miles north?"

"That's a good idea," said Casey, the wireless man off duty. "We needn't give any name—only a jumble of letters that spell nothing."

"How far can you send with what you've got?" asked Jenkins.

"With those aërials," answered Casey, glancing aloft at the long gridiron of wires, "about fifty miles."

"Not much good, I'm afraid," said Jenkins. "Lord knows where we are, but we're more than fifty miles from land."

"That as far as you can reason?" broke in Forsythe. "Jenkins, you're handy at a knockdown, but if you can't use what brain you've got, you'd better resign command here. I don't know who elected you, anyhow."

"Are you looking for more, Forsythe?" asked Jenkins, taking a step toward him. "If you are, you can have it. If not, get down to your studies, and find out where this craft is, so we can get somewhere."

Forsythe, hiding his emotions under a forced grin, retreated toward the fore-hatch.

"I can give you the latitude," he said, before descending, "by a meridian observation this noon. I picked up the method in one lesson this morning. But I tell you fellows, I'm tired of getting knocked down."

Jenkins watched him descend, then said to Casey: "Fake up a message claiming to be from some ship with a jumbled name, as you say, and be ready to send it if he gets our position."

"Then you think well of it?"

"Certainly. Forsythe has brains. The only trouble with him is that he wants to run things too much."

Casey, a smooth-faced, keen-eyed Irish-American, descended to consult with his *confrère*, Munson; and Forsythe appeared, swinging a book. Laying this on the bridge stairs, he passed Jenkins and walked aft.

"Where are you going?" asked the latter.

Forsythe turned, white with rage, and answered slowly and softly:

"Down to the officers' quarters to get a sextant or a quadrant. I found that book on navigation in the pilot-house, but I need the instrument, and a nautical almanac. That is as far as my studies have progressed."

"You stay out of the officers' quarters," said Jenkins. "There's a man there who'll eat you alive if you show yourself. You want a sextant and nautical almanac. Anything else?"

"That is all."

"I'll get them, and, remember, you and the rest are to stay away from the after end of the boat."

Forsythe made no answer as Jenkins passed him on the way aft, but muttered: "Eat me alive? We'll see."

Riley, one of the machinists, appeared from the engine-room hatch and came forward, halting before Forsythe.

"Say," he grumbled, "what call has that big lobster to bullyrag this crowd the way he's been doin'? I heard him just now givin' you hell, and he gave me hell yesterday when I spoke of the short oil."

"Short oil?" queried Forsythe. "Do you mean that——"

"I mean that the oil won't last but a day longer. We've been storming along at forty knots, and eating up oil. What'll we do?"

"God knows," answered Forsythe, reflectively. "Without oil, we stop—in mid-ocean. What then?"

"What then?" queried Riley. "Well, before then we must hold up some craft and get the oil—also grub and water, if I guess right. This bunch is hard on the commissary."

"Riley," said Forsythe, impressively, "will you stand by me?"

"Yes; if you can bring that big chump to terms."

"All right. Talk to your partners. Something must be done—and he can't do it. Wait a little."

As though to verify Riley and uphold him in his contention, Daniels, the cook, came forward from the galley, and said: "Just about one week's whack o' grub and water left. We'll have to go on an allowance." Then he passed on, but was called back.

"One week's grub left?" asked Forsythe. "Sure o' that, Daniels?"

"Surest thing you know. Plenty o' beans and hard-tack; but who wants beans and hard-tack?"

"Have you spoken to Jenkins about it?"

"No, but we meant to. Something's got to be done. Where is he now?"

"Down aft," said Forsythe, reflectively. "What's keeping him?"

Riley sank into the engine room, and Daniels went forward to the forecastle, reappearing before Forsythe had reached a conclusion.

"Come aft with me, Daniels," he said. "Let's find out what's doing."

Together they crept aft, and peered down the wardroom skylight. They saw Denman and Jenkins locked in furious embrace, and watched while Jenkins sank down, helpless and impotent. They saw Denman bind him, disappear from sight, and reappear with the irons, then they listened to his parting lecture to Jenkins.

"Come," said Forsythe, "down below with us, quick."

They descended the galley companion, from which a passage led aft to the petty officers' quarters, which included the armroom, and thence to the forward door of the wardroom. Here they halted, and listened to Denman's movements while he armed himself and climbed the companion stairs. They could also see through the keyhole.

"He's heeled!" cried Forsythe. "Where did he get the guns?"

"Where's the armroom? Hereabouts somewhere. Where is it?"

They hurriedly searched, and found the armroom; it contained cumbersome rifles, cutlasses, and war heads, but no pistols.

"He's removed them all. Can we break in that door?" asked Forsythe, rushing toward the bulkhead.

"No, hold on," said Daniels. "We'll watch from the companion, and when he's forward we'll sneak down the other, and heel ourselves."

"Good."

So, while Denman crept up and walked forward, glancing right and left, the two watched him from the galley hatch, and, after he had bound the two engineers and the helmsman, they slipped aft and descended the wardroom stairs. Here they looked at Jenkins, vainly trying to speak, but ignored him for the present.

They hurried through the quarters, and finally found Denman's room with its arsenal of loaded revolvers. They belted and armed themselves, and carefully climbed the steps just in time to see Denman drive the forecastle contingent to the deck. Then Forsythe, taking careful aim, sent the bullet which knocked Denman unconscious to the deck.

CHAPTER VIII

Forsythe and Daniels ran forward, while Billings, the cook off watch, followed from the galley hatch, and Casey came up from the wireless room. Each asked questions, but nobody answered at once. There were eight bound men lying upon the deck, and these must first be released, which was soon done.

Denman, lying prone with a small pool of blood near his head, was next examined, and pronounced alive—he was breathing, but dazed and shocked; for a large-caliber bullet glancing upon the skull has somewhat the same effect as the blow of a cudgel. He opened his eyes as the men examined them, and dimly heard what they said.

"Now," said Forsythe, when these preliminaries were concluded, "here we are, miles at sea, with short store of oil, according to Riley, and a short store of grub, according to Daniels. What's to be done? Hey? The man who has bossed us so far hasn't seen this, and is now down in the wardroom—knocked out by this brass-buttoned dudeling. What are you going to do, hey?"

Forsythe flourished his pistols dramatically, and glared unspeakable things at the "dudeling" on the deck.

"Well, Forsythe," said old Kelly, the gunner's mate, "you've pretended to be a navigator. What do you say?"

"I say this," declared Forsythe: "I'm not a navigator, but I can be. But I want it understood. There has got to be a leader—a commander. If you fellows agree, I'll master the navigation and take this boat to the African coast. But I want no half-way work; I want my orders to go, just as I give them. Do you agree? You've gone wrong under Jenkins. Take your choice."

"You're right, Forsythe," said Casey, the wireless man of the starboard watch. "Jenkins is too easy—too careless. Take the job, I say."

"Do you all agree?" yelled Forsythe wildly in his excitement.

"Yes, yes," they acclaimed. "Take charge, and get us out o' these seas. Who wants to be locked up?"

"All right," said Forsythe. "Then I'm the commander. Lift that baby down to the skipper's room with the sick woman, and let them nurse each other. Lift Jenkins out of the wardroom, and stow him in a forecastle bunk. Riley, nurse your engines and save oil, but keep the dynamo going for the wireless; and you, Casey, have you got that message cooked up?"

"I have. All I want is the latitude and longitude to send it from."

"I'll give it to you soon. Get busy, now, and do your share. I must study a little."

The meeting adjourned. Denman, still dazed and with a splitting headache, was assisted aft and below to the spare berth in the captain's quarters, where he sank into unconsciousness with the moaning of the stricken woman in his ears.

Casey went down to his partner and his instruments; Riley and King, with their confrères of the other watch, went down to the engines to "nurse them"; and Forsythe, after Jenkins had been lifted out of the wardroom and forward to a forecastle bunk, searched the bookshelves and the desks of the officers, and, finding what he wanted, went forward to study.

He was apt; he was a high-school graduate who only needed to apply himself to produce results. And Forsythe produced them. As he had promised, he took a meridian observation that day, and in half an hour announced the latitude—thirty-five degrees forty minutes north.

"Now, Casey," he called, after he had looked at a track chart. "Got your fake message ready?"

"Only this," answered Casey, scanning a piece of paper. "Listen:

"Stolen destroyer bound north. Latitude so and so, longitude so and so."

"That'll do, or anything like it. Send it from latitude forty north, fifty-five west. That's up close to the corner of the Lanes, and if it's caught up it'll keep 'em busy up there for a while."

"What's our longitude?"

"Don't know, and won't until I learn the method. But just north of us is the west-to-east track of outbound low-power steamers, which, I take it, means tramps and tankers. Well, we'll have good use for a tanker."

"You mean we're to hold up one for oil?"

"Of course, and for grub if we need it."

"Piracy, Forsythe."

"Have pirates got anything on us, now?" asked Forsythe. "What are we? Mutineers, convicts, strong-arm men, thieves—or just simply pirates. Off the deck with you, Casey, and keep your wires hot. Forty north, forty-five west for a while, then we'll have it farther north."

Casey jotted down the figures, and departed to the wireless room, where, at intervals through the day he sent out into the ether the radiating waves, which, if picked up within fifty miles by a craft beyond the horizon, might be relayed on.

The success of the scheme could not be learned by any tangible signs, but for the next few days, while the boat lay with quiet engines and Forsythe studied navigation, they remarked that they were not pursued or noticed by passing craft.

And as the boat, with dead engines, rolled lazily in the long Atlantic swell, while the men—all but Forsythe, the two cooks, and the two wireless experts—lolled lazily about the deck, the three invalids of the ship's company were convalescing in different degrees.

Jenkins, dumb and wheezy, lay prone in a forecastle bunk, trying to wonder how it happened. His mental faculties, though apprising him that he was alive, would hardly carry him to the point of wonder; for wonder predicates imagination, and what little Jenkins was born with had been shocked out of him.

Still he struggled, and puzzled and guessed, weakly, as to what had happened to him, and when a committee from the loungers above visited him, and asked what struck him, he could only point suggestively to his throat, and wag his head. He could not even whisper; and so they left him, pondering upon the profanely expressed opinion of old Kelly that it was a "visitation from God."

The committee went aft to the skipper's quarters, and here loud talk and profanity ceased; for there was a woman below, and, while these fellows were not gentlemen—as the term is understood—they were men—bad men, but men.

On the way down the stairs, Kelly struck, bare-handed, his watch mate Hawkes for expressing an interest in the good looks of the woman; and

Sampson, a giant, like his namesake, smote old Kelly, hip and thigh, for qualifying his strictures on the comment of Hawkes.

Thus corrected and enjoined, with caps in hand, they approached the open door of the starboard room, where lay the injured woman in a berth, fully clothed in her now dried garments, and her face still hidden in Denman's bandage.

"Excuse me, madam," said Sampson, the present chairman of the committee, "can we do anything for you?"

"I cannot see you," she answered, faintly. "I do not know where I am, nor what will happen to me. But I am in need of attention. One man was kind to me, but he has not returned. Who are you—you men?"

"We're the crew of the boat," answered Sampson, awkwardly. "The skipper's forward, and I guess the man that was kind to you is our prisoner. He's not on the job now, but—what can we do?"

"Tell me where I am, and where I am going. What boat is this? Who are you?"

"Well, madam," broke in old Kelly, "we're a crowd o' jail-breakers that stole a torpedo-boat destroyer, and put to sea. We got you off a burned and sinking yacht, and you're here with us; but I'm blessed if I know what we'll do with you. Our necks are in the halter, so to speak—or rather, our hands and ankles are in irons for life, if we're caught. You've got to make the best of it until we get caught, and if we don't, you've got to make the best of it, too. Lots o' young men among us, and you're no spring chicken, by the looks o' you."

Old Kelly went down before a fist blow from Hawkes, who thus strove to rehabilitate himself in the good opinion of his mates, and Hawkes went backward from a blow from Sampson, who, as yet unsullied from unworthy thought, held his position as peacemaker and moralist. And while they were recovering from the excitement, Denman, with blood on his face from the wound in his scalp, appeared among them.

"Are you fellows utterly devoid of manhood and self-respect," he said, sternly, "that you appear before the door of a sickroom and bait a woman who cannot defend herself even by speech? Shame upon you! You have crippled me, but I am recovering. If you cannot aid this woman, leave her to me. She is burned, scalded, disfigured—she hardly knows her name, or where she came from. You have saved her from the wreck, and have since neglected her. Men, you are jailbirds as you say, but you are American seamen. If you cannot help her, leave her. Do not insult her. I am helpless; if I had power I would decree further relief from the medicine-chest. But I am a prisoner—restricted."

Sampson squared his big shoulders. "On deck with you fellows—all of you. Git—quick!"

They filed up the companion, leaving Sampson looking at Denman.

"Lieutenant," he said, "you take care o' this poor woman, and if any one interferes, notify me. I'm as big a man as Jenkins, who's knocked out, and a bigger man than Forsythe, who's now in command. But we're fair—understand? We're fair—the most of us."

"Yes, yes," answered Denman, as he staggered back to a transom seat.

"Want anything yourself?" asked Sampson, as he noted the supine figure of Denman. "You're still Lieutenant Denman, of the navy—understand?"

"No, I do not. Leave me alone."

Sampson followed his mates.

Denman sat a few moments, nursing his aching head and trying to adjust himself to conditions. And as he sat there, he felt a hand on his shoulder and heard a weak voice saying:

"Are you Lieutenant Denman—Billie Denman?"

He looked up. The bandaged face of the woman was above him. Out of the folds of the bandage looked two serious, gray eyes; and he knew them.

"Florrie!" he said, in a choke. "Is this you—grown up? Florrie Fleming! How—why—what brings you here?"

"I started on the trip, Billie," she said, calmly, "with father on a friend's yacht bound for the Bermudas. We caught fire, and I was the only one saved, it seems; but how are you here, subordinate to these men? And you are injured, Billie—you are bleeding! What has happened?"

"The finger of Fate, Florrie, or the act of God," answered Denman, with a painful smile. "We must have the conceit taken out of us on occasions, you know. Forsythe, my schoolmate, is in command of this crowd of jail-breakers and pirates."

"Forsythe—your conqueror?" She receded a step. "I had— Do you know, Mr. Denman, that you were my hero when I was a child, and that I never forgave Jack Forsythe? I had hoped to hear—"

"Oh, I know," he interrupted, hotly, while his head throbbed anew with the surge of emotion. "I know what you and the whole town expected. But—well, I knocked him down on deck a short time back, and the knockdown stands; but they would not allow a finish. Then he shot me when I was not looking."

"I am glad," she answered, simply, "for your sake, and perhaps for my own, for I, too, it seems, am in his power."

He answered her as he could, incoherently and meaninglessly, but she went to her room and closed the door.

CHAPTER IX

Down the wardroom companion came Forsythe, followed by Sampson, who edged alongside of him as he peered into the after compartment, where Denman sat on the transom.

"What do you want down here with me?" asked Forsythe, in a snarl, as he looked sidewise at Sampson.

"To see that you act like a man," answered the big machinist. "There's a sick woman here."

"And a more or less sick man," answered Forsythe, "that if I hadn't made sick would ha' had you in irons. Get up on deck. All I want is a chronometer."

"Under the circumstances," rejoined Sampson, coolly, "though I acknowledge your authority as far as governing this crew is concerned, when it comes to a sick woman defended only by a wounded officer, I shift to the jurisdiction of the officer. If Lieutenant Denman asks that I go on deck, I will go. Otherwise, I remain."

"Wait," said Denman, weakly, for he had lost much blood. "Perhaps Forsythe need not be antagonized or coerced. Forsythe, do you remember a little girl at home named Florrie Fleming? Well, that woman is she. I appeal to whatever is left of your boyhood ideals to protect this woman, and care for her."

"Yes, I remember her," answered Forsythe, with a bitter smile. "She thought you were a little tin god on wheels, and told me after you'd gone that you'd come back and thrash me. You didn't, did you?" His speech ended in a sneer.

"No, but I will when the time comes," answered Denman; but the mental transition from pity to anger overcame him, and he sank back.

"Now, this is neither here nor there, Forsythe," said Sampson, sternly. "You want a chronometer. When you get it, you've no more business here than I have, and I think you'd better use your authority like a man, or I'll call a meeting of the boys."

"Of course," answered Forsythe, looking at the big shoulders of Sampson. "But, inasmuch as I knew this fellow from boyhood, and knew this little girl when a child, the best care I can give her is to remove this chap from her vicinity. We'll put him down the fore peak, and let one o' the cooks feed her and nurse her."

"We'll see about that on deck," said Sampson, indignantly. "I'll talk—"

"Yes," broke in Denman, standing up. "Forsythe is right. It is not fitting that I should be here alone with her. Put me anywhere you like, but take care of her, as you are men and Americans."

Forsythe made no answer, but Sampson gave Denman a troubled, doubtful look, then nodded, and followed Forsythe to the various rooms until he had secured what he wanted; then they went on deck together.

But in an hour they were back; and, though Denman had heard nothing of a conclave on deck, he judged by their faces that there had been one, and that Forsythe had been overruled by the influence of Sampson. For Sampson smiled and Forsythe scowled, as they led Denman into the wardroom to his own berth, and locked him in with the assurance that the cooks would feed him and attend to the wants of himself and the woman.

Billings soon came with arnica, plaster, and bandages, and roughly dressed his wound; but he gave him no information of their plans. However, Denman could still look out through a deadlight.

A few hours after the boat's engines had started, he could see a steamer on the horizon, steering a course that would soon intercept that of the destroyer.

She was a one-funneled, two-masted craft, a tramp, possibly, a working boat surely; but he only learned when her striped funnel came to view that she belonged to a regular line. She made no effort to avoid them, but held on until within hailing distance, when he heard Forsythe's voice from the bridge.

"Steamer ahoy!" he shouted. "What's your cargo?"

"Oil," answered a man on the steamer's bridge. "What are you holding me up for?"

"Oil," answered Forsythe. "How is it stowed—in cases, or in bulk?"

"In bulk, you doggoned fool."

"Very good. We want some of that oil."

"You do, hey? Who are you? You look like that runaway destroyer I've heard so much about. Who's going to recompense the company for the oil you want? Hey? Where do I come in? Who pays the bill?"

"Send it to the United States Government, or send it to the devil. Pass a hose over the side, and dip your end into the tank."

"Suppose I say no?"

"Then we'll send a few shells into your water line."

"Is that straight? Are you pirates that would sink a working craft?"

"As far as you are concerned we are. Pass over your hose, and stop talking about it. All we want is a little oil."

"Will you give me a written receipt?"

"Of course. Name your bill. We'll toss it up on a drift bolt. Pass over the hose."

"All right. Hook on your own reducer and suck it full with your pump; then it will siphon down."

"Got reducers, Sampson?"

"Got several. Guess we can start the flow."

The two craft drew close together, a hose was flung from the tanker to the destroyer, and the four machinists worked for a while with wrenches and pump fittings until the connection was made; then they started the pump, filled the hose, and, disconnecting, dropped their end into the tanks.

The oil, by the force of gravity, flowed from one craft to the other until the gauges showed a full supply. Then a written receipt for one hundred and twenty-five tons of oil was signed by the leaders, tied to a piece of iron, and tossed aboard the tanker, and the two craft separated, the pirate heading south, as Denman could see by the telltale.

Denman, his wounded scalp easier, lay down in his berth and smoked while he thought out his plans. Obviously the men were pirates, fully committed; they would probably repeat the performance; and as obviously they would surely be caught in time. There was nothing that he could do, except to heal his wound and wait.

He could not even assist Miss Florrie, no matter what peril might menace her; then, as he remembered a bunch of duplicate keys given him when he joined as executive officer, he thought that perhaps he might. They were in his desk, and, rolling out, he secured them.

He tried them in turn on his door lock, and finally found the one that fitted. This he took off the ring and secured with his own bunch of keys, placing the others—which he easily surmised belonged to all the locking doors in the boat—in another pocket. Then he lay back to finish his smoke. But Sampson opened his door, and interrupted.

"You'll excuse me, sir," he began, while Denman peered critically at him through the smoke. "But I suppose you know what we've just done?"

"Yes," he answered. "I could see a little and hear more. You've held up and robbed an oil steamer."

"And is it piracy, sir, in the old sense—a hanging matter if we're caught?"

"Hardly know," said Denman, after a moment's reflection. "Laws are repealed every now and then. Did you kill any one?"

"No, sir."

"Well, I judge that a pirate at sea is about on the same plane as a burglar on shore. If he kills any one while committing a felony, he is guilty of murder in the first degree. Better not kill any fellow men, then you'll only get a long term—perhaps for life—when you're nabbed."

"Thank you, Mr. Denman. They're talking big things on deck, but—there'll be no killing. Forsythe is something of a devil and will stop at nothing, but I'll—"

"Pardon me," said Denman, lazily, "he'll stop at me if you release me."

"Not yet, sir. It may be necessary, but at present we're thinking of ourselves."

"All right. But, tell me, how did you get a key to my door? How many keys are there?"

"Oh, from Billings, sir. Not with Forsythe's knowledge, however. Billings, and some others, think no more of him than I do."

"That's right," responded Denman. "I knew him at school. Look out for him. By the way, is the lady aft being attended to?"

"Yes, sir. Daniels, the other cook, brings her what she needs. She is not locked up, though."

"That's good. Give her the run of the deck, and take care of her."

"Yes, sir, we will," answered Sampson, as respectfully as though it were a legitimate order—for force of habit is strong. Then he left the room, locking the door behind him.

Denman smoked until he had finished the cigar, and, after he had eaten a supper brought by Billings, he smoked again until darkness closed down. And with the closing down of darkness came a plan.

CHAPTER X

Tossing his cigar through the opened deadlight, Denman arose and unlocked his door, passing into the small and empty wardroom. First, he tried the forward door leading into the petty officers' quarters and to the armroom, and, finding it locked, sought for the key which opened it, and passed through, closing the door softly behind him.

Farther forward he could hear the voice of Billings, singing cheerfully to himself in the galley; and, filtering through the galley hatch and open deadlights, the voice of Forsythe, uttering angry commands to some one on deck.

He had no personal design upon Billings, nor at present upon Forsythe, so he searched the armroom. As Forsythe and Daniels had found, there was nothing there more formidable than cutlasses, rifles, and torpedo heads; the pistols had been removed to some other place. So Denman went back and searched the wardroom, delving into closets and receptacles looking for arms; but he found none, and sat down on a chair to think. Presently he arose and tapped on the glazed glass door of the captain's apartment.

"Florrie," he said, in a half whisper. "Florrie, are you awake?"

There was no answer for a moment; then he saw a shadow move across the door.

"Florrie," he repeated, "are you awake?"

"Who is this?" came an answering whisper through the door.

"Denman—Billie Denman," he answered. "If you are awake and clothed, let me in. I have a key, and I want to talk with you."

"All right—yes. Come in. But—I have no key, and the door is locked."

Denman quickly found the key and opened the door. She stood there, with her face still tied up in cloths, and only her gray eyes showing in the light from the electric bulbs of the room.

"Florrie," he said, "will you do your part toward helping us out of our present trouble?"

"I'll do what I can, Billie; but I cannot do much."

"You can do a lot," he responded. "Just get up on deck, with your face tied up, and walk around. Speak to any man you meet, and go forward to the bridge. Ask any one you see, any question you like, as to where we are going, or what is to be done with us—anything at all which will justify your presence on deck. Just let them see that you are on deck, and will be on deck again. Will you, Florrie?"

"My face is still very bad, Billie; and the wind cuts like a knife. Why must I go up among those men?"

"I'll tell you afterward. Go along, Florrie. Just show yourself, and come down."

"I am in the dark. Why do you not tell me what is ahead? I would rather stay here and go to bed."

"You can go to bed in ten minutes," said Denman. "But go up first and show yourself, and come down. I will do the rest."

"Well, Billie, I will. I do not like to, but you seem to have some plan which you do not tell me of, so—well, all right. I will go up."

She put on a cloak and ascended the companion stairs, and Denman sat down to wait. He heard nothing, not even a voice of congratulation, and after a few moments Florrie came down.

"I met them all," she said, "and they were civil and polite. What more do you want of me, Billie?"

"Your cloak, your hat, and your skirt. I will furnish the bandage."

"What?"

"Exactly. I will go up, dressed like you, and catch them unawares, one by one."

"But, Billie, they will kill you, or—hurt you. Don't do it, Billie."

"Now, here, Florrie girl," he answered firmly. "I'll go into the wardroom, and you toss in the materials for my disguise. Then you go to bed. If I get into trouble they will return the clothes."

"But suppose they kill you! I will be at their mercy. Billie, I am alone here without you."

"Florrie, they are sailors; that means that they are men. If I win, you are all right, of course. Now let me have the things. I want to get command of this boat."

"Take them, Billie; but return to me and tell me. Don't leave me in suspense."

"I won't. I'll report, Florrie. Just wait and be patient."

He passed into the wardroom, and soon the skirt, hat, and cloak were thrown to him. He had some trouble in donning the garments; for, while the length of the skirt did not matter, the width certainly did, and he must needs piece out the waistband with a length of string, ruthlessly punching holes to receive it. The cloak was a tight squeeze for his broader shoulders, but he managed it; and, after he had thoroughly masked his face with bandages, he tried the hat. There were hatpins sticking to it, which he knew the utility of; but, as she had furnished him nothing of her thick crown of hair, he jabbed these through the bandage, and surveyed himself in the skipper's large mirror.

"Most ladylike," he muttered, squinting through the bandages. Then he went on deck.

His plan had progressed no further than this—to be able to reach the deck unrecognized, so that he could watch, listen to the talk, and decide what he might do later on.

Billings still sang cheeringly in the galley, and the voices forward were more articulate; chiefly concerned, it seemed, with the replenishing of the water and food supply, and the necessity of Forsythe's pursuing his studies so that they could know where they were. The talk ended by their driving their commander below; and, when the watches were set, Denman himself went down. He descended as he had come up, by the captain's companion, reported his safety to Florrie through the partly opened stateroom door, and also requested that, each night as she retired, she should toss the hat, cloak, and skirt into the wardroom. To this she agreed, and he discarded the uncomfortable rig and went to his room, locking the captain's door behind him, also his own.

His plan had not progressed. He had only found a way to see things from the deck instead of through a deadlight; and he went to sleep with the troubled thought that, even though he should master them all, as he had once nearly succeeded in doing, he would need to release them in order that they should "work ship." To put them on parole was out of the question.

The sudden stopping of the turbines woke him in the morning, and the sun shining into his deadlight apprised him that he had slept late. He looked out and ahead, and saw a large, white steam yacht resting quietly on the rolling ground swell, apparently waiting for the destroyer to creep up to her.

"Another holdup," he said; "and for grub and water this time, I suppose."

Wishing to see this from the deck, he rushed aft to the captain's room and tapped on the door, meanwhile fumbling for his keys. There was no answer, and, tapping again, he opened the door and entered.

"Florrie," he called, in a whisper, "are you awake?"

She did not reply, but he heard Sampson's voice from the deck.

"This is your chance, miss," he said. "We're going to get stores from that yacht; but no doubt she'll take you on board."

"Is she bound to New York, or some port where I may reach friends?" asked the girl.

"No; bound to the Mediterranean."

"Will you release Mr. Denman as well?"

"No. I'm pretty sure the boys will not. He knows our plans, and is a naval officer, you see, with a strong interest in landing us. Once on shore, he would have every warship in the world after us."

"Then I stay here with Mr. Denman. He is wounded, and is my friend."

Denman was on the point of calling up—to insist that she leave the yacht; but he thought, in time, that it would reveal his position, and leave him more helpless, while, perhaps, she might still refuse to go. He heard Sampson's footsteps going forward, and called to her softly; but she, too, had moved forward, and he went back to his deadlight.

It was a repetition of the scene with the oil steamer. Forsythe, loudly and profanely announcing their wants, and calling the yacht's attention to two twelve-pounders aimed at her water line. She was of the standard type, clipper-bowed, square-sterned, with one funnel and two masts; and from the trucks of these masts stretched the three-wire grid of a wireless outfit.

Forward was a crowd of blue-clad sailors, on the bridge an officer and a helmsman, and aft, on the fantail, a number of guests; while amidships, conversing earnestly, were two men, whose dress indicated that they were the owner and sailing master.

In the door of a small deck house near them stood another man in uniform, and to this man the owner turned and spoke a few words. The man disappeared inside, and Denman, straining his ears, heard the rasping sound of a wireless "sender," and simultaneously Casey's warning shout to Forsythe:

"He's calling for help, Forsythe. Stop him."

Then came Forsythe's vibrant voice.

"Call that man out of the wireless room," he yelled, "or we'll send a shell into it. Train that gun, Kelly, and stand by for the word. Call him out," he continued. "Stop that message."

The rasping sound ceased, and the operator appeared; then, with their eyes distended, the three ran forward.

"Any one else in that deck house?" called Forsythe.

"No," answered the sailing master. "What are you going to do?"

"Kelly," said Forsythe, "aim low, and send a shell into the house. Aim low, so as to smash the instruments."

Kelly's reply was inarticulate, but in a moment the gun barked, and the deck house disintegrated into a tangle of kindling from which oozed a cloud of smoke. Women screamed, and, forward and aft, the yacht's people crowded toward the ends of the craft.

"What in thunder are you trying to do?" roared the sailing master, shaking his fist. "Are you going to sink us?"

"Not unless necessary," replied Forsythe; "but we want grub—good grub, too—and water. We want water through your own hose, because ours is full of oil. Do you agree?"

There was a short confab between the owner and the sailing master, ending with the latter's calling out: "We'll give you water and grub, but don't shoot any more hardware at us. Come closer and throw a heaving line, and send your boat, if you like, for the grub. Our boats are all lashed down."

"That's reasonable," answered Forsythe. "Hawkes, Davis, Daniels, Billings—you fellows clear away that boat of ours, and stand by to go for the grub."

The two craft drew together, and for the rest it was like the other holdup. The hose was passed, and, while the tanks were filling, the boat passed back and forth, making three trips, heavily laden with barrels, packages, and boxes. Then, when Forsythe gave the word, the hose was drawn back, the boat hoisted and secured, and the two craft separated without another word of threat or protest.

CHAPTER XI

"Fully committed," muttered Denman, as he drew back from the deadlight. "They'll stop at nothing now."

He was about to open his door to visit Florrie, if she had descended, when it was opened from without by Billings, who had brought his breakfast.

"We'll have better grub for a while, sir," he said, as he deposited the tray on the desk. "Suppose you know what happened?"

"Yes, and I see life imprisonment for all of you, unless you are killed in the catching."

"Can't help it, sir," answered Billings, with a deprecatory grin. "We're not going back to jail, nor will we starve on the high seas. All we're waiting for is the course to the African coast—unless—" He paused.

"Unless what?" demanded Denman, leaning over his breakfast.

"Well—unless the vote is to stay at sea. We've got a good, fast boat under us."

"What do you mean? Continued piracy?"

"I can't tell you any more, sir," answered Billings, and he went off, after carefully locking the door behind him.

When Denman had finished his breakfast, he quietly let himself out. Tapping on the after door, he saw Florrie's shadow on the translucent glass, and opened it.

She stood before him with the bandages removed, and he saw her features for the first time since she had come aboard. They were pink, and here and there was a blister that had not yet disappeared; but, even so handicapped, her face shone with a beauty that he had never seen in a woman nor imagined in the grown-up child that he remembered. The large, serious, gray eyes were the same; but the short, dark ringlets had developed to a wealth of hair that would have suitably crowned a queen.

Denman stood transfixed for a moment, then found his tongue.

"Florrie," he said, softly, so as not to be heard from above, "is this really you? I wouldn't have known you."

"Yes, I know," she answered, with a smile, which immediately changed to a little grimace of pain. "I was badly scalded, but I had to take off the cloth to eat my breakfast."

"No," he said. "I didn't mean that. I mean you've improved so. Why, Florrie, you've grown up to be a beauty. I never imagined you—you—looking so fine."

"Don't talk like that, Billie Denman. I'm disfigured for life, I know. I can never show my face again."

"Nonsense, Florrie. The redness will go away. But, tell me, why didn't you go aboard that yacht? I overheard you talking to Sampson. Why didn't you go, and get away from this bunch?"

"I have just told you," she answered, while a tint overspread her pink face that did not come of the scalding. "There were women on that yacht. Do you think I want to be stared at, and pitied, and laughed at?"

"I never thought of that," said Denman; "but I suppose it is a very vital reason for a woman. Yet, it's too bad. This boat is sure to be captured, and there may be gun fire. It's a bad place for you. But, Florrie—let me tell you. Did you see what came on board from the yacht?"

"Boxes, and barrels, and the water."

"Yes, and some of those boxes contained whisky and brandy. Whisky and brandy make men forget that they are men. Have you a key for your door?"

"No; I never saw one."

Denman tried his bunch of keys on the stateroom door until he found the right one. This he took off the ring and inserted in the lock.

"Lock your door every time you go in there," he said, impressively; "and, Florrie, another thing—keep that pretty face of yours out of sight of these men. Go right in there now and replace the bandages. Then, after a while, about nine o'clock, go on deck for a walk around, and then let me have your rig. I want a daylight look at things."

She acquiesced, and he went back to his room, locking himself in, just in time to escape the notice of Billings, who had come for the tray.

"Are you fellows going to deprive me of all exercise?" he demanded. "Even a man in irons is allowed to walk the deck a little."

"Don't know, sir," answered Billings. "Forsythe is the man to talk to."

"I'll do more than talk to him," growled Denman between his teeth. "Carry my request for exercise to him. Say that I demand the privileges of a convict."

"Very good, sir," answered Billings as he went out.

In a few moments he was back with the news that Forsythe had profanely denied the request. Whereat Denman's heart hardened the more.

He remained quiet until two bells—nine o'clock—had struck, then went out and approached the after door, just in time to see Florrie's shadow pass across the glass as she mounted the stairs. He waited, and in about five minutes she came down, and, no doubt seeing his shadow on the door, tapped gently. He promptly opened it, and she said:

"Leave the door open and I will throw you my things in a minute. They are drinking up there."

"Drinking!" he mused, as he waited. "Well, perhaps I can get a gun if they drink to stupidity."

Soon Florrie's hand opened the door, and the garments came through. Denman had little trouble now in donning them, and, with his head tied up as before, he passed through the captain's apartment to the deck. It was a mild, sunshiny morning, with little wind, and that from the northeast. White globes of cloud showed here and there, and Denman knew them for the unmistakable sign of the trade winds. But he was more interested in matters on deck. All hands except Billings, who was singing in the galley, and Munson, one of the wireless men, were clustered around the forward funnel; and there were several bottles circulating around. Forsythe, with a sextant in his hand, was berating them.

"Go slow, you infernal ginks," he snarled at them, "or you'll be so drunk in an hour that you won't know your names. Ready—in there, Munson?"

"Yes," answered Munson from the pilot-house.

Forsythe put the sextant to his eye, and swept it back and forth for a few moments.

"Time," he called suddenly, and, lowering the sextant, looked in on Munson.

"Got it?" asked Munson.

"Yes; and have it down in black and white." Forsythe made a notation from the sextant on a piece of paper.

"Now, again," said Forsythe, and again he took a sight, shouted, "Time," and made another notation.

Then he went into the pilot-house and Munson came out and made the shortest cut to the nearest bottle.

"He's taken chronometer sights," mused Denman, as he leaned against the companion hood. "Well, he's progressing fast, but there never was a doubt that he is a scholar."

He went down, and through a crack of the door obtained Miss Florrie's permission to keep the cloak and skirt for the morning, as he wanted to see later how the drinking was progressing. Florrie consented, and he went to his room to wait.

As he waited, the sounds above grew ominous. Oaths and loud laughter, shouts, whoops, and grumblings, mingled with Forsythe's angry voice of command, came down to him through the open deadlight. Soon he heard the thumping of human bodies on deck, and knew there was a fight going on.

A fight always appealed to him; and, yielding to this unworthy curiosity, Denman again passed through the captain's quarters, making sure on the way that Florrie was locked in, and reached the deck.

There were two fights in progress, one a stand-up-and-knock-down affair near the pilot-house; the other a wrestling match amidships. He could not recognize the contestants, and, with the thought that perhaps Forsythe was one of them, stepped forward a few feet to observe.

At this moment Billings—the cheerful Billings—came up the galley hatch, no longer cheerful, but morose of face and menacing of gait, as is usual with this type of man when drunk. He spied Denman in his skirt, cloak, hat, and bandage, and, with a clucking chuckle in his throat and a leering grin on his face, made for him.

"Say, old girl," he said, thickly. "Let's have a kiss."

Denman, anxious about his position and peculiar privilege, backed away; but the unabashed pursuer still pursued, and caught him at the companion. He attempted to pass his arm around Denman, but did not succeed. Denman pushed him back a few feet; then, with the whole weight of his body behind it, launched forth his fist, and struck the suitor squarely between the eyes.

Billings was lifted off his feet and hurled backward his whole length before he reached the deck; then he lay still for a moment, and as he showed signs of life, Denman darted down to the wardroom, where he shed his disguise as quickly as possible. Then he roused Florrie, passed the garments in to her, warned her to keep her door locked, and went to his own room, locking the doors behind him.

He waited and listened, while the shouts and oaths above grew less, and finally silent, though at times he recognized Forsythe's threatening voice. He supposed that by now all of them except Forsythe were stupidly drunk, and was much surprised when, at eight bells, Billings opened the door with his dinner, well cooked and savory. He was not quite sober, but as sober as a drunken man may become who has had every nerve, sinew, and internal organ shocked as by the kick of a mule.

"Bad times on deck, sir," he said. "This drinkin's all to the bad." He leered comically through his closed and blackened eyelids, and tried to smile; but it was too painful, and his face straightened.

"Why, what has happened?" inquired Denman. "I heard the row, but couldn't see."

"Nothin' serious, sir," answered Billings, "except to me. Say, sir—that woman aft. Keep away from her. Take it from me, sir, she's a bad un. Got a punch like a battering-ram. Did you ever get the big end of a handspike jammed into your face by a big man, sir? Well, that's the kind of a punch she has."

Billings departed, and Denman grinned maliciously while he ate his dinner; and, after Billings had taken away the dishes—with more comments on the woman's terrible punch—Denman went out into the wardroom, intending to visit Miss Florrie. A glance overhead stopped him, and sent him back. The lubber's point on the telltale marked due west northwest.

CHAPTER XII

He sat down to think it out. Sampson had hinted at big things talked about. Billings had spoken of a vote—to stay at sea or not. However, there could have been no vote since Billings' last visit because of their condition. But Forsythe had indubitably taken chronometer sights in the morning, and, being most certainly sober, had doubtless worked them out and ascertained the longitude, which, with a meridian observation at noon, would give him the position of the yacht.

The "big things" requiring a vote were all in Forsythe's head, and he had merely anticipated the vote. Not knowing their position himself, except as indicated by the trade-wind clouds, Denman could only surmise that a west northwest course would hit the American coast somewhere between Boston and Charleston. But what they wanted there was beyond his comprehension.

He gave up the puzzle at last, and visited Florrie, finding her dressed, swathed in the bandage, and sitting in the outer apartment, reading. Briefly he explained the occurrences on deck, and, as all was quiet now, asked her to step up and investigate. She did so, and returned.

"Forsythe is steering," she said, "and two or three are awake, but staggering around, and several others are asleep on the deck."

"Well," he said, hopefully, "Forsythe evidently can control himself, but not the others. If they remain drunk, or get drunker, I mean to do something to-night. No use trying now."

"What will you do, Billie?" she asked, with concern in her voice.

"I don't know. I'll only know when I get at it. I hope that Forsythe will load up, too. Hello! What's up? Run up, Florrie, and look."

The engine had stopped, and Forsythe's furious invective could be heard. Florrie ran up the steps, peeped out, and returned.

"He is swearing at some one," she said.

"So it seems," said Denman. "Let me have a look."

He ascended, and carefully peeped over the companion hood. Forsythe was looking down the engine-room hatch, and his voice came clear and distinct as he anathematized the engineers below.

"Shut off your oil, you drunken mutts," he vociferated. "If the whole four of you can't keep steam on the steering-gear, shut it off—all of it, I say. Shut off every burner and get into your bunks till you're sober."

Then Sampson's deep voice arose from the hatch. "You'll stop talking like that to me, my lad, before long," he said, "or I'll break some o' your bones."

"Shut off the oil—every burner," reiterated Forsythe. "We'll drift for a while."

"Right you are," sang out another voice, which Denman recognized as Dwyer's. "And here, you blooming crank, take a drink and get into a good humor."

"Pass it up, then. I need a drink by this time. *But shut off that oil.*"

Denman saw Forsythe reach down and bring up a bottle, from which he took a deep draught. The electric lights slowly dimmed in the cabin, indicating the slowing down of the dynamo engine; then they went out.

Denman descended, uneasy in mind, into the half darkness of the cabin. He knew, from what he had learned of Forsythe, that the first drink would lead to the second, and the third, and that his example would influence the rest to further drinking; but he gave none of his fears to Florrie. He simply bade her to go into her room and lock the door. Then he went to his own room against the possible advent of Billings at supper-time.

But there was no supper for any that evening. Long before the time for it pandemonium raged above; and the loudest, angriest voice was that of Forsythe, until, toward the last, Sampson's voice rose above it, and, as a dull thud on the deck came to Denman's ears, he knew that his fist had silenced it. Evidently the sleeping men had wakened to further potations; and at last the stumbling feet of some of them approached the stern. Then again came Sampson's voice.

"Come back here," he roared. "Keep away from that companion, the lot of you, or I'll give you what I gave Forsythe."

A burst of invective and malediction answered him, and then there were the sounds of conflict, even the crashing of fists as well as the thuds on the deck, coming to Denman through the deadlight.

"Forrard wi' you all," continued Sampson between the sounds of impact; and soon the shuffling of feet indicated a retreat. Denman, who had opened his door, ready for a rush to Florrie's defense, now went aft to reassure her. She opened the door at his tap and his voice through the keyhole.

"It's all right for the present, Florrie," he said. "While Sampson is sober they won't come aft again."

"Oh, Billie," she gasped. "I hope so. Don't desert me, Billie."

"Don't worry," he said, reassuringly. "They'll all be stupid before long, and then—to-night—there will be something doing on our side. Now, I must be in my room when Billings comes, or until I'm sure he will not come. And you stay here. I'll be on hand if anything happens."

He went back to his room, but Billings did not come with his supper. And one by one the voices above grew silent, and the shuffling footsteps ended in thuds, as their owners dropped to the deck; and when darkness had closed down and all above was still, Denman crept out to reconnoiter. He reached the door leading to the captain's room, and was just about to open it when a scream came to his ears.

"Billie! Billie—come—come quick! Help!"

Then a tense voice:

"Shut up your noise in there and open the door. I only want to have a talk with you."

Denman was into the room before the voice had ceased, and in the darkness barely made out the figure of a man fumbling at the knob of the stateroom door. He knew, as much by intuition as by recognition of the voice, that it was Forsythe, and, without a word of warning, sprang at his throat.

With an oath Forsythe gripped him, and they swayed back and forth in the small cabin, locked together in an embrace that strained muscles and sinews to the utmost. Forsythe expended breath and energy in curses.

Denman said nothing until Florrie screamed again, then he found voice to call out:

"All right, Florrie, I've got him."

She remained silent while the battle continued. At first it was a wrestling match, each with a right arm around the body of the other, and with Denman's left hand gripping Forsythe's left wrist. Their left hands swayed about, above their heads, to the right, to the left, and down between the close pressure of their chests.

Denman soon found that he was the stronger of arm, for he twisted his enemy's arm around as he pleased; but he also found that he was not stronger of fingers, for suddenly Forsythe broke away from his grip and seized tightly the wrist of Denman.

Thus reversed, the battle continued, and as they reeled about, chairs, table, and desk were overturned, making a racket as the combatants stumbled around over and among them that would have aroused all hands had they been but normally asleep.

As it was, there was no interruption, and the two battled on in the darkness to an end. It came soon. Forsythe suddenly released his clasp on Denman's wrist and gripped his throat, then as suddenly he brought his right hand up, and Denman felt the pressure of his thumb on his right eyeball. He was being choked and gouged; and, strangely enough, in this exigency there came to him no thought of the trick by which he had mastered Jenkins. But instead, he mustered his strength, pushed Forsythe from him, and struck out blindly.

It was a lucky blow, for his eyes were filled with lights of various hue, and he could not see; yet his fist caught Forsythe on the chin, and Denman heard him crash back over the upturned table.

Forsythe uttered no sound, and when the light had gone out of his eyes, Denman groped for him, and found him, just beginning to move. He groaned and sat up.

CHAPTER XIII

"No, you don't," said Denman, grimly. "Fair play is wasted on you, so back you go to the Land of Nod."

He drew back his right fist, and again sent it crashing on the chin of his victim, whom he could just see in the starlight from the companion, and Forsythe rolled back.

Like Jenkins, he had arrayed himself in an officer's uniform, and there was no convenient neckerchief with which to bind him; but Denman took his own, and securely tied his hands behind his back, and with another string tie from his room tied his ankles together. Then only did he think of Florrie, and called to her. She answered hysterically.

"It's all right, Florrie girl," he said. "It was Forsythe, but I've knocked him silly and have him tied hand and foot. Go to sleep now."

"I can't go to sleep, Billie," she wailed. "I can't. Don't leave me alone any more."

"I must, Florrie," he answered. "I'm going on deck to get them all. I'll never have a better chance. Keep quiet and don't come out, no matter what you hear."

"But come back soon, Billie," she pleaded.

"I will, soon as I can. But stay quiet in there until I do."

He stole softly up the stairs and looked forward. The stars illuminated the deck sufficiently for him to see the prostrate forms scattered about, but not enough for him to distinguish one from another until he had crept close. The big machinist, Sampson, he found nearest to the companion, as though he had picked this spot to guard, even in drunken sleep, the sacred after cabin. Denman's heart felt a little twinge of pain as he softly untied and withdrew the big fellow's neckerchief and bound his hands behind him. Sampson snored on through the process.

The same with the others. Kelly, Daniels, and Billings lay near the after funnel; Munson, Casey, Dwyer, and King were in the scuppers amidships; Riley, Davis, and Hawkes were huddled close to the pilot-house; and not a man moved in protest as Denman bound them, one and all, with their own neckerchiefs. There was one more, the stricken Jenkins in the forecastle; and Denman descended and examined him by the light of a match. He was awake, and blinked and grimaced at Denman, striving to speak.

"Sorry for you, Jenkins," said Billie. "You'll get well in time, but you'll have to wait. You're harmless enough now, however."

There was more to do before he felt secure of his victory. He must tie their ankles; and, as neckerchiefs had run out, he sought, by the light of matches, the "bos'n's locker" in the fore peak. Here he found spun yarn, and, cutting enough lengths of it, he came up and finished the job, tying knots so hard and seamanly that the strongest fingers of a fellow prisoner could not untie them. Then he went aft.

Forsythe was still unconscious. But he regained his senses while Denman dragged him up the steps and forward beside his enemy, Sampson; and he emitted various sulphurous comments on the situation that cannot be recorded here.

Denman wanted the weapons; but, with engines dead, there was no light save from his very small supply of matches, and for the simple, and perhaps very natural, desire to save these for his cigar lights, he forbore a search for them beyond an examination of each man's pockets. He found nothing, however. It seemed that they must have agreed upon disarmament before the drinking began. But from Forsythe he secured a bunch of keys, which he was to find useful later on.

All else was well. Each man was bound hand and foot, Jenkins was still a living corpse; and Forsythe, the soberest of the lot, had apparently succumbed to the hard knocks of the day, and gone to sleep again. So Denman went down, held a jubilant conversation with Florrie through the keyhole, and returned to the deck, where, with a short spanner in his hand—replevined from the engine room for use in case of an emergency—he spent the night on watch; for, with all lights out, a watch was necessary.

But nothing happened. The men snored away their drunkenness, and at daylight most of them were awake and aware of their plight. Denman paid no attention to their questions; but, when the light permitted, went on a search for the arms and irons, which he found in the forecastle, carefully stowed in a bunk.

He counted the pistols, and satisfied himself that all were there; then he carried them aft to his room, belted himself with one of them, and returned for the cutlasses, which he hid in another room.

But the irons he spread along the deck, and, while they cursed and maligned him, he replaced the silk and spun-yarn fetters with manacles of steel. Next he dragged the protesting prisoners from forward and aft until he had them bunched amidships, and then, walking back and forth before them, delivered a short, comprehensive lecture on the unwisdom of stealing torpedo-boat destroyers and getting drunk.

Like all lecturers, he allowed his audience to answer, and when he had refuted the last argument, he unlocked the irons of Billings and Daniels and sternly ordered them to cook breakfast.

They meekly arose and went to the galley, from which, before long, savory odors arose. And, while waiting for breakfast, Denman aroused Miss Florrie and brought her on deck, clothed and bandaged, to show her his catch.

"And what will you do now, Billie?" she asked, as she looked at the unhappy men amidships.

"Haven't the slightest idea. I've got to think it out. I'll have to release some of them to work the boat, and I'll have to shut down and iron them while I sleep, I suppose. I've already freed the two cooks, and we'll have breakfast soon."

"I'm glad of that," she answered. "There was no supper last night."

"And I'm hungry as a wolf myself. Well, they are hungry, too. We'll have our breakfast on deck before they get theirs. Perhaps the sight will bring them to terms."

"Why cannot I help, Billie?" asked the girl. "I could watch while you were asleep, and wake you if anything happened."

"Oh, no, Florrie girl. Of course I'll throw the stuff overboard, but I wouldn't trust some of them, drunk or sober."

Billings soon reported breakfast ready, and asked how he should serve the captives.

"Do not serve them at all," said Denman, sharply. "Bring the cabin table on deck, and place it on the starboard quarter. Serve breakfast for two, and you and Daniels eat your own in the galley."

"Very good, sir," answered the subdued Billings, with a glance at the long, blue revolver at Denman's waist. He departed, and with Daniels' help arranged the breakfast as ordered.

Florrie was forced to remove her bandage; but as she faced aft at the table her face was visible to Denman only. He faced forward, and while he ate he watched the men, who squirmed as the appetizing odors of broiled ham, corn bread, and coffee assailed their nostrils. On each countenance, besides the puffed, bloated appearance coming of heavy and unaccustomed drinking, was a look of anxiety and disquiet. But they were far from being conquered—in spirit, at least.

Breakfast over, Denman sent Florrie below, ordered the dishes and table below, and again put the irons on Billings and Daniels. Then he went among them.

"What do you mean to do?" asked Forsythe, surlily, as Denman looked down on him. "Keep us here and starve us?"

"I will keep you in irons while I have the power," answered Denman, "no matter what I may do with the others. Sampson," he said to the big machinist, "you played a man's part last night, and I feel strongly in favor of releasing you on parole. You understand the nature of parole, do you not?"

"I do, sir," answered the big fellow, thickly, "and if I give it, I would stick to it. What are the conditions, sir?"

"That you stand watch and watch with me while we take this boat back to Boston; that you aid me in keeping this crowd in subjection; that you do your part in protecting the lady aft from annoyance. In return, I promise you my influence at Washington. I have some, and can arouse more. You will, in all probability, be pardoned."

"No, sir," answered Sampson, promptly. "I am one of this crowd—you are not one of us. I wouldn't deserve a pardon if I went back on my mates—even this dog alongside of me. He's one of us, too; and, while I have smashed him, and will smash him again, I will not accept my liberty while he, or any of the others, is in irons."

Denman bowed low to him, and went on. He questioned only a few—those who seemed trustworthy—but met with the same response, and he left them, troubled in mind.

CHAPTER XIV

He sat down in a deck chair and lighted a cigar as an aid to his mental processes. Three projects presented themselves to his mind, each of which included, of course, the throwing overboard of the liquor and the secure hiding of the arms, except a pistol for himself, and one for Florrie.

The first was to release them all, and, backed by his pistol, his uniform, and the power of the government, to treat them as mutineers, and shoot them if they defied or disobeyed him.

To this was the logical objection that they were already more than mutineers—that there was no future for them; that, even though he overawed and conquered them, compelling them to work the boat shoreward, each passing minute would find them more keen to revolt; and that, if they rushed him in a body, he could only halt a few—the others would master him.

The second plan was born of his thoughts before breakfast. It was to release one cook, one engineer, and one helmsman at a time; to guard them until sleep was necessary, then to shut off steam, lock them up, and allow the boat to drift while they slept. Against this plan was the absolute necessity, to a seaman's mind, of a watch—even a one-man watch—and this one man could work mischief while he slept—could even, if handy with tools, file out a key that would unlock the shackles.

The third plan was to starve them into contrition and subjection, torturing them the while with the odors of food cooked for himself and Florrie. But this was an inhuman expedient, only to be considered as a last resource; and, besides, it would not affect the man doing the cooking, who could keep himself well fed and obdurate. And, even though they surrendered and worked their way back toward prison, would their surrender last beyond a couple of good meals? He thought not. Yet out of this plan came another, and he went down the companion.

"Florrie," he called, "can you cook?"

She appeared at the stateroom door without her bandages, smiling at his query, and for the moment Denman forgot all about his plans. Though the pink tinge still overspread her face, the blisters were gone, and, in the half light of the cabin, it shone with a new beauty that had not appeared to him in the garish sunlight when at breakfast—when he was intent upon watching the men. His heart gave a sudden jump, and his voice was a little unsteady as he repeated the question.

"Why, yes, Billie," she answered, "I know something about cooking—not much, though."

"Will you cook for yourself and me?" he asked. "If so, I'll keep the men locked up, and we'll wait for something to come along."

"I will," she said; "but you must keep them locked up, Billie."

"I'll do that, and fit you out with a pistol, too. I'll get you one now."

He brought her a revolver, fully loaded, with a further supply of cartridges, and fitted the belt around her waist. Then, his heart still jumping, he went on deck.

"Love her?" he mused, joyously. "Of course. Why didn't I think of it before?"

But there was work to be done, and he set himself about it. He searched the storerooms and inspected the forecastle. In the first he found several cases of liquor—also a barrel of hard bread. In the forecastle he found that the water supply was furnished by a small faucet on the after bulkhead. Trying it, he found a clear flow. Then he selected from his bunch of keys the one belonging to the forecastle door, and put it in the lock—outside. Next, with a few cautionary remarks to the men, he unlocked their wrist irons one by one; and, after making each man place his hands in front, relocked the irons.

"Now, then," he said, standing up over the last man, "you can help yourselves and Jenkins to bread and water. One by one get up on your feet and pass into the forecastle. If any man needs help, I will assist him."

Some managed to scramble to their feet unaided, while others could not. These Denman helped; but, as he assisted them with one hand, holding his pistol in the other, there was no demonstration against him with doubled fists—which is possible and potential. Mumbling and muttering, they floundered down the small hatch and forward into the forecastle. The last in the line was Sampson, and Denman stopped him.

"I've a job for you, Sampson," he said, after the rest had disappeared. "You are the strongest man in the crowd. Go down the hatch, but aft to the storeroom, and get that barrel of hard bread into the forecastle. You can do it without my unlocking you."

"Very good, sir," answered Sampson, respectfully, and descended.

Denman watched him from above, as, with his manacled hands, he twirled the heavy barrel forward and into the men's quarters.

"Shut the door, turn the key on them, and come aft here," he commanded.

Sampson obeyed.

"Now, lift up on deck and then toss overboard every case of liquor in that storeroom."

"Very good, sir." And up came six cases, as easily in his powerful grip as though they had been bandboxes, and then he hoisted his own huge bulk to the deck.

"Over the side with them all," commanded Denman.

Sampson picked them up, and, whether or not it came from temper, threw them from where he stood, above and beyond the rail; but the fifth struck the rail, and fell back to the deck. He advanced and threw it over.

"Carry the other one," said Denman, and Sampson lifted it up. It was a low, skeleton rail, and, as the big man hobbled toward it, somehow—neither he nor Denman ever knew how—his foot slipped, and he and the box went overboard together. The box floated, but when Sampson came to the surface it was out of his reach.

"Help!" he gurgled. "I can't swim."

Without a thought, Denman laid his pistol on the deck, shed his coat, and dove overboard, reaching the struggling man in three strokes.

"Keep still," he commanded, as he got behind and secured a light but secure grip on Sampson's hair. "Tread water if you can, but don't struggle. I'll tow you back to the boat."

But, though Sampson grew quiet and Denman succeeded in reaching the dark, steel side, there was nothing to catch hold of—not a trailing rope, nor eyebolt, nor even the open deadlights, for they were high out of reach. The crew were locked in the forecastle, and there was only Florrie. There was no wind, and only the long, heaving ground swell, which rolled the boat slightly, but not enough to bring those tantalizing deadlights within reach; and at last, at the sound of dishes rattling in the galley, Denman called out.

"Florrie!" he shouted. "Florrie, come on deck. Throw a rope over. Florrie—oh, Florrie!"

CHAPTER XV

She came hurriedly, and peered over the rail with a startled, frightened expression. Then she screamed.

"Can you see any ropes lying on deck, Florrie?" called Denman. "If you can, throw one over."

She disappeared for a moment, then came back, and cried out frantically: "No, there is nothing—no ropes. What shall I do?"

"Go down and get the tablecloth," said Denman, as calmly as he could, with his nose just out of water and a big, heavy, frightened man bearing him down.

Florrie vanished, and soon reappeared with the tablecloth of the morning's breakfast. It was a cloth of generous size, and she lowered it over.

"Tie one corner to the rail, Florrie," said Denman, while he held the irresponsible Sampson away from the still frail support. She obeyed him, tying the knot that all women tie but which no sailor can name, and then Denman led his man up to it.

Sampson clutched it with both hands, drew it taut, and supported his weight on it. Fortunately the knot did not slip. Denman also held himself up by it until he had recovered his breath, then cast about for means of getting on board. He felt that the tablecloth would not bear his weight and that of his water-soaked clothing, and temporarily gave up the plan of climbing it.

Forward were the signal halyards; but they, too, were of small line, and, even if doubled again and again until strong enough, he knew by experience the wonderful strength of arm required in climbing out of the water hand over hand. This thought also removed the tablecloth from the problem; but suggested another by its association with the necessity of feet in climbing with wet clothes.

He remembered that forward, just under the anchor davit, was a small, fixed ladder, bolted into the bow of the boat for use in getting the anchor. So, cautioning Sampson not to let go, he swam forward, with Florrie's frightened face following above, and, reaching the ladder, easily climbed on board. He was on the high forecastle deck, but the girl had reached it before him.

"Billie," she exclaimed, as she approached him. "Oh, Billie—"

He caught her just as her face grew white and her figure limp, and forgot Sampson for the moment. The kisses he planted on her lips and cheek forestalled the fainting spell, and she roused herself.

"I thought you would drown, Billie," she said, weakly, with her face of a deeper pink than he had seen. "Don't drown, Billie—don't do that again. Don't leave me alone."

"I won't, Florrie," he answered, stoutly and smilingly. "I'm born to be hanged, you know. I won't drown. Come on—I must get Sampson."

They descended—Denman picking up his pistol on the way—and found Sampson quietly waiting at the end of the tablecloth. With his life temporarily safe, his natural courage had come to him.

"I'm going to tow you forward to the anchor ladder, Sampson. You'll have to climb it the best way you can; for there isn't a purchase on board that will bear your weight. Hold tight now."

He untied Florrie's knot, and slowly dragged the big man forward, experiencing a check at the break of the forecastle, where he had to halt and piece out the tablecloth with a length of signal halyards, but finally got Sampson to the ladder. Sampson had some trouble in mounting, for his shackles would not permit one hand to reach up to a rung without letting go with the other; but he finally accomplished the feat, and floundered over the rail, where he sat on deck to recover himself. Finally he scrambled to his feet.

"Mr. Denman," he said, "you've saved my life for me, and whatever I can do for you, except"—his face took on a look of embarrassment—"except going back on my mates, as I said, I will do, at any time of my life."

"That was what I might have suggested," answered Denman, calmly, "that you aid me in controlling this crew until we reach Boston."

"I cannot, sir. There is prison for life for all of us if we are taken; and this crowd will break out, sir—mark my words. You won't have charge very long. But—in that case—I mean—I might be of service. I can control them all, even Forsythe, when I am awake."

"Forsythe!" grinned Denman. "You can thank Forsythe for your round-up. If he hadn't remained sober enough to attempt to break into Miss Fleming's room while you were all dead drunk, I might not have knocked him out, and might not have roused myself to tie you all hand and foot."

"Did he do that, sir?" asked Sampson, his rugged features darkening.

"He did; but I got there in time to knock him out."

"Well, sir," said Sampson, "I can promise you this much. I must be locked up, of course—I realize that. But, if we again get charge, I must be asleep part of the time, and so I will see to it that you retain possession of your gun—and the lady, too, as I see she carries one; also, sir, that you will have the run of the deck—on parole, of course."

"That is kind of you," smiled Denman; "but I don't mean to let you take charge. It is bread and water for you all until something comes along to furnish me a crew. Come on, Sampson—to the forecastle."

Sampson preceded him down the steps, down the hatch, and to the forecastle door, through which Denman admitted him; then relocked the door and bunched the key with his others. Then he joined Florrie, where she had waited amidships.

"Now, then, Florrie girl," he said, jubilantly, "you can have the use of the deck, and go and come as you like. I'm going to turn in. You see, I was awake all night."

"Are they secured safely, Billie?" she asked, tremulously.

"Got them all in the forecastle, in double irons, with plenty of hard-tack and water. We needn't bother about them any more. Just keep your eyes open for a sail, or smoke on the horizon; and if you see anything, call me."

"I will," she answered; "and I'll have dinner ready at noon."

"That's good. A few hours' sleep will be enough, and then I'll try and polish up what I once learned about wireless. And say, Florrie. Next time you go below, look in the glass and see how nice you look."

She turned her back to him, and he went down. In five minutes he was asleep. And, as he slipped off into unconsciousness, there came to his mind the thought that one man in the forecastle was not manacled; and when Florrie wakened him at noon the thought was still with him, but he dismissed it. Jenkins was helpless for a while, unable to move or speak, and need not be considered.

CHAPTER XVI

Florrie had proved herself a good cook, and they ate dinner together, then Denman went on deck. The boat was still rolling on a calm sea; but the long, steady, low-moving hills of blue were now mingled with a cross swell from the northwest, which indicated a push from beyond the horizon not connected with the trade wind. And in the west a low bank of cloud rose up from, and merged its lower edge with, the horizon; while still higher shone a "mackerel sky," and "mare's tail" clouds—sure index of coming wind. But there was nothing on the horizon in the way of sail or smoke; and, anticipating another long night watch, he began preparations for it.

Three red lights at the masthead were needed as a signal that the boat—a steamer—was not under command. These he found in the lamp room. He filled, trimmed, and rigged them to the signal halyards on the bridge, ready for hoisting at nightfall. Then, for a day signal of distress, he hoisted an ensign—union down—at the small yard aloft.

Next in his mind came the wish to know his position, and he examined the log book. Forsythe had made an attempt to start a record; and out of his crude efforts Denman picked the figures which he had noted down as the latitude and longitude at noon of the day before. He corrected this with the boat's course throughout the afternoon until the time of shutting off the oil feed, and added the influence of a current, which his more expert knowledge told him of. Thirty-one, north, and fifty-five, forty, west was the approximate position, and he jotted it down.

This done, he thought of the possibility of lighting the boat through the night, and sought the engine room. He was but a theoretical engineer, having devoted most of his studies to the duties of a line officer; but he mastered in a short time the management of the small gas engine that worked the dynamo, and soon had it going. Electric bulbs in the engine room sprang into life; and, after watching the engine for a short time, he decided that it required only occasional inspection, and sought the deck.

The cross sea was increasing, and the bank to the northwest was larger and blacker, while the mare's tails and mackerel scales had given way to cirrus clouds that raced across the sky. Damp gusts of wind blew, cold and heavy, against his cheek; and he knew that a storm was coming that would try out the low-built craft to the last of its powers. But before it came he would polish up his forgotten knowledge of wireless telegraphy, and searched the wireless room for books.

He found everything but what he wanted most—the code book, by which he could furbish up on dots and dashes. Angry at his bad memory, he studied the apparatus, found it in working order, and left the task to go on deck.

An increased rolling of the boat threatened the open deadlights. Trusting that the men in the forecastle would close theirs, he attended to all the others, then sought Florrie in the galley, where she had just finished the washing of the dishes. Her face was not pale, but there was a wild look in her eyes, and she was somewhat unsteady on her feet.

"Oh, Billie, I'm sick—seasick," she said, weakly. "I'm a poor sailor."

"Go to bed, little girl," he said, gently. "We're going to have some bad weather, but we're all right. So stay in bed."

He supported her aft through the wardroom to her stateroom door in the after cabin. "I'll get supper, Florrie, and, if you can eat, I'll bring you some. Lie down now, and don't get up until I call you, or until you feel better."

He again sought the deck. The wind now came steadily, while the whole sky above and the sea about were assuming the gray hue of a gale. He closed all hatches and companions, taking a peep down into the engine room before closing it up. The dynamo was buzzing finely.

A few splashes of rain fell on him, and he clothed himself in oilskins and rubber boots to watch out the gale, choosing to remain aft—where his footsteps over her might reassure the seasick girl below—instead of the bridge, where he would have placed himself under normal conditions.

The afternoon wore on, each hour marked by a heavier pressure of the wind and an increasing height to the seas, which, at first just lapping at the rail, now lifted up and washed across the deck. The boat rolled somewhat, but not to add to his discomfort or that of those below; and there were no loose articles on deck to be washed overboard.

So Denman paced the deck, occasionally peeping down the engine-room hatch at the dynamo, and again trying the drift by the old-fashioned chip-and-reel log at the stern. When tired, he would sit down in the deck chair, which he had wedged between the after torpedo and the taffrail, then resume his pacing.

As darkness closed down, he sought Florrie's door, and asked her if she would eat something. She was too ill, she said; and, knowing that no words could comfort her, he left her, and in the galley ate his own supper—tinned meat, bread, and coffee.

Again the deck, the intermittent pacing, and resting in the chair. The gale became a hurricane in the occasional squalls; and at these times the seas were beaten to a level of creamy froth luminous with a phosphorescent glow, while the boat's rolling motion would give way to a stiff inclination to starboard of fully ten degrees. Then the squalls would pass, the seas rise the higher for their momentary suppression, and the boat resume her wallowing, rolling both rails under, and practically under water, except for the high forecastle deck, the funnels, and the companions.

Denman did not worry. With the wind northwest, the storm center was surely to the north and east-ward of him; and he knew that, according to the laws of storms in the North Atlantic, it would move away from him and out to sea.

And so it continued until about midnight, when he heard the rasping of the companion hood, then saw Florrie's face peering out. He sprang to the companion.

"Billie! Oh, Billie!" she said, plaintively. "Let me come up here with you?"

"But you'll feel better lying down, dear," he said. "Better go back."

"It's so close and hot down there. Please let me come up."

"Why, yes, Florrie, if you like; but wait until I fit you out. Come down a moment."

They descended, and he found rubber boots, a sou'wester, and a long oilskin coat, which she donned in her room. Then he brought up another chair, lashed it—with more neckties—to his own, and seated her in it.

"Don't be frightened," he said, as a sea climbed on board and washed aft, nearly flooding their rubber boots and eliciting a little scream from the girl. "We're safe, and the wind will blow out in a few hours."

He seated himself beside her. As they faced to leeward, the long brims of the sou'westers sheltered their faces from the blast of rain and spume, permitting conversation; but they did not converse for a time, Denman only reaching up inside the long sleeve of her big coat to where her small hand nestled, soft and warm, in its shelter. He squeezed it gently, but there was no answering pressure, and he contented himself with holding it.

He was a good sailor, but a poor lover, and—a reeling, water-washed deck in a gale of wind is an embarrassing obstacle to love-making. Yet he squeezed again, after ten minutes of silence had gone by and several seas had bombarded their feet. Still no response in kind, and he spoke.

"Florrie," he said, as gently as he could when he was compelled to shout, "do you remember the letter you sent me the other day?"

"The other day," she answered. "Why, it seems years since then."

"Last week, Florrie. It made me feel like—like thirty cents."

"Why, Billie?"

"Oh, the unwritten roast between the lines, little girl. I knew what you thought of me. I knew that I'd never made good."

"How—what do you mean?"

"About the fight—years ago. I was to come back and lick him, you know, and didn't—that's all."

"Are you still thinking of that, Billie? Why, you've won. You are an officer, while he is a sailor."

"Yes, but he licked me at school, and I know you expected me to come back."

"And you did not come back. You never let me hear from you. You might have been dead for years before I could know it."

"Is that it, Florrie?" he exclaimed, in amazement. "Was it me you thought of? I supposed you had grown to despise me."

She did not answer this; but when he again pressed her hand she responded. Then, over the sounds of the storm, he heard a little sob; and, reaching over, drew her face close to his, and kissed her.

"I'm sorry, Florrie, but I didn't know. I've loved you all these years, but I did not know it until a few days ago. And I'll never forget it, Florrie, and I promise you—and myself, too—that I'll still make good, as I promised before."

Poor lover though he was, he had won. She did not answer, but her own small hand reached for his.

And so they passed the night, until, just as a lighter gray shone in the east, he noticed that one of the red lamps at the signal yard had gone out. As the lights were still necessary, he went forward to lower them; but, just as he was about to mount the bridge stairs, a crashing blow from two heavy fists sent him headlong and senseless to the deck.

When he came to, he was bound hand and foot as he had bound the men—with neckerchiefs—and lay close to the forward funnel, with the whole thirteen, Jenkins and all, looking down at him. But Jenkins was not speaking. Forsythe, searching Denman's pockets, was doing all that the occasion required.

CHAPTER XVII

When Sampson had entered the forecastle after his rescue by Denman, he found a few of his mates in their bunks, the rest sitting around in disconsolate postures, some holding their aching heads, others looking indifferently at him with bleary eyes. The apartment, long and triangular in shape, was dimly lighted by four deadlights, two each side, and for a moment Sampson could not distinguish one from another.

"Where's my bag?" he demanded, generally. "I want dry clothes."

He groped his way to the bunk he had occupied, found his clothes bag, and drew out a complete change of garments.

"Who's got a knife?" was his next request; and, as no one answered, he repeated the demand in a louder voice.

"What d'you want of a knife?" asked Forsythe, with a slight snarl.

"To cut your throat, you hang-dog scoundrel," said Sampson, irately. "Forsythe, you speak kindly and gently to me while we're together, or I'll break some o' your small bones. Who's got a knife?"

"Here's one, Sampson," said Hawkes, offering one of the square-bladed jackknives used in the navy.

"All right, Hawkes. Now, will you stand up and rip these wet duds off me? I can't get 'em off with the darbies in the way."

Hawkes stood up and obeyed him. Soon the dripping garments fell away, and Sampson rubbed himself dry with a towel, while Hawkes sleepily turned in.

"What kept you, and what happened?" asked Kelly. "Did he douse you with a bucket o' water?"

Sampson did not answer at once—not until he had slashed the side seams of a whole new suit, and crawled into it. Then, as he began fastening it on with buttons and strings, he said, coldly:

"Worse than that. He's made me his friend."

"His friend?" queried two or three.

"His friend," repeated Sampson. "Not exactly while he has me locked up," he added; "but if I ever get out again—that's all. And his friend in some ways while I'm here. D'you hear that, Forsythe?"

Forsythe did not answer, and Sampson went on: "And not only his friend, but the woman's too. Hear that, Forsythe?"

Forsythe refused to answer.

"That's right, and proper," went on Sampson, as he fastened the last button. "Hide your head and saw wood, you snake-eyed imitation of a man."

"What's up, Sampson?" wearily asked Casey from a bunk. "What doused you, and what you got on Forsythe now?"

"I'll tell you in good time," responded Sampson. "I'll tell you now about Denman. I threw all the booze overboard at his orders. Then *I* tumbled over; and, as I can't swim, would ha' been there yet if he hadn't jumped after me. Then we couldn't get up the side, and the woman come with a tablecloth, that held me up until I was towed to the anchor ladder. That's all. I just want to hear one o' you ginks say a word about that woman that she wouldn't like to hear. That's for you all—and for *you*, Forsythe, a little more in good time."

"Bully for the woman!" growled old Kelly. "Wonder if we treated her right."

"We treated her as well as we knew how," said Sampson; "that is, all but one of us. But I've promised Denman, and the woman, through him, that they'll have a better show if we get charge again."

"Aw, forget it!" grunted Forsythe from his bunk. "She's no good. She's been stuck on that baby since she was a kid."

Sampson went toward him, seized him by the shirt collar, and pulled him bodily from the bunk. Then, smothering his protesting voice by a grip on his throat, slatted him from side to side as a farmer uses a flail, and threw him headlong against the after bulkhead and half-way into an empty bunk. Sampson had uttered no word, and Forsythe only muttered as he crawled back to his own bunk. But he found courage to say:

"What do you pick on me for? If you hadn't all got drunk, you wouldn't be here."

"You mean," said Sampson, quietly, "that if you hadn't remained sober enough to find your way into the after cabin and frighten the woman, we wouldn't ha' been here; for that's what roused Denman."

A few oaths and growls followed this, and men sat up in their bunks, while those that were out of their bunks stood up. Sampson sat down.

"Is that so, Sampson?" "Got that right, old man?" "Sure of it?" they asked, and then over the hubbub of profane indignation rose Forsythe's voice.

"Who gave you that?" he yelled. "Denman?"

"Yes—Denman," answered Sampson.

"He lied. I did nothing of the—"

"You lie yourself, you dog. You're showing on your chin the marks of Denman's fist."

"You did that just now," answered Forsythe, fingering a small, bleeding bruise.

"I didn't hit you. I choked you. Denman knocked you out."

"Well," answered Forsythe, forgetting the first accusation in the light of this last, "it was a lucky blow in the dark. He couldn't do it in the daylight."

"Self-convicted," said Sampson, quietly.

Then, for a matter of ten minutes, the air in the close compartment might have smelled sulphurous to one strange to forecastle discourse. Forsythe, his back toward them, listened quietly while they called him all the names, printable and unprintable, which angry and disgusted men may think of.

But when it had ended—when the last voice had silenced and the last man gone to the water faucet for a drink before turning in, Forsythe said:

"I'll even things up with you fellows if I get on deck again."

Only a few grunts answered him, and soon all were asleep.

They wakened, one by one, in the afternoon, to find the electric bulbs glowing, and the boat rolling heavily, while splashes of rain came in through the weather deadlights. These they closed; and, better humored after their sleep, and hungry as well, they attacked the barrel of bread and the water faucet.

"He's started the dynamo," remarked Riley, one of the engineers. "Why don't he start the engine and keep her head to the sea?"

"Because he knows too much," came a hoarse whisper, and they turned to Jenkins, who was sitting up, regarding them disapprovingly.

"Because he knows too much," he repeated, in the same hoarse whisper. "This is a so-called seagoing destroyer; but no one but a fool would buck one into a head sea; and that's what's coming, with a big blow, too. Remember the English boat that broke her back in the North Sea?"

"Hello, Jenkins—you alive?" answered one, and others asked of his health.

"I'm pretty near all right," he said to them. "I've been able to move and speak a little for twenty-four hours, but I saved my energy. I wasn't sure of myself, though, or I'd ha' nabbed Denman when he came in here for the pistols."

"Has he got them?" queried a few, and they examined the empty bunk.

"He sure has," they continued. "Got 'em all. Oh, we're in for it."

"Not necessarily," said Jenkins. "I've listened to all this powwow, and I gather that you got drunk to the last man, and he gathered you in."

"That's about it, Jenkins," assented Sampson. "We all got gloriously drunk."

"And before you got drunk you made this pin-headed, educated rat"—he jerked his thumb toward Forsythe—"your commander."

"Well—we needed a navigator, and you were out of commission, Jenkins."

"I'm in commission now, though, and when we get on deck, we'll still have a navigator, and it won't be Denman, either."

"D'you mean," began Forsythe, "that you'll take charge again, and make"

"Yes," said Jenkins, "make you navigate. Make you navigate under orders and under fear of punishment. You're the worst-hammered man in this crowd; but hammering doesn't improve you. You'll be keelhauled, or triced up by the thumbs, or spread-eagled over a boiler—but you'll navigate. Now, shut up."

There was silence for a while, then one said: "You spoke about getting on deck again, Jenkins. Got any plan?"

"Want to go on deck now and stand watch in this storm?" Jenkins retorted.

"No; not unless necessary."

"Then get into your bunk and wait for this to blow over. If there is any real need of us, Denman will call us out."

This was good sailorly logic, and they climbed back into their bunks, to smoke, to read, or to talk themselves to sleep again. As the wind and sea arose they closed the other two deadlights, and when darkness closed down they turned out the dazzling bulbs, and slept through the night as only sailors can.

Just before daylight Jenkins lifted his big bulk out of the bunk, and, taking a key from his pocket, unlocked the forecastle door. He stepped into the passage, and found the hatch loose on the coamings, then came back and quietly wakened them all.

"I found this key on the deck near the door first day aboard," he volunteered; "but put it in my pocket instead of the door."

They softly crept out into the passage and lifted the hatch; but it was the irrepressible and most certainly courageous Forsythe who was first to climb up. He reached the deck just in time to dodge into the darkness behind the bridge ladder at the sight of Denman coming forward to attend to the lamps; and it was he who sent both fists into the side of Denman's face with force enough to knock him senseless. Then came the others.

CHAPTER XVIII

"That'll do, Forsythe," said Sampson, interrupting the flow of billingsgate. "We'll omit prayers and flowers at this funeral. Stand up."

Forsythe arose, waving two bunches of keys and Denman's revolver.

"Got him foul," he yelled, excitedly. "All the keys and his gun."

"All right. Just hand that gun to me—what! You won't?"

Forsythe had backed away at the command; but Sampson sprang upon him and easily disarmed him.

"Now, my lad," he said, sternly, "just find the key of these darbies and unlock us."

Forsythe, muttering, "Got one good smash at him, anyhow," found the key of the handcuffs, and, first unlocking his own, went the rounds. Then he found the key of the leg irons, and soon all were free, and the manacles tossed down the hatch to be gathered up later. Then big Jenkins reached his hand out to Forsythe—but not in token of amnesty.

"The keys," he said, in his hoarse whisper.

"Aren't they safe enough with me?" queried Forsythe, hotly.

Jenkins still maintained the outstretched hand, and Forsythe looked irresolutely around. He saw no signs of sympathy. They were all closing in on him, and he meekly handed the two bunches to Jenkins, who pocketed them.

Meanwhile, Sampson had lifted Denman to his feet; and, as the boat still rolled heavily, he assisted him to the bridge stairs, where he could get a grip on the railing with his fettered hands. Daylight had come, and Denman could see Florrie, still seated in the deck chair, looking forward with frightened eyes.

"Jenkins, step here a moment," said Sampson; "and you other fellows—keep back."

Jenkins drew near.

"Did you hear, in the fo'castle," Sampson went on, "what I said about Mr. Denman saving my life, and that I promised him parole and the possession of his gun in case we got charge again?"

Jenkins nodded, but said: "He broke his parole before."

"So would you under the same provocation. Forsythe called him a milk-fed thief. Wouldn't you have struck out?"

Jenkins nodded again, and Sampson continued:

"All right. My proposition is to place Mr. Denman under parole once more, to give him and the lady the run of the deck abaft the galley hatch, and to leave them both the possession of their guns for self-defense, in case"—he looked humorously around at the others—"these inebriates get drunk again."

"But the other guns. He has them somewhere. We want power of self-defense, too."

"Mr. Denman," said Sampson, turning to the prisoner, "you've heard the conditions. Will you tell us where the arms are, and will you keep aft of the galley hatch, you and the lady?"

"I will," answered Denman, "on condition that you all, and particularly your navigator, keep forward of the galley hatch."

"We'll do that, sir; except, of course, in case of working or fighting ship. Now, tell us where the guns are, and we'll release you."

"Haven't we something to say about this?" inquired Forsythe, while a few others grumbled their disapproval of the plan.

"No; you have not," answered Jenkins, his hoarse whisper becoming a voice. "Not a one of you. Sampson and I will be responsible for this."

"All right, then," responded Forsythe. "But I'll carry my gun all the time. I'm not going to be shot down without a white man's chance."

"You'll carry a gun, my son," said Sampson, "when we give it to you—and then it won't be to shoot Mr. Denman. It's on your account, remember, that we're giving him a gun. Now, Mr. Denman, where are the pistols and toothpicks?"

"The pistols are in my room, the cutlasses in the room opposite. You have the keys."

"Aft all hands," ordered Jenkins, fumbling in his pockets for the keys, "and get the weapons."

Away they trooped, and crowded down the wardroom companion, Sampson lifting his cap politely to the girl in the chair. In a short time they reappeared, each man loaded down with pistols and cutlasses. They placed them in the forecastle, and when they had come up Sampson released Denman's bonds.

"Now, sir," he said, "you are free. We'll keep our promises, and we expect you to keep yours. Here is your gun, Mr. Denman."

"Thank you, Sampson," said Denman, pocketing the revolver and shaking his aching hands to circulate the blood. "Of course, we are to keep our promises."

"Even though you see things done that will raise your hair, sir."

"What do you mean by that?" asked Denman, with sudden interest.

"Can't tell you anything, sir, except what you may know, or will know. This boat is *not* bound for the African coast. That's all, sir."

"Go below the watch," broke in Jenkins' husky voice. "To stations, the rest."

CHAPTER XIX

"What happened, Billie?" asked Florrie as Denman joined her.

"Not much, Florrie," he replied, as cheerfully as was possible in his mood. "Only a physical and practical demonstration that I am the two ends and the bight of a fool."

"You are not a fool, Billie; but what happened? How did they get out?"

"By picking the lock of the door, I suppose; or, perhaps, they had a key inside. That's where the fool comes in. I should have nailed the door on them."

"And what do they mean to do?"

"Don't know. They have some new project in mind. But we're better off than before, girl. We're at liberty to carry arms, and to go and come, provided we stay this side of the galley hatch. They are to let us alone and stay forward of the hatch. By the way," he added. "In view of the rather indeterminate outlook, let's carry our hardware outside."

He removed his belt from his waist and buckled it outside his oilskin coat. Then, when he had transferred the pistol from his pocket to the scabbard, he assisted the girl.

"There," he said, as he stood back and looked at her, admiringly, "with all due regard for your good looks, Florrie, you resemble a cross between a cowboy and a second mate."

"No more so than you," she retorted; "but I've lost my place as cook, I think." She pointed at the galley chimney, from which smoke was arising. Denman looked, and also became interested in an excited convention forward.

Though Jenkins had sent the watch below and the rest to stations, only the two cooks had obeyed. The others, with the boat still rolling in the heavy sea, had surrounded Jenkins, and seemed to be arguing with him. The big man, saving his voice, answered only by signs as yet; but the voices of the others soon became audible to the two aft.

"I tell you it's all worked out, Jenkins—all figured out while you were dopy in your bunk."

Jenkins shook his head.

Then followed an excited burst of reason and flow of words from which Denman could only gather a few disjointed phrases: "Dead easy, Jenkins—Run close and land—Casey's brother—Can hoof it to—Might get a job, which'd be better—Got a private code made up—Don't need money—Can beat his way in—My brother has a wireless—Take the dinghy; we don't need it—I'll take the chance if you have a life-buoy handy—Chance of a lifetime—Who wants beach combing in Africa—You see, he'll watch the financial news—I'll stow away in her—I tell you, Jenkins, there'll be no killing. I've made my mind up to that, and will see to it."

The last speech was from Sampson; and, on hearing it, Jenkins waved them all away. Then he used his voice.

"Get to stations," he said. "I'll think it out. Forsythe, take the bridge and dope out where we are."

They scattered, and Forsythe mounted to the bridge, while Jenkins, still a sick man, descended to the forecastle.

"What does it all mean, Billie?" asked the girl.

"Haven't the slightest idea," answered Denman, as he seated himself beside her. "They've been hinting at big things; and Sampson said that they might raise my hair. However, we'll know soon. The wind is going down. This was the outer fringe of a cyclone."

"Why don't they go ahead?"

"Too much sea. These boats are made for speed, not strength. You can break their backs by steaming into a head sea."

Daniels, the cook, came on deck and aft to the limits of the hatch, indicating by his face and manner that he wished to speak to Denman.

Denman arose and approached him.

"Will you and the lady eat breakfast together, sir?" he asked.

"I believe so," answered Denman. Then, turning to Florrie: "How will it be? May I eat breakfast with you this morning?"

She nodded.

"Then, sir," said Daniels, "I'll have to serve it in the after cabin."

"Why not the wardroom? Why not keep out of Miss Fleming's apartment?"

"Because, Mr. Denman, our work is laid out. Billings attends to the wardroom, and swears he won't serve this lady, or get within reach of her."

"Serve it in the after cabin, then," said Denman, turning away to hide the coming smile, and Daniels departed.

Not caring to agitate the girl with an account of Billings' drunken overtures and his own vicarious repulse of them, he did not explain to her Billings' trouble of mind; but he found trouble of his own in explaining his frequent bursts of laughter while they ate their breakfast in the cabin. And Florrie found trouble in accepting his explanations, for they were irrelevant, incompetent, and inane.

After breakfast they went on deck without oilskins, for wind and sea were going down. There was a dry deck; and above, a sky which, still gray with the background of storm cloud, yet showed an occasional glimmer of blue, while to the east the sun shone clear and unobstructed; but on the whole clean-cut horizon there was not a sign of sail or smoke.

Eight bells having struck, the watches were changed; but except possibly a man in the engine room getting up steam—for smoke was pouring out of the four funnels—no one was at stations. The watch on deck was scattered about forward; and Forsythe had given way to Jenkins, who, with his eye fixed to a long telescope, was scanning the horizon from the bridge.

Denman, for over forty-eight hours without sleep, would have turned in had not curiosity kept him awake. So he waited until nine o'clock, when Forsythe, with Munson's help, took morning sights, and later until ten, when Forsythe handed Jenkins a slip of paper on which presumably he had jotted the boat's approximate position. Immediately Jenkins rang the engine bells, and the boat forged ahead.

Denman watched her swing to a starboard wheel; and, when the rolling gave way to a pitching motion as she met the head sea, he glanced at the after binnacle compass.

"Northwest by north, half north," he said. "Whatever their plan is, Jenkins has been won over. Florrie, better turn in. I'm going to. Lock your door and keep that gun handy."

But they were not menaced—not even roused for dinner; for Daniels had gone below, and Billings, on watch for the morning, could not wake Denman, and would not approach Miss Florrie's door. So it was late in the afternoon when they again appeared on deck.

The weather had cleared, the sea was smoothing, and the boat surging along under the cruising turbines; while Hawkes had the wheel, and Forsythe, still in officer's uniform, paced back and forth.

Evidently Jenkins, in the light of his physical and mental limitations, had seen the need of an assistant. Old Kelly, the gunner's mate, was fussing around a twelve-pounder; the rest were out of sight.

Denman concluded that some kind of sea discipline had been established while he slept, and that Kelly had been put in charge of the gunnery department and been relieved from standing watch; otherwise, by the former arrangement, Kelly would have been below while Forsythe and Hawkes were on deck.

The horizon was dotted with specks, some showing smoke, others, under the glass, showing canvas. Denman examined each by the captain's binoculars, but saw no signs of a government craft—all were peaceably going their way.

"Why is it," asked Florrie, as she took the glass from Denman, "that we see so many vessels now, when we lay for days without seeing any?"

"We were in a pocket, I suppose," answered Denman. "Lane routes, trade routes, for high and low-powered craft, as well as for sailing craft, are so well established these days that, if you get between them, you can wait for weeks without seeing anything."

"Do you think there is any chance of our being rescued soon?"

"I don't know, Florrie; though we can't go much nearer the coast without being recognized. In fact, I haven't thought much about it lately—the truth is, I'm getting interested in these fellows. This is the most daring and desperate game I ever saw played, and how they'll come out is a puzzle. Hello! Eight bells."

The bell was struck on the bridge, and the watches changed, except that Jenkins, after a short talk with Forsythe, did not relieve him, but came aft to the engine-room hatch, where he held another short talk with Sampson and Riley, who, instead of going below, had waited.

Only a few words came to Denman's ears, and these in the hoarse accents of Jenkins as he left them: "Six days at cruising speed, you say, and two at full steam? All right."

Jenkins continued aft, but halted and called the retreating Sampson, who joined him; then the two approached the galley hatch and hailed Denman.

"Captain Jenkins can't talk very well, sir," said Sampson, with a conciliatory grin; "but he wants me to ask you what you did to him. He says he bears no grudge."

"Can't tell you," answered Denman, promptly. "It is a trick of Japanese jujutsu, not taught in the schools, and known only to experts. I learned it in Japan when my life was in danger."

Jenkins nodded, as though satisfied with the explanation, and Sampson resumed:

"Another thing we came aft for, Mr. Denman, is to notify you that we must search the skipper's room and the wardroom for whatever money there is on board. There may be none, but we want the last cent."

"What on earth," exclaimed Denman, "do you want with money?" Then, as their faces clouded, he added: "Oh, go ahead. Don't turn my room upside-down. You'll find my pile in a suit of citizen's clothes hanging up. About four and a half."

"Four and a half is a whole lot, sir," remarked Sampson as they descended the wardroom hatch.

"Got any money down below, Florrie?" inquired Denman, joining the girl.

She shook her head. "No. I lost everything but what I wear."

The tears that started to her eyes apprised Denman that hers was more than a money loss; but there is no comfort of mere words for such loss, and he went on quickly:

"They are going through the cabin for money. They'll get all I've got. Did you see any cash in the captain's desk?"

"Why, yes, Billie," she said, hesitatingly. "I wanted a place to put my combs when I wore the bandage, and I saw some money in the upper desk. It was a roll."

"He's lost it, then. Always was a careless man. Did you count it?"

"No. I had no right to."

But the question in Denman's mind was answered by Sampson when he and Jenkins emerged from the hatch. "Five hundred," he said. "Fine! He won't need a quarter of it, Jenkins."

"Five hundred!" repeated Denman to the girl. "Jail-breaking, stealing government property, mutiny—against me—piracy, and burglary. Heaven help them when they are caught!"

"But will they be?"

"Can't help but be caught. I know nothing of their plans; but I do know that they are running right into a hornet's nest. If a single one of those craft on the horizon recognizes this boat and can wireless the nearest station, we'll be surrounded tomorrow."

But, as it happened, they were not recognized, though they took desperate chances in charging through a coasting fleet in daylight. And at nightfall Jenkins gave the order for full speed.

CHAPTER XX

For an hour Denman remained with Florrie to witness the unusual spectacle of a forty-knot destroyer in a hurry.

The wind was practically gone, though a heavy ground swell still met the boat from the northwest; and as there was no moon, nor starlight, and as all lights were out but the white masthead and red and green side lights, invisible from aft, but dimly lighting the sea ahead, the sight presented was unusual and awe-inspiring.

They seemed to be looking at an ever-receding wall of solid blackness, beneath which rose and spread from the high bow, to starboard and port, two huge, moving snowdrifts, lessening in size as the bow lifted over the crest of a sea it had climbed, and increasing to a liquid avalanche of foam that sent spangles up into the bright illumination of the masthead light when the prow buried itself in the base of the next sea.

Astern was a white, self-luminous wake that narrowed to a point in the distance before it had lost its phosphorescent glow.

Florrie was interested only in the glorious picture as a whole. Denman, equally impressed, was interested in the somewhat rare spectacle of a craft meeting at forty knots a sea running at twenty; for not a drop of water hit the deck where they stood.

They went below at last; but Denman, having slept nearly all day, was long in getting to sleep. A curious, futile, and inconsequential thought bothered him—the thought that the cheerful Billings had ceased his singing in the galley.

The monotonous humming of the turbines brought sleep at last; but he awakened at daylight from a dream in which Billings, dressed in a Mother Hubbard and a poke bonnet, was trying to force a piece of salt-water soap into his mouth, and had almost succeeded when he awoke. But it was the stopping of the turbines that really had wakened him; and he dressed hurriedly and went on deck.

There was nothing amiss. No one was in sight but Jenkins, who leaned lazily against the bridge rail. In the dim light that shone, nothing could be seen on the horizon or within it.

So, a little ashamed of his uncalled-for curiosity, he hurried down and turned in, "all standing," to wait for breakfast and an explanation.

But no explanation was given him, either by events or the attitude of the men. Those on deck avoided the after end of the boat—all except old Kelly, whose duties brought him finally to the after guns and tubes; but, while civilly lifting his cap to Miss Florrie, he was grouchy and taciturn in his manner until his work was done, then he halted at the galley hatch on his way forward to lean over and pronounce anathema on the heads of the cooks because of the quality of the food.

While waiting for breakfast, Denman had listened to an angry and wordy argument between the two cooks, in which Daniels had voiced his opinion of Billings for waking him from his watch below to serve the prisoners.

When the watches were changed at eight bells that morning, he had heard Hawkes and Davis, the two seamen of the deck department, protesting violently to Jenkins at the promotion of Forsythe and Kelly, which left them to do all the steering.

Jenkins had not answered orally, but his gestures overruled the protest. Even Casey and Munson argued almost to quarreling over various "tricks of their trade," which Denman, as he listened, could only surmise were to form a part of the private code they had spoken of when haranguing Jenkins.

There was a nervous unrest pervading them all which, while leaving Florrie and Denman intact, even reached the engine room.

At noon Sampson and Dwyer were relieved, and the former turned back to shout down the hatch:

"I told you to do it, and that goes. We've over-hauled and cleaned it. You two assemble and oil it up this afternoon, or you'll hear from me at eight bells."

The voice of Riley—who was nearly as large a man as Sampson—answered hotly but inarticulately, and Denman could only ascribe the row to a difference of opinion concerning the condition of some part of the engines.

Sampson, though possibly a lesser engineer than the others of his department, yet dominated them as Jenkins dominated them all—by pure force of personality. He had made himself chief engineer, and his orders were obeyed, as evidenced by the tranquil silence that emanated from the engine room when Sampson returned at four in the afternoon.

All day the boat lay with quiet engines and a bare head of steam, rolling slightly in a swell that now came from the east, while the sun shone brightly overhead from east to west, and only a few specks appeared on the horizon, to remain for a time, and vanish.

Meanwhile Florrie worried Denman with questions that he could not answer.

"Forsythe took sights in the morning," he explained at length, "and a meridian observation at noon. He has undoubtedly found another 'pocket,' as I call these triangular spaces between the routes; but I do not know where we are, except that, computing our yesterday and last night's run, we are within from sixty to a hundred miles of New York."

He was further mystified when, on going into his room for a cigar after supper, he found his suit of "citizen's clothes" missing from its hook.

"Not the same thief," he grumbled. "Sampson and Jenkins are too big for it."

He did not mention his loss to Florrie, not wishing to arouse further feminine speculation; and when, at a later hour in this higher latitude, darkness had come, and full speed was rung to the engine room, he induced her to retire.

"I don't know what's up," he said; "but—get all the sleep you can. I'll call you if anything happens."

He did not go to sleep himself, but smoked and waited while the humming turbines gathered in the miles—one hour, two hours, nearly three—until a quarter to eleven o'clock, when speed was reduced.

Remembering his embarrassment of the morning, Denman did not seek the deck, but looked through his deadlight. Nothing but darkness met his eye; it was a black night with rain.

He entered the lighted wardroom and looked at the telltale above; it told him that the boat was heading due north. Then he entered an opposite room—all were unlocked now—from which, slantingly through the deadlight, he saw lights. He threw open the thick, round window, and saw more clearly. Lights, shore lights, ahead and to port.

He saw no land; but from the perspective of the lights he judged that they ran east and west. Then he heard the call of the lead: "A quarter seventeen;" and a little later: "By the deep seventeen," delivered in a sing-song voice by Hawkes.

"The coast of Long Island," muttered Denman. "Well, for picked-up, school-book navigation, it is certainly a feat—to run over six hundred miles and stop over soundings."

The boat went on at reduced speed until Hawkes had called out: "By the mark ten," when the engines stopped, and there was a rush of footsteps on deck, that centered over the open deadlight, above which was slung to the davits the boat called by them the dinghy, but which was only a very small gasoline launch.

"In with you, Casey," said Jenkins, in his low, hoarse voice, "and turn her over. See about the bottom plug, too. Clear away those guys fore and aft, you fellows."

In a few moments came the buzzing of the small engine; then it stopped, and Casey said: "Engine's all right, and—so is the plug. Shove out and lower away."

"Got everything right, Casey? Got your money? Got the code?"

"Got everything," was the impatient answer.

"Well, remember—you're to head the boat out from the beach, pull the bottom plug, and let her sink in deep water. Make sure your wheel's amidships."

"Shove out and lower away," retorted Casey. "D'you think I never learned to run a naphtha launch?"

Denman heard the creaking sound of the davits turning in their beds, then the slackening away of the falls, their unhooking by Casey, and the chugging of the engine as the launch drew away.

"Good luck, Casey!" called Jenkins.

"All right!" answered Casey from the distance. "Have your life-buoys handy."

Denman had ducked out of sight as the launch was lowered, and he did not see Casey; but, on opening a locker in his room for a fresh box of cigars, he noticed that his laundry had been tampered with. Six shirts and twice as many collars were gone. On looking further, he missed a new derby hat that he had prized more than usual, also his suitcase.

"Casey and I are about the same size," he muttered. "But what the deuce does it all mean?"

He went to sleep with the turbines humming full speed in his ears; but he wakened when they were reduced to cruising speed. Looking at his watch in the light from the wardroom, he found that it was half-past two; and, on stepping out for a look at the telltale, he found the boat heading due south.

"Back in the pocket," he said, as he returned to his room.

But the engines did not stop, as he partly expected; they remained at half speed, and the boat still headed south when he wakened at breakfast-time.

CHAPTER XXI

After breakfast, King, one of the machinists, and a pleasant-faced young man, came aft with an ensign, a hammer, chisel, and paint pot.

"This is work, sir," he said, as he passed, tipping his cap politely to Miss Florrie. "Should have been done before."

He went to the taffrail, and, leaning over with the hammer and chisel, removed the raised letters that spelled the boat's name. Then he covered the hiatus with paint, and hoisted the ensign to the flagstaff.

"Now, sir," he remarked, as he gathered up his tools and paint pot, "she's a government craft again."

"I see," commented Denman; and then to Florrie as King went forward: "They're getting foxy. We're steaming into the crowd again, and they want to forestall inspection and suspicion. I wonder if our being allowed on deck is part of the plan? A lady and an officer aft look legitimate."

At noon every man was dressed to the regulations, in clean blue, with neckerchief and knife lanyard, while Jenkins and Forsythe appeared in full undress uniform, with tasteful linen and neckwear.

That this was part of the plan was proven when, after a display of bunting in the International Signal Code from the yard up forward, they ranged alongside of an outbound tank steamer that had kindly slowed down for them.

All hands but one cook and one engineer had mustered on deck, showing a fair semblance of a full-powered watch; and the one cook—Billings—displayed himself above the hatch for one brief moment, clad in a spotless white jacket.

Then, just before the two bridges came together, Jenkins hurried down the steps and aft to Denman to speak a few words, then hasten forward. It was sufficiently theatrical to impress the skipper of the tanker, but what Jenkins really said to Denman was: "You are to remember your parole, sir, and not hail that steamer."

To which Denman had nodded assent.

"Steamer ahoy!" shouted Forsythe, through a small megaphone. "You are laden with oil, as you said by signal. We would like to replenish our supply, which is almost exhausted."

"Yes, sir," answered the skipper; "but to whom shall I send the bill?"

"To the superintendent of the Charlestown Navy Yard. It will very likely be paid to your owners before you get back. We want as much as a hundred tons. I have made out a receipt for that amount. Throw us a heaving line to take our hose, and I will send it up on the bight."

"Very well, sir. Anything else I can do for you, sir?"

"Yes; we want about two hundred gallons of water. Been out a long time."

"Certainly, sir—very glad to accommodate you. Been after that runaway torpedo boat?"

"Yes; any news of her on shore? Our wireless is out of order."

"Well, the opinion is that she was lost in the big blow a few days ago. She was reported well to the nor'ard; and it was a St. Lawrence Valley storm. Did you get any of it?"

"Very little," answered Forsythe. "We were well to the s'uth'ard."

"A slight stumble in good diction there, Mr. Forsythe," muttered the listening Denman. "Otherwise, very well carried out."

But the deluded tank skipper made no strictures on Forsythe's diction; and, while the pleasant conversation was going on, the two lines of hose were passed, and the receipt for oil and water sent up to the steamer.

In a short time the tanks were filled, the hose hauled back, and the starting bells run in both engine rooms.

The destroyer was first to gather way; and, as her stern drew abreast of the tanker's bridge, the skipper lifted his cap to Florrie and Denman, and called out: "Good afternoon, captain, I'm very glad that I was able to accommodate you."

To which Denman, with all hands looking expectantly at him, only replied with a bow—as became a dignified commander with two well-trained officers on his bridge to attend to the work.

The boat circled around, headed northwest, and went on at full speed until, not only the tanker, but every other craft in view, had sunk beneath the horizon. Then the engines were stopped, and the signal yard sent down.

"Back in the pocket again," said Denman to Florrie. "What on earth can they be driving at?"

"And why," she answered, with another query, "did they go to all that trouble to be so polite and nice, when, as you say, they are fully committed to piracy, and robbed the other vessels by force?"

"This seems to show," he said, "the master hand of Jenkins, who is a natural-born gentleman, as against the work of Forsythe, who is a natural-born brute."

"Yet he is a high-school graduate."

"And Jenkins is a passed seaman apprentice."

"What is that?"

"One who enters the navy at about fifteen or sixteen to serve until he is twenty-one, then to leave the navy or reënlist. They seldom reënlist, for they are trained, tutored, and disciplined into good workmen, to whom shore life offers better opportunities. Those who do reënlist have raised the standard of the navy sailor to the highest in the world; but those that don't are a sad loss to the navy. Jenkins reënlisted. So did Forsythe."

"But do you think the training and tutoring that Jenkins received equal to an education like Forsythe's—or yours?"

"They learn more facts," answered Denman. "The training makes a man of a bad boy, and a gentleman of a good one. What a ghastly pity that, because of conservatism and politics, all this splendid material for officers should go to waste, and the appointments to Annapolis be given to good high-school scholars, who might be cowardly sissies at heart, or blackguards like Forsythe!"

"But that is how you received your appointment, Billie Denman," said the girl, warmly; "and you are neither a sissy nor a blackguard."

"I hope not," he answered, grimly. "Yet, if I had first served my time as seaman apprentice before being appointed to Annapolis, I might be up on that bridge now, instead of standing supinely by while one seaman apprentice does the navigating and another the bossing."

"There is that man again. I'm afraid of him, Billie. All the others, except Forsythe, have been civil to me; but he looks at me—so—so hatefully."

Billings, minus his clean white jacket, had come up the hatch and gone forward. He came back soon, showing a sullen, scowling face, as though his cheerful disposition had entirely left him.

As he reached the galley hatch, he cast upon the girl a look of such intense hatred and malevolence that Denman, white with anger, sprang to the hatch, and halted him.

"If ever again," he said, explosively, "I catch you glaring at this lady in that manner, parole or no parole, I'll throw you overboard."

Billings' face straightened; he saluted, and, without a word, went down the hatch, while Denman returned to the girl.

"He is an enlisted man," he said, bitterly, "not a passed seaman apprentice; so I downed him easily with a few words."

And then came the thought, which he did not express to Florrie, that his fancied limitations, which prevented him from being on the bridge, also prevented him from enlightening the morbid Billings as to the real source of the "terrible punch" he had received; for, while he could justify his silence to Florrie, he could only, with regard to Billings, feel a masculine dread of ridicule at dressing in feminine clothing.

CHAPTER XXII

At supper that evening they were served with prunes, bread without butter, and weak tea, with neither milk nor sugar.

"Orders from for'a'd, sir," said Daniels, noticing Denman's involuntary look of surprise. "All hands are to be on short allowance for a while—until something comes our way again."

"But why," asked Denman, "do you men include us in your plans and economies? Why did you not rid yourself of us last night, when you sent one of your number ashore?"

Daniels was a tall, somber-faced man—a typical ship's cook—and he answered slowly: "I cannot tell you, sir. Except that both you and the lady might talk about this boat."

"Oh, well," said Denman, "I was speaking for this lady, who doesn't belong with us. My place is right here."

"Yes, sir," agreed Daniels; "but I am at liberty to say, sir, to you and the lady, that you'd best look out for Billings. He seems to be goin' batty. I heard him talking to himself, threatening harm to this lady. I don't know what he's got against her myself—"

"Tell him," said Denman, sharply, "that if he enters this apartment, or steps one foot abaft the galley hatch on deck, the parole is broken, and I'll put a bullet through his head. You might tell that to Jenkins, too."

Daniels got through the wardroom door before answering: "I'll not do that, sir. Jenkins might confine him, and leave all the work to me. But I think Billings needs a licking."

Whether Daniels applied this treatment for the insane to Billings, or whether Billings, with an equal right to adjudge Daniels insane, had applied the same treatment to him, could not be determined without violation of the parole; but when they had finished supper and reached the deck, sounds of conflict came up from the galley hatch, unheard and uninterrupted by those forward. It was a series of thumps, oaths, growlings, and the rattling of pots and pans on the galley floor. Then there was silence.

"You see," said Denman to Florrie, with mock seriousness, "the baleful influence of a woman aboard ship! It never fails."

"I can't help it," she said, with a pout and a blush—her blushes were discernible now, for the last vestige of the scalding had gone—"but I mean to wear a veil from this on. I had one in my pocket."

"I think that would be wise," answered Denman, gravely. "These men are—"

"You see, Billie," she interrupted. "I've got a new complexion—brand new; peaches and cream for the first time in my life, and I'm going to take care of it."

"That's right," he said, with a laugh. "But I'll wager you won't patent the process. Live steam is rather severe as a beautifier!"

But she kept her word. After the meager breakfast next morning—which Daniels served with no explanation of the row—she appeared on deck with her face hidden, and from then on wore the veil.

There was a new activity among the men—a partial relief from the all-pervading nervousness and irritability. Gun and torpedo practice—which brought to drill every man on board except Munson, buried in his wireless room, and one engineer on duty—was inaugurated and continued through the day.

Their natty blue uniforms discarded, they toiled and perspired at the task; and when, toward the end of the afternoon, old Kelly decided that they could be depended upon to fire a gun or eject a torpedo, Jenkins decreed that they should get on deck and lash to the rail in their chocks four extra torpedoes.

As there was one in each tube, this made eight of the deadliest weapons of warfare ready at hand; and when the task was done they quit for the day, the deck force going to the bridge for a look around the empty horizon, the cooks to the galley, and the machinists to the engine room.

Denman, who with doubt and misgiving had watched the day's preparations, led Florrie down the companion.

"They're getting ready for a mix of some kind; and there must be some place to put you away from gun fire. How's this?"

He opened a small hatch covered by the loose after edge of the cabin carpet, and disclosed a compartment below which might have been designed for stores, but which contained nothing, as a lighted electric bulb showed him. Coming up, he threw a couple of blankets down, and said:

"There's a cyclone cellar for you, Florrie, below the water line. If we're fired upon jump down, and don't come up until called, or until water comes in."

Then he went to his room for the extra store of cartridges he had secreted, but found them gone. Angrily returning to Florrie, he asked for her supply; and she, too, searched, and found nothing. But both their weapons were fully loaded.

"Well," he said, philosophically, as they returned to the deck, "they only guaranteed us the privilege of carrying arms. I suppose they feel justified from their standpoint."

But on deck they found something to take their minds temporarily off the loss. Sampson, red in the face, was vociferating down the engine-room hatch.

"Come up here," he said, loudly and defiantly. "Come up here and prove it, if you think you're a better man than I am. Come up and square yourself, you flannel-mouthed mick."

The "flannel-mouthed mick," in the person of Riley, white of face rather than red, but with eyes blazing and mouth set in an ugly grin, climbed up.

It was a short fight—the blows delivered by Sampson, the parrying done by Riley—and ended with a crashing swing on Riley's jaw that sent him to the deck, not to rise for a few moments.

"Had enough?" asked Sampson, triumphantly. "Had enough, you imitation of an ash cat? Oh, I guess you have. Think it out."

He turned and met Jenkins, who had run aft from the bridge.

"Now, Sampson, this'll be enough of this."

"What have *you* got to say about it?" inquired Sampson, irately.

"Plenty to say," answered Jenkins, calmly.

"Not much, you haven't. You keep away from the engine room and the engine-room affairs. I can 'tend to my department. You 'tend to yours."

"I can attend to yours as well when the time comes. There's work ahead for—"

"Well, attend to me now. You've sweated me all day like a stoker at your work; now go on and finish it up. I'll take a fall out o' you, Jenkins, right here."

"No, you won't! Wait until the work's done, and I'll accommodate you."

Jenkins went forward; and Sampson, after a few moments of scarcely audible grumbling, followed to the forecastle. Then Riley got up, looked after him, and shook his fist.

"I'll git even wi' you for this," he declared, with lurid profanity. "I'll have yer life for this, Sampson."

Then he went down the hatch, while Forsythe on the bridge, who had watched the whole affair with an evil grin, turned away from Jenkins when the latter joined him. Perhaps he enjoyed the sight of some one beside himself being knocked down.

"It looks rather bad, Florrie," said Denman, dubiously; "all this quarreling among themselves. Whatever job they have on hand they must hold together, or we'll get the worst of it. I don't like to see Jenkins and Sampson at it, though the two cooks are only a joke."

But there was no more open quarreling for the present. As the days wore on, a little gun and torpedo drill was carried out; while, with steam up, the boat made occasional darts to the north or south to avoid too close contact with passing craft, and gradually—by fits and starts—crept more to the westward. And Jenkins recovered complete control of his voice and movements, while Munson, the wireless man, grew haggard and thin.

At last, at nine o'clock one evening, just before Denman went down, Munson ran up with a sheet of paper, shouting to the bridge:

"Caught on—with the United—night shift."

Then, having delivered the sheet to Jenkins, he went back, and the rasping sound of his sending instrument kept up through the night.

But when Denman sought the deck after breakfast, it had stopped; and he saw Munson, still haggard of face, talking to Jenkins at the hatch.

"Got his wave length now," Denman heard him say. "Took all night, but that and the code'll fool 'em all."

From then on Munson stood watch at his instrument only from six in the evening until midnight, got more sleep thereby, and soon the tired, haggard look left his face, and it resumed its normal expression of intelligence and cheerfulness.

CHAPTER XXIII

After supper about a week later, Denman and Florrie sat in the deck chairs, watching the twilight give way to the gloom of the evening, and speculating in a desultory manner on the end of this never-ending voyage, when Munson again darted on deck, and ran up the bridge stairs with a sheet of paper, barely discernible in the gathering darkness, and handed it to Jenkins, who peered over it in the glow from the binnacle.

Then Jenkins blew on a boatswain's whistle—the shrill, trilling, and penetrating call that rouses all hands in the morning, but is seldom given again throughout the day except in emergencies.

All hands responded. Both cooks rushed up from the galley, the engineers on watch shut off all burners and appeared, and men tumbled up from the forecastle, all joining Jenkins and Munson on the bridge.

Denman strained his ears, but could hear nothing, though he saw each man bending over the paper in turn.

Then they quickly went back to their places below or on deck; and, as the bells were given to the engine room, the rasping of the wireless could be heard.

As the two cooks came aft, Denman heard them discussing excitedly but inaudibly the matter in hand; and, his curiosity getting the better of his pride, he waited only long enough to see the boat steadied at east-northeast, then went down and forward to the door leading into the passage that led to the galley.

Billings was doing most of the talking, in a high-pitched, querulous tone, and Daniels answered only by grunts and low-pitched monosyllables.

"*Gigantia*—ten to-morrow—five million," were a few of the words and phrases Denman caught; and at last he heard the concluding words of the talk.

"Dry up," said Daniels, loudly and threateningly. "Yes, thirteen is an unlucky number; but, if you don't shut up and clear off these dishes, I'll make our number twelve. Glad you've got something to think about besides that woman, but—shut up. You make me tired."

Denman went back to Florrie somewhat worried, but no longer puzzled; yet he gave the girl none of his thoughts that evening—he waited until morning, when, after a look around a bright horizon dotted with sail and steam, he said to her as she came up:

"Eat all the breakfast you can this morning, Florrie, for it may be some time before we'll eat again."

"Why, Billie, what is the matter?" asked the girl.

"We've traveled at cruising speed all night," he answered, "and now must be up close to the 'corner,' as they call the position where the outbound liners change to the great circle course."

"Well?" she said, inquiringly.

"Did you ever hear of the *Gigantia*?"

"Why, of course—you mean the new liner?"

"Yes; the latest and largest steamship built. She was on her maiden passage when this boat left port, and is about due to start east again. Florrie, she carries five million in bullion, and these fellows mean to hold her up."

"Goodness!" exclaimed the girl. "You mean that they will rob her—a big steamship?"

"She's big enough, of course, to tuck this boat down a hatchway; but these passenger boats carry no guns except for saluting, while this boat could sink her with the armament she carries. Look at those torpedoes—eight altogether, and more below decks. Eight compartments could be flooded, and bulkheads are not reliable. But will they dare? Desperate though they are, will they dare fire on a ship full of passengers?"

"How did you learn this, Billie? It seems impossible—incredible."

"Remember the gun and torpedo drill!" said Denman, softly, yet excitedly. "Our being in these latitudes is significant. They put Casey ashore the other night and robbed the captain and me to outfit him. I overheard some of the talk. He has reached New York, secured a position as night operator in a wireless station, studied the financial news, and sent word last night that the *Gigantia* sails at ten this morning with five million in gold."

"And where do you think she is now?" asked the girl, glancing around the horizon.

"At her dock in New York. She'll be out here late in the afternoon, I think. But, heavens, what chances!—to wait all day, while any craft that comes along may recognize this boat and notify the nearest station! Why didn't they intercept the lane route out at sea, where there is no crowd like this? I can only account for it by the shortage of stores. Yes; that's it. No sane pirate would take such risks. We've plenty of oil and water, but little food."

That Denman had guessed rightly was partly indicated by the action of the men and the boat that day.

All hands kept the deck, and their first task was to discard the now useless signal mast, which might help identify the boat as the runaway destroyer.

Two engineers sawed nearly through the mast at its base, while the others cleared away the light shrouds and forestay. Then a few tugs on the lee shroud sent it overboard, while the men dodged from under. Beyond smashing the bridge rail it did no damage.

The dodging tactics were resumed. A steamer appearing on the east or west horizon, heading so as to pass to the northward or southward, was given a wider berth by a dash at full speed in the opposite direction.

Every face—even Florrie's and Denman's—wore an anxious, nervous expression, and the tension increased as the hours went by.

Dinner was served, but brought no relief. Men spoke sharply to one another; and Jenkins roared his orders from the bridge, bringing a culmination to the strain that no one could have foreseen.

The sudden appearance of an inbound steamer out of a haze that had arisen to the east necessitated immediate full speed. Riley was in charge of the engine room, but Sampson stood at the hatch exercising an unofficial supervision; and it was he that received Jenkins' thundering request for more steam.

Sampson, in a voice equally loud, and with more profanity, admonished Jenkins to descend to the lower regions and attend to his own affairs.

Jenkins yielded. Leaving Forsythe in charge of the bridge, he came down the stairs and aft on the run. Not a word was spoken by either; but, with the prescience that men feel at the coming of a fight, the two cooks left their dishes and the engineers their engines to crowd their heads into the hatches. Riley showed his disfigured face over the heads of the other two; and on the bridge Forsythe watched with the same evil grin.

But few blows were passed, then the giants locked, and, twisting and writhing, whirled about the deck. Florrie screamed, but Denman silenced her.

"Nothing can be done," he said, "without violating the parole; and even if—"

He stopped, for the two huge forms, tightly embraced, had reeled like one solid object to the rail, which, catching them at just above the knees, had sent them overboard, exactly as Sampson had gone before.

"Man overboard!" yelled Denman, uselessly, for all had seen. But he threw a life-buoy fastened to the quarter, and was about to throw another, when he looked, and saw that his first was a hundred feet this side of the struggling men.

He turned to glance forward. Men were running about frantically, and shouting, but nothing was done, and the boat still held at a matter of forty knots an hour. Riley grinned from the hatch; and, forward on the bridge,

Forsythe turned his now sober face away, to look at the compass, and at the steamer fast disappearing in the haze that followed her.

Then, more as an outlet for his anger and disgust than in the hope of saving life, Denman threw the second life-buoy high in air over the stern, and led the shocked and hysterical Florrie down the stairs.

"Rest here a while," he said, gently, "and try to forget it. I don't know what they'll do now, but—keep your pistol with you at all times."

He went up with a grave face and many heartfelt misgivings; for, with Forsythe and Riley now the master spirits, things might not go well with them.

CHAPTER XXIV

In about ten minutes Forsythe ground the wheel over and headed back; but, though Denman kept a sharp lookout, he saw nothing of the two men or the life-buoys. He could feel no hope for Sampson, who was unable to swim. As for Jenkins, possibly a swimmer, even should he reach a life-buoy, his plight would only be prolonged to a lingering death by hunger and thirst; for there was but one chance in a million that he would be seen and picked up.

After ten minutes on the back track, the boat was logically in about the same position as when she had fled from the steamer; but Forsythe kept on for another ten minutes, when, the haze having enveloped the whole horizon, he stopped the engines, and the boat lost way, rolling sluggishly in the trough.

There was no wind, and nothing but the long ground swell and the haze to inconvenience them; the first in making it difficult to sight a telescope, the second in hiding everything on the horizon, though hiding the boat herself.

But at last Forsythe fixed something in the glass, gazing long and intently at a faint spot appearing to the northwest; and Denman, following suit with the binoculars, saw what he was looking at—a huge bulk coming out of the haze carrying one short mast and five funnels. Then he remembered the descriptions he had read of the mighty *Gigantia*—the only ship afloat with five funnels since the *Great Eastern.*

Forsythe called, and all hands flocked to the bridge, where they discussed the situation; and, as Denman judged by the many faces turned his way, discussed him and Florrie. But whatever resulted from the latter came to nothing.

They suddenly left the bridge, to disappear in the forecastle for a few moments, then to reappear—each man belted and pistoled, and one bringing an outfit to Forsythe on the bridge.

Two engineers went to the engines, Forsythe rang full speed to them, and the rest, cooks and all, swung the four torpedo tubes to port and manned the forward one.

The big ship seemed to grow in size visibly as her speed, plus the destroyer's, brought them together. In a few moments Denman made out details—six parallel lines of deadlights, one above the other, and extending from bow to stern, a length of a thousand feet; three tiers of deck houses, one above the other amidships; a line of twenty boats to a side along the upper deck, and her after rails black with passengers; while as many as six uniformed officers stood on her bridge—eighty feet above the water line.

The little destroyer rounded to alongside, and slowed down to a little more than the speed of the larger ship, which permitted her to creep along the huge, black side, inch by inch, until the bridges were nearly abreast. Then a white-whiskered man on the high bridge hailed:

"Steamer ahoy! What do you want?"

"Want all that bullion stowed in your strong room," answered Forsythe through a megaphone; "and, if you please, speak more distinctly, for the wash of your bow wave prevents my hearing what you say."

The officer was handed a megaphone, and through it his voice came down like a thunderclap.

"You want the bullion stowed in our strong room, do you? Anything else you want, sir?"

"Yes," answered Forsythe. "We want a boat full of provisions. Three barrels of flour, the rest in canned meats and vegetables."

"Anything else?" There was as much derision in the voice as can carry through a megaphone.

"That is all," answered Forsythe. "Load your gold into one of your own boats, the provisions in another. Lower them down and let the falls unreeve, so that they will go adrift. We will pick them up."

"Well, of all the infernal impudence I ever heard, yours is the worst. I judge that you are that crew of jail-breakers we've heard of that stole a government boat and turned pirates."

"You are right," answered Forsythe; "but don't waste our time. Will you give us what we asked for, or shall we sink you?"

"Sink us, you scoundrel? You can't, and you'd better not try, or threaten to. Your position is known, and three scouts started this morning from Boston and New York."

"That bluff don't go," answered Forsythe. "Will you cough up?"

"No; most decidedly *no*!" roared the officer, who might, or might not, have been the captain.

"Kelly," said Forsythe, "send that Whitehead straight into him."

Whitehead torpedoes, be it known, are mechanical fish of machined steel, self-propelling and self-steering, actuated by a small air engine, and carrying in their "war heads" a charge of over two hundred pounds of guncotton, and in their blunt noses a detonating cap to explode it on contact.

At Forsythe's word, Kelly turned a lever on the tube, and the contained torpedo dived gently overboard.

Denman, looking closely, saw it appear once on the surface, porpoiselike, before it dived to its indicated depth.

"The inhuman devil!" he commented, with gritting teeth.

A muffled report came from the depths. A huge mound of water lifted up, to break into shattered fragments and bubbles. Then these bubbles burst, giving vent to clouds of brown and yellow smoke; while up through the ventilators and out through the opened lower deadlights came more of this smoke, and the sound of human voices, screaming and groaning. These sounds were drowned in the buzzing of thousands of other voices on deck as men, women, and children fought their way toward the stern.

"Do you agree?" yelled Forsythe, through the megaphone. "Do you agree, or shall we unload every torpedo we've got into your hull?"

Old Kelly had calmly marshaled the crew to the next torpedo, and looked up to Forsythe for the word. But it did not come.

Instead, over the buzzing of the voices, came the officer's answer, loud and distinct:

"We agree. We understand that your necks are in the halter, and that you have nothing to lose, even though you should fill every compartment and drown every soul on board this ship. So we will accede to your demands. We will fill one boat with the bullion and another with provisions, and cast them adrift. But do not fire again, for God's sake!"

"All right," answered Forsythe. "Bear a hand."

Breast to breast, the two craft charged along, while two boats were lowered to the level of the main deck, and swiftered in to the rail. Sailors appeared from the doors in pairs, each carrying a box that taxed their strength and made them stagger. There were ten in all, and they slowly and carefully ranged them along the bottom of one of the boats, so as to distribute their weight.

While this was going on, stewards and galley helpers were filling the other boat with provisions—in boxes, barrels, and packages. Then the word was given, and the boats were cast off and lowered, the tackles of the heavier groaning mightily under the strain.

When they struck the water, the falls were instantly let go; and, as the boats drifted astern, the tackles unrove their long length from the blocks, and were hauled on board again.

Forsythe stopped the engines, and then backed toward the drifting boats. As the destroyer passed the stern of the giant steamer, a shout rang out; but only Denman heard it above the buzzing of voices. And it seemed that only he saw Casey spring from the high rail of the mammoth into the sea; for the rest were busy grappling for the boat's painters, and Forsythe was looking aft.

When the painters were secured and the boats drawn alongside, Forsythe rang for half speed; and the boat, under a port wheel, swung away from the *Gigantia*, and went ahead.

"There is your man Casey," yelled Denman, excitedly. "Are you going to leave him?"

Forsythe, now looking dead ahead, seemed not to hear; but Riley spoke from the hatch:

"Hold yer jaw back there, or ye'll get a passage, too."

With Casey's cries in his ears—sick at heart in the belief that not even a life-buoy would avail, for the giant steamship had not stopped her engines throughout the whole transaction, and was now half a mile away, Denman went down to Florrie, obediently waiting, yet nervous and frightened.

He told her nothing of what had occurred—but soothed and quieted her with the assurance that they would be rescued soon.

CHAPTER XXV

The engine stopped; and, climbing the steps to look forward, Denman saw the bridge deserted, and the whole ten surrounding an equal number of strong boxes, stamped and burned with official-looking letters and numbers. Farther along were the provision; and a peep astern showed Denman the drifting boats.

The big *Gigantia* had disappeared in the haze that hid the whole horizon; but up in the western sky was a portent—a black silhouette of irregular outline, that grew larger as he looked.

It was a monoplane—an advance scout of a scout boat—and Denman recognized the government model. It seemed to have sighted the destroyer, for it came straight on with a rush, circled overhead, and turned back.

There was no signal made; and, as it dwindled away in the west, Denman's attention was attracted to the men surrounding the boxes; only Munson was still watching the receding monoplane. But the rest were busy. With hammers and cold chisels from the engine room they were opening the boxes of treasure.

"Did any one see that fellow before?" demanded Munson, pointing to the spot in the sky.

A few looked, and the others answered with oaths and commands: "Forget it! Open the boxes! Let's have a look at the stuff!"

But Munson spoke again. "Forsythe, how about the big fellow's wireless? We didn't disable it. He has sent the news already. What do you think?"

"Oh, shut up!" answered Forsythe, irately. "I didn't think of it. Neither did any one. What of it? Nothing afloat can catch us. Open the box. Let's have a look, and we'll beat it for Africa."

"I tell you," vociferated Munson, "that you'd better start now—at full speed, too. That's a scout, and the mother boat isn't far away."

"Will you shut up, or will I shut you up?" shouted Forsythe.

"You'll not shut me up," retorted Munson. "You're the biggest fool in this bunch, in spite of your bluff. Why don't you go ahead and get out o' this neighborhood?"

A box cover yielded at this juncture, and Forsythe did not immediately answer. Instead, with Munson himself, and Billings the cook—insanely emitting whoops and yelps as he danced around for a peep—he joined the others in tearing out excelsior from the box. Then the bare contents came to view.

"Lead!" howled Riley, as he stood erect, heaving a few men back with his shoulders. "Lead it is, if I know wan metal from another."

"Open them all," roared Forsythe. "Get the axes—pinch bars—anything."

"Start your engine!" yelled Munson; but he was not listened to.

With every implement that they could lay their hands on they attacked the remaining boxes; and, as each in turn disclosed its contents, there went up howls of disappointment and rage. "Lead!" they shouted at last. "All lead! Was this job put up for us?"

"No," yelled Munson, "not for us. Every steamer carrying bullion also carries lead in the same kind of boxes. I've read of it many a time. It's a safeguard against piracy. We've been fooled—that's all."

Forsythe answered profanely and as coherently as his rage and excitement would permit.

Munson replied by holding his fist under Forsythe's nose.

"Get up on the bridge," he said. "And you, Riley, to your engines."

Riley obeyed the call of the exigency; but Forsythe resisted. He struck Munson's fist away, but received it immediately full in the face. Staggering back, he pulled his revolver; and, before Munson could meet this new antagonism, he aimed and fired. Munson lurched headlong, and lay still.

Then an uproar began. The others charged on Forsythe, who retreated, with his weapon at arm's length. He held them off until, at his command, all but one had placed his pistol back in the scabbard. The dilatory one was old

Kelly; and him Forsythe shot through the heart. Then the pistols were redrawn, and the shooting became general.

How Forsythe, single-handed against the eight remaining men, won in that gun fight can only be explained by the fact that the eight were too wildly excited to aim, or leave each other free to attempt aiming; while Forsythe, a single target, only needed to shoot at the compact body of men to make a hit.

It ended soon with Hawkes, Davis, and Daniels writhing on the deck, and Forsythe hiding, uninjured, behind the forward funnel; while Riley, King, and Dwyer, the three engineers, were retreating into their engine room.

"Now, if you've had enough," shouted Forsythe, "start the engine when I give you the bells." Then he mounted to the bridge and took the wheel.

But, though the starting of the engines at full speed indicated that the engineers had had enough, there was one man left who had not. It was Billings, who danced around the dead and the wounded, shrieking and laughing with the emotions of his disordered brain. But he did not fire on Forsythe, and seemed to have forgotten the animus of the recent friction.

He drifted aft, muttering to himself, until suddenly he stopped, and fixed his eyes on Denman, who, with gritting teeth, had watched the deadly fracas at the companion.

"I told you so. I told you so," rang out the crazed voice of Billings. "A woman aboard ship—a woman aboard ship. Always makes trouble. There, take it!"

He pulled his revolver and fired; and Denman, stupefied with the unexpected horror of it all, did not know that Florrie had crept up beside him in the companion until he heard her scream in conjunction with the whiz of the bullet through her hair. Then Denman awoke.

After assuring himself of the girl's safety, and pushing her down the companion, he drew his revolver; and, taking careful aim, executed Billings with the cold calmness of a hangman.

A bullet, nearly coincident with the report of a pistol, came from the bridge; and there was Forsythe, with one hand on the wheel, facing aft and taking second aim at him.

Denman accepted the challenge, and stepped boldly out of the companion. They emptied their revolvers, but neither did damage; and, as Forsythe reloaded, Denman cast a momentary glance at a black spot in the southern sky.

Hurriedly sweeping the upper horizon, he saw still another to the east; while out of the haze in the northwest was emerging a scout cruiser; no doubt the "mother" of the first monoplane. She was but two miles away, and soon began spitting shot and shell, which plowed up the water perilously near.

"You're caught, Forsythe," called out Denman, pointing to the south and east. "Will you surrender before we're sunk or killed?"

Forsythe's answer was another shot.

"Florrie," called Denman down the companion, "hand me your gun and pass up the tablecloth; then get down that hatch out of the way. We're being fired at."

She obeyed him; and, with Forsythe's bullets whistling around his head, he hoisted the flag of truce and surrender to the flagstaff. But just a moment too late. A shell entered the boat amidships and exploded in her vitals, sending up through the engine-room hatch a cloud of smoke and white steam, while fragments of the shell punctured the deck from below. But there were no cries of pain or calls for help from the three men in the engine room.

Forsythe left the bridge. Breathing vengeance and raging like a madman, he rushed aft.

"I'll see you go first!" he shrieked. He fired again and again as he came; then, realizing that he had but one bullet left in his pistol, he halted at the galley hatch, took careful aim, and pulled the trigger for the last time.

There are tricks of the fighting trade taught to naval officers that are not included in the curriculum at Annapolis. Denman, his loaded revolver hanging in his right hand at his side, had waited for this final shot. Like a duelist he watched, not his opponent's hand, but his eye; and, the moment that eye gave him the unconcealable signal to the trigger finger, he ducked his head, and the bullet sped above.

"Now, Forsythe," he said, as he covered the chagrined marksman, "you should have aimed lower and to the right—but that's all past now. This boat is practically captured, and I'm not going to kill you; for, even though it would not be murder, there is no excuse in my conscience for it. Whether the boat sinks or not, we will be taken off in time, for that fellow over yonder is coming, and has ceased firing. But before you are out of my hands I want to settle an old score with you—one dating from our boyhood, which you'll perhaps remember. Toss that gun forward and step aft a bit."

Forsythe, his face working convulsively, obeyed him.

"Florrie!" called Denman down the hatch. "Come up now. We're all right."

She came, white in the face, and stood beside him.

"Off with your coat, Forsythe, and stand up to me. We'll finish that old fight. Here, girl, hold this gun."

Florrie took the pistol, and the two men discarded their jackets and faced each other.

There is hardly need of describing in detail the fist fight that followed. It was like all such, where one man is slightly the superior of the other in skill, strength, and agility.

In this case that one was Denman; and, though again and again he felt the weight of Forsythe's fist, and reeled to the deck occasionally, he gradually tired out his heavier, though weaker, adversary; and at last, with the whole weight of his body behind it, dealt a crashing blow on Forsythe's chin.

Denman's old-time foe staggered backward and fell face upward. He rolled his head to the right and to the left a few times, then sank into unconsciousness.

Denman looked down on him, waiting for a movement, but none came. Forsythe had been knocked out, and for the last time. Florrie's scream aroused Denman.

"Is the boat sinking, Billie?"

He looked, and sprang for a life-buoy, which he slipped over Florrie's head. The bow of the boat was flush with the water, which was lapping at the now quiet bodies of the dead and wounded men forward. He secured another life-buoy for himself; and, as he donned the cork ring, a hail came from abeam.

"Jump!" it said. "Jump, or you'll be carried down with the wash."

The big scout ship was but a few lengths away, and a boat full of armed men was approaching.

Hand in hand they leaped into the sea; and Denman, towing the girl by the becket of her life-buoy, paid no attention to the sinking hull until satisfied that they were safe from the suction.

When he looked, the bow was under water, the stern rising in the air, higher and higher, until a third of the after body was exposed; then it slid silently, but for the bursting of huge air bubbles, out of sight in the depths.

About a year later, Lieutenant Denman received a letter with a Paris postmark, which he opened in the presence of his wife. In it was a draft on a Boston bank, made out to his order.

"Good!" he exclaimed, as he glanced down the letter. "Listen, Florrie, here's something that pleases me as much as my exoneration by the Board of Inquiry." Then he read to her the letter:

> "DEAR SIR: Inasmuch as you threw two life-buoys over for us you may be glad, even at this late period, to know that we got them. The fight stopped when we hit the water, and since then Sampson and myself have been chums. I saw both buoys thrown and held Sampson up while I swam with him to the first; then, from the top of a sea, I saw the other, and,

getting it, returned to him. We were picked up by a fisherman next day, but you will not mind, sir, if I do not tell you where we landed, or how we got here, or where we'll be when this letter reaches you. We will not be here, and never again in the United States. Yet we want to thank you for giving us a chance for our lives.

"We read in the Paris *Herald* of your hearing before the Board of Inquiry, and the story you told of the mess Forsythe made of things, and the final sinking of the boat. Of course we were sorry for them, for they were our mates; but they ought not to have gone back on Casey, even though they saw fit to leave Sampson and me behind. And, thinking this way, we are glad that you licked Forsythe, even at the last minute.

"We inclose a draft for five hundred and fifty dollars, which we would like you to cash, and pay the captain, whose name we do not know, the money we took from his desk. We hope that what is left will square up for the clothes and money we took from your room. You see, as we did not give Casey but a little of the money, and it came in mighty handy for us two when we got ashore, it seems that we are obligated to return it. I will only say, to conclude, that we got it honestly.

"Sampson joins with me in our best respects to Miss Fleming and yourself.

"Truly yours,

"HERBERT JENKINS."

"Oh, I'm glad, Billie!" she exclaimed. "They are honest men, after all."

"Honest men?" repeated Denman, quizzically. "Yet they stole a fine destroyer from Uncle Sam!"

"I don't care," she said, stoutly. "I'm glad they were saved. And, Billie boy"—her hands were on his shoulders—"if they hadn't stolen that fine destroyer, I wouldn't be here to-day looking into your eyes."

And Billie, gathering her into his arms, let it go at that.

BEYOND THE SPECTRUM

The long-expected crisis was at hand, and the country was on the verge of war. Jingoism was rampant. Japanese laborers were mobbed on the western slope, Japanese students were hazed out of colleges, and Japanese children stoned away from playgrounds. Editorial pages sizzled with burning words of patriotism; pulpits thundered with invocations to the God of battles and prayers for the perishing of the way of the ungodly. Schoolboy companies were formed and paraded with wooden guns; amateur drum-corps beat time to the throbbing of the public pulse; militia regiments, battalions, and separate companies of infantry and artillery, drilled, practiced, and paraded; while the regular army was rushed to the posts and garrisons of the Pacific Coast, and the navy, in three divisions, guarded the Hawaiian Islands, the Philippines, and the larger ports of western America. For Japan had a million trained men, with transports to carry them, battle-ships to guard them; with the choice of objective when she was ready to strike; and she was displaying a national secrecy about her choice especially irritating to molders of public opinion and lovers of fair play. War was not yet declared by either side, though the Japanese minister at Washington had quietly sailed for Europe on private business, and the American minister at Tokio, with several consuls and clerks scattered around the ports of Japan, had left their jobs hurriedly, for reasons connected with their general health. This was the situation when the cabled news from Manila told of the staggering into port of the scout cruiser *Salem* with a steward in command, a stoker at the wheel, the engines in charge of firemen, and the captain, watch-officers, engineers, seamen gunners, and the whole fighting force of the ship stricken with a form of partial blindness which in some cases promised to become total.

The cruiser was temporarily out of commission and her stricken men in the hospital; but by the time the specialists had diagnosed the trouble as amblyopia, from some sudden shock to the optic nerve—followed in cases by complete atrophy, resulting in amaurosis—another ship came into Honolulu in the same predicament. Like the other craft four thousand miles away, her deck force had been stricken suddenly and at night. Still another, a battle-ship, followed into Honolulu, with fully five hundred more or less blind men groping around her decks; and the admiral on the station called in all the outriders by wireless. They came as they could, some hitting sand-bars or shoals on the way, and every one crippled and helpless to fight. The diagnosis was the same—amblyopia, atrophy of the nerve, and incipient amaurosis; which in plain language meant dimness of vision increasing to blindness.

Then came more news from Manila. Ship after ship came in, or was towed in, with fighting force sightless, and the work being done by the "black gang" or the idlers, and each with the same report—the gradual dimming of lights and outlines as the night went on, resulting in partial or total blindness by sunrise. And now it was remarked that those who escaped were the lower-deck workers, those whose duties kept them off the upper deck and away from gunports and deadlights. It was also suggested that the cause was some deadly attribute of the night air in these tropical regions, to which the Americans succumbed; for, so far, the coast division had escaped.

In spite of the efforts of the Government, the Associated Press got the facts, and the newspapers of the country changed the burden of their pronouncements. Bombastic utterances gave way to bitter criticism of an inefficient naval policy that left the ships short of fighters in a crisis. The merging of the line and the staff, which had excited much ridicule when inaugurated, now received more intelligent attention. Former critics of the change not only condoned it, but even demanded the wholesale granting of commissions to skippers and mates of the merchant service; and insisted that surgeons, engineers, paymasters, and chaplains, provided they could still see to box the compass, should be given command of the torpedo craft and smaller scouts. All of which made young Surgeon Metcalf, on waiting orders at San Francisco, smile sweetly and darkly to himself: for his last appointment had been the command of a hospital ship, in which position, though a seaman, navigator, and graduate of Annapolis, he had been made the subject of newspaper ridicule and official controversy, and had even been caricatured as going into battle in a ship armored with court-plaster and armed with hypodermic syringes.

Metcalf had resigned as ensign to take up the study and practice of medicine, but at the beginning of the war scare had returned to his first love, relinquishing a lucrative practice as eye-specialist to tender his services to the Government. And the Government had responded by ranking him with his class as junior lieutenant, and giving him the aforesaid command, which he was glad to be released from. But his classmates and brother officers had not responded so promptly with their welcome, and Metcalf found himself combating a naval etiquette that was nearly as intolerant of him as of other appointees from civil life. It embittered him a little, but he pulled through; for he was a likable young fellow, with a cheery face and pleasant voice, and even the most hide-bound product of Annapolis could not long resist his personality. So he was not entirely barred out of official gossip and speculations, and soon had an opportunity to question some convalescents sent home from Honolulu. All told the same story and described the same symptoms, but one added an extra one. An itching and burning of the face had accompanied the attack, such as is produced by sunburn.

"And where were you that night when it came?" asked Metcalf, eagerly.

"On the bridge with the captain and watch-officers. It was all hands that night. We had made out a curious light to the north'ard, and were trying to find out what it was."

"What kind of a light?"

"Well, it was rather faint, and seemed to be about a mile away. Sometimes it looked red, then green, or yellow, or blue."

"And then it disappeared?"

"Yes, and though we steamed toward it with all the searchlights at work, we never found where it came from."

"What form did it take—a beam or a glow?"

"It wasn't a glow—radiation—and it didn't seem to be a beam. It was an occasional flash, and in this sense was like a radiation—that is, like the spokes of a wheel, each spoke with its own color. But that was at the beginning. In three hours none of us could have distinguished colors."

Metcalf soon had an opportunity to question others. The first batch of invalid officers arrived from Manila, and these, on being pressed, admitted that they had seen colored lights at the beginning of the night. These, Metcalf remarked, were watch-officers, whose business was to look for strange lights and investigate them. But one of them added this factor to the problem.

"And it was curious about Brainard, the most useless and utterly incompetent man ever graduated. He was so near-sighted that he couldn't see the end of his nose without glasses; but it was he that took the ship in, with the rest of us eating with our fingers and asking our way to the sick-bay."

"And Brainard wore his glasses that night?'" asked Metcalf.

"Yes; he couldn't see without them. It reminds me of Nydia, the blind girl who piloted a bunch out of Pompeii because she was used to the darkness. Still, Brainard is hardly a parallel."

"Were his glasses the ordinary kind, or pebbles?"

"Don't know. Which are the cheapest? That's the kind."

"The ordinary kind."

"Well, he had the ordinary kind—like himself. And he'll get special promotion. Oh, Lord! He'll be jumped up a dozen numbers."

"Well," said Metcalf, mysteriously, "perhaps not. Just wait."

Metcalf kept his counsel, and in two weeks there came Japan's declaration of war in a short curt note to the Powers at Washington. Next day the papers burned with news, cabled *via* St. Petersburg and London, of the sailing of the Japanese fleet from its home station, but for where was not given—in all probability either the Philippines or the Hawaiian Islands. But when, next day, a torpedo-boat came into San Francisco in command of the cook, with his mess-boy at the wheel, conservatism went to the dogs, and bounties were offered for enlistment at the various navy-yards, while commissions were made out as fast as they could be signed, and given to any applicant who could even pretend to a knowledge of yachts. And Surgeon George Metcalf, with the rank of junior lieutenant, was ordered to the torpedo-boat above mentioned, and with him as executive officer a young graduate of the academy, Ensign Smith, who with the enthusiasm and courage of youth combined the mediocrity of inexperience and the full share of the service prejudice against civilians.

This prejudice remained in full force, unmodified by the desperate situation of the country; and the unstricken young officers filling subordinate positions on the big craft, while congratulating him, openly denied his moral right to a command that others had earned a better right to by remaining in the service; and the old jokes, jibes, and satirical references to syringes and sticking-plaster whirled about his head as he went to and fro, fitting out his boat and laying in supplies. And when they learned—from young Mr. Smith—that among these supplies was a large assortment of plain-glass spectacles, of no magnifying power whatever, the ridicule was unanimous and heartfelt; even the newspapers taking up the case from the old standpoint and admitting that the line ought to be drawn at lunatics and foolish people. But Lieutenant Metcalf smiled and went quietly ahead, asking for and receiving orders to scout.

He received them the more readily, as all the scouts in the squadron, including the torpedo-flotilla and two battle-ships, had come in with blinded crews. Their stories were the same—they had all seen the mysterious colored lights, had gone blind, and a few had felt the itching and tingling of sunburn. And the admiral gleaned one crew of whole men from the fleet, and with it manned his best ship, the *Delaware*.

Metcalf went to sea, and was no sooner outside the Golden Gate than he opened his case of spectacles, and scandalized all hands, even his executive officer, by stern and explicit orders to wear them night and day, putting on a pair himself as an example.

A few of the men attested good eyesight; but this made no difference, he explained. They were to wear them or take the consequences, and as the first man to take the consequences was Mr. Smith, whom he sent to his room for twenty-four hours for appearing on deck without them five minutes afterward, the men concluded that he was in earnest and obeyed the order, though with smiles and silent ridicule. Another explicit command they received more readily: to watch out for curious-looking craft, and for small objects such as floating casks, capsized tubs or boats, et cetera. And this brought results the day after the penitent Smith was released. They sighted a craft without spars steaming along on the horizon and ran down to her. She was a sealer, the skipper explained, when hailed, homeward bound under the auxiliary. She had been on fire, but the cause of the fire was a mystery. A few days before a strange-looking vessel had passed them, a mile away. She was a whaleback sort of a hull, with sloping ends, without spars or funnels, only a slim pole amidships, and near its base a projection that looked like a liner's crow's-nest. While they watched, their foremast burst into flames, and while they were rigging their hose the mainmast caught fire. Before this latter was well under way they noticed a round hole burnt deeply into the mast, of about four inches diameter. Next, the topsides caught fire, and they had barely saved their craft, letting their masts burn to do so.

"Was it a bright, sunshiny day?" asked Metcalf.

"Sure. Four days ago. He was heading about sou'west, and going slow."

"Anything happen to your eyesight?"

"Say—yes. One of my men's gone stone blind. Thinks he must have looked squarely at the sun when he thought he was looking at the fire up aloft."

"It wasn't the sun. Keep him in utter darkness for a week at least. He'll get well. What was your position when you met that fellow?"

"About six hundred miles due nor'west from here."

"All right. Look out for Japanese craft. War is declared."

Metcalf plotted a new course, designed to intercept that of the mysterious craft, and went on, so elated by the news he had heard that he took his gossipy young executive into his confidence.

"Mr. Smith," he said, "that sealer described one of the new seagoing submersibles of the Japanese, did he not?"

"Yes, sir, I think he did—a larger submarine, without any conning-tower and the old-fashioned periscope. They have seven thousand miles' cruising radius, enough to cross the Pacific."

By asking questions of various craft, and by diligent use of a telescope, Metcalf found his quarry three days later—a log-like object on the horizon, with the slim white pole amidships and the excrescence near its base.

"Wait till I get his bearing by compass," said Metcalf to his chief officer, "then we'll smoke up our specs and run down on him. Signal him by the International Code to put out his light, and to heave to, or we'll sink him."

Mr. Smith bowed to his superior, found the numbers of these commands in the code book, and with a string of small flags at the signal-yard, and every man aboard viewing the world darkly through a smoky film, the torpedo-boat approached the stranger at thirty knots. But there was no blinding glare of light in their eyes, and when they were within a hundred yards of the submersible, Metcalf removed his glasses for a moment's distinct vision. Head and shoulders out of a hatch near the tube was a man waving a white handkerchief. He rang the stopping bells.

"He surrenders, Mr. Smith," he said, joyously, "and without firing a torpedo!"

He examined the man through the telescope and laughed.

"I know him," he said. Then funneling his hands, he hailed:

"Do you surrender to the United States of America?"

"I surrender," answered the man. "I am helpless."

"Then come aboard without arms. I'll send a boat."

A small dinghy-like boat was dispatched, and it returned with the man, a Japanese in lieutenant's uniform, whose beady eyes twinkled in alarm as Metcalf greeted him.

"Well, Saiksi, you perfected it, didn't you?—my invisible searchlight, that I hadn't money to go on with."

The Jap's eyes sought the deck, then resumed their Asiatic steadiness.

"Metcalf—this you," he said, "in command? I investigated and heard you had resigned to become a doctor."

"But I came back to the service, Saiksi. Thanks to you and your light—my light, rather—I am in command here in place of men you blinded. Saiksi, you deserve no consideration from me, in spite of our rooming together at Annapolis. You took—I don't say stole—my invention, and turned it against the country that educated you. You, or your *confrères*, did this before a declaration of war. You are a pirate, and I could string you up to my signal-yard and escape criticism."

"I was under orders from my superiors, Captain Metcalf."

"They shall answer to mine. You shall answer to me. How many boats have you equipped with my light?"

"There are but three. It is very expensive."

"One for our Philippine squadron, one for the Hawaiian, and one for the coast. You overdid things, Saiksi. If you hadn't set fire to that sealer the other day, I might not have found you. It was a senseless piece of work that did you no good. Oh, you are a sweet character! How do you get your ultraviolet rays—by filtration or prismatic dispersion?"

"By filtration."

"Saiksi, you're a liar as well as a thief. The colored lights you use to attract attention are the discarded rays of the spectrum. No wonder you investigated me before you dared flash such a decoy! Well, I'm back in the navy, and I've been investigating you. As soon as I heard of the first symptom of sunburn, I knew it was caused by the ultraviolet rays, the same as from the sun; and I knew that nothing but my light could produce those rays at night time. And as a physician I knew what I did not know as an inventor—the swift amblyopia that follows the impact of this light on the retina. As a physician, too, I can inform you that your country has not permanently blinded a single American seaman or officer. The effects wear off."

The Jap gazed stolidly before him while Metcalf delivered himself of this, but did not reply.

"Where is the Japanese fleet bound?" he asked, sternly.

"I do not know."

"And would not tell, whether you knew or not. But you said you were helpless. What has happened to you? You can tell that."

"A simple thing, Captain Metcalf. My supply of oil leaked away, and my engines must work slowly. Your signal was useless; I could not have turned on the light."

"You have answered the first question. You are far from home without a mother-ship, or she would have found you and furnished oil before this. You have come thus far expecting the fleet to follow and strike a helpless coast before your supplies ran out."

Again the Jap's eyes dropped in confusion, and Metcalf went on.

"I can refurnish your boat with oil, my engineer and my men can handle her, and I can easily learn to manipulate your—or shall I say *our*—invisible searchlight. Hail your craft in English and order all hands on deck unarmed, ready for transshipment to this boat. I shall join your fleet myself."

A man was lounging in the hatchway of the submersible, and this man Saiksi hailed.

"Ae-hai, ae-hai, Matsu. We surrender. We are prisoner. Call up all men onto the deck. Leave arms behind. We are prisoner."

They mustered eighteen in all, and in half an hour they were ironed in a row along the stanchioned rail of the torpedo-boat.

"You, too, Saiksi," said Metcalf, coming toward him with a pair of jingling handcuffs.

"Is it not customary, Captain Metcalf," said the Jap, "to parole a surrendered commander?"

"Not the surrendered commander of a craft that uses new and deadly weapons of war unknown to her adversary, and before the declaration of war. Hold up your hands. You're going into irons with your men. All Japs look alike to me, now."

So Lieutenant Saiksi, of the Japanese navy, was ironed beside his cook and meekly sat down on the deck. With the difference of dress, they really did look alike.

Metcalf had thirty men in his crew. With the assistance of his engineer, a man of mechanics, he picked eighteen of this crew and took them and a barrel of oil aboard the submersible. Then for three days the two craft lay together, while the engineer and the men familiarized themselves with her internal economy—the torpedo-tubes, gasoline-engines, storage-batteries, and motors; and the vast system of pipes, valves, and wires that gave life and action to the boat—and while Metcalf experimented with the mysterious searchlight attached to the periscope tube invented by himself, but perfected by others. Part of his investigation extended into the night. Externally, the light resembled a huge cup about two feet in diameter, with a thick disk fitted around it in a vertical plane. This disk he removed; then, hailing Smith to rig his fire-hose and get off the deck, he descended the hatchway and turned on the light, viewing its effects through the periscope. This, be it known, is merely a perpendicular, non-magnifying telescope that, by means of a reflector at its upper end, gives a view of the seascape when a submarine boat is submerged. And in the eyepiece at its base Metcalf beheld a thin thread of light, of such dazzling brilliancy as to momentarily blind him, stretch over the sea; but he put on his smoked glasses and turned the apparatus, tube and all, until the thin pencil of light touched the end of the torpedo-boat's signal-yard. He did not need to bring the two-inch beam to a focus; it burst into flame and he quickly shut off the light and shouted to Smith to put out the fire—which Smith promptly did, with open comment to his handful of men on this destruction of Government property.

"Good enough!" he said to Smith, when next they met. "Now if I'm any good I'll give the Japs a taste of their own medicine."

"Take me along, captain," burst out Smith in sudden surrender. "I don't understand all this, but I want to be in it."

"No, Mr. Smith. The chief might do your work, but I doubt that you could do his. I need him; so you can take the prisoners home. You will undoubtedly retain command."

"Very good, sir," answered the disappointed youngster, trying to conceal his chagrin.

"I don't want you to feel badly about it. I know how you all felt toward me. But I'm on a roving commission. I have no wireless apparatus and no definite instructions. I've been lampooned and ridiculed in the papers, and

I'm going to give them my answer—that is, as I said, if I'm any good. If I'm not I'll be sunk."

So when the engineer had announced his mastery of his part of the problem, and that there was enough of gasoline to cruise for two weeks longer, Smith departed with the torpedo-boat, and Metcalf began his search for the expected fleet.

It was more by good luck than by any possible calculation that Metcalf finally found the fleet. A steamer out of San Francisco reported that it had not been heard from, and one bound in from Honolulu said that it was not far behind—in fact had sent a shot or two. Metcalf shut off gasoline, waited a day, and saw the smoke on the horizon. Then he submerged to the awash condition, which in this boat just floated the searchlight out of water; and thus balanced, neither floating nor sinking nor rolling, but rising and falling with the long pulsing of the ground-swell, he watched through the periscope the approach of the enemy.

It was an impressive spectacle, and to a citizen of a threatened country a disquieting one. Nine high-sided battle-ships of ten-gun type—nine floating forts, each one, unopposed, able to reduce to smoking ruin a city out of sight of its gunners; each one impregnable to the shell fire of any fortification in the world, and to the impact of the heaviest torpedo yet constructed—they came silently along in line-ahead formation, like Indians on a trail. There were no compromises in this fleet. Like the intermediate batteries of the ships themselves, cruisers had been eliminated and it consisted of extremes, battle-ships, and torpedo-boats, the latter far to the rear. But between the two were half a dozen colliers, repair, and supply ships.

Night came down before they were near enough for operations, and Metcalf turned on his invisible light, expanding the beam to embrace the fleet in its light, and moved the boat to a position about a mile away from its path. It was a weird picture now showing in the periscope: each gray ship a bluish-green against a background of black marked here and there by the green crest of a breaking sea. Within Metcalf's reach were the levers, cranks, and worms that governed the action of the periscope and the light; just before him were the vertical and horizontal steering-wheels; under these a self-illuminating compass, and at his ear a system of push-buttons, speaking-tubes, and telegraph-dials that put him in communication with every man on the boat, each one of whom had his part to play at the proper moment, but not one of whom could see or know the result. The work to be done was in Metcalf's hands and brain, and, considering its potentiality, it was a most undramatic performance.

He waited until the leading flag-ship was within half a mile of being abreast; then, turning on a hanging electric bulb, he held it close to the eyepiece of the periscope, knowing that the light would go up the tube through the lenses and be visible to the fleet. And in a moment he heard faintly through the steel walls the sound transmitted by the sea of a bugle-call to quarters. He shut off the bulb, watched a wandering shaft of light from the flag-ship seeking him, then contracted his own invisible beam to a diameter of about three feet, to fall upon the flag-ship, and played it back and forth, seeking gun ports and apertures and groups of men, painting all with that blinding light that they could not see, nor immediately sense. There was nothing to indicate that he had succeeded; the faces of the different groups were still turned his way, and the futile searchlight still wandered around, unable to bring to their view the white tube with its cup-like base.

Still waving the wandering beam of white light, the flag-ship passed on, bringing along the second in line, and again Metcalf turned on his bulb. He heard her bugle-call, and saw, in varied shades of green, the twinkling red and blue lights of her masthead signals, received from the flag-ship and passed down the line. And again he played that green disk of deadly light upon the faces of her crew. This ship, too, was seeking him with her searchlight, and soon, from the whole nine, a moving network of brilliant beams flashed and scintillated across the sky; but not one settled upon the cause of their disquiet.

Ship after ship passed on, each with its bugle-call to quarters, each with its muster of all hands to meet the unknown emergency—the menace on a hostile coast of a faint white light on the port beam—but not one firing a shot or shell; there was nothing to fire at. And with the passing of the last of the nine Metcalf listened to a snapping and a buzzing overhead that told of the burning out of the carbons in the light.

"Good work for the expenditure," he murmured, wearily. "Let's see—two carbons and about twenty amperes of current, against nine ships at ten millions apiece. Well, we'll soon know whether or not it worked."

While an electrician rigged new carbons he rested his eyes and his brain; for the mental and physical strain had been severe. Then he played the light upon the colliers and supply ships as they charged by, disposing of them in the same manner, and looked for other craft of larger menace. But there were none, except the torpedo contingent, and these he decided to leave alone. There were fifteen of them, each as speedy and as easily handled as his own craft; and already, apprised by the signaled instructions from ahead, they were spreading out into a fan-like formation, and coming on, nearly abreast.

"The jig's up, chief," he called through a tube to the engineer. "We'll get forty feet down until the mosquitoes get by. I'd like to take a chance at them but there are too many. We'd get torpedoed, surely."

Down went the diving rudder, and, with a kick ahead of the engine, the submersible shot under, heading on a course across the path of the fleet, and in half an hour came to the surface. There was nothing in sight, close by, either through the periscope or by direct vision, and Metcalf decided to make for San Francisco and report.

It was a wise decision, for at daylight he was floundering in a heavy sea and a howling gale from the northwest that soon forced him to submerge again for comfort. Before doing so, however, he enjoyed one good look at the Japanese fleet, far ahead and to port. The line of formation was broken, staggered, and disordered; and, though the big ships were making good weather of it, they were steering badly, and on one of them, half-way to the signal-yard, was the appeal for help that ships of all nations use and recognize—the ensign, upside-down. Under the lee of each ship was snuggled a torpedo-boat, plunging, rolling, and swamped by the breaking seas that even the mighty bulk to windward could not protect them from. And even as Metcalf looked, one twisted in two, her after funnels pointing to port, her forward to starboard, and in ten seconds had disappeared.

Metcalf submerged and went on at lesser speed, but in comfort and safety. Through the periscope he saw one after the other of the torpedo-craft give up the fight they were not designed for, and ship after ship hoist that silent prayer for help. They yawed badly, but in some manner or other managed to follow the flag-ship, which, alone of that armada, steered fairly well. She kept on the course for the Golden Gate.

Even submerged Metcalf outran the fleet before noon, and at night had dropped it, entering the Golden Gate before daylight, still submerged, not only on account of the troublesome turmoil on the surface, but to avoid the equally troublesome scrutiny of the forts, whose searchlights might have caught him had he presented more to their view than a slim tube painted white. Avoiding the mines, he picked his way carefully up to the man-of-war anchorage, and arose to the surface, alongside the *Delaware*, now the flag-ship, as the light of day crept upward in the eastern sky.

"We knew they were on the coast," said the admiral, a little later, when Metcalf had made his report on the quarter-deck of the *Delaware*. "But about this light? Are you sure of all this? Why, if it's so, the President will rank you over us all. Mr. Smith came in with the prisoners, but he said nothing of an invisible light—only of a strong searchlight with which you set fire to the signal-yard."

"I did not tell him all, admiral," answered Metcalf, a little hurt at the persistence of the feeling. "But I'm satisfied now. That fleet is coming on with incompetents on the bridge."

"Well, we'll soon know. I've only one ship, but it's my business to get out and defend the United States against invaders, and as soon as I can steam against this gale and sea I'll go. And I'll want you, too. I'm short-handed."

"Thank you, sir. I shall be glad to be with you. But wouldn't you like to examine the light?"

"Most certainly," said the admiral; and, accompanied by his staff, he followed Metcalf aboard the submersible.

"It is very simple," explained Metcalf, showing a rough diagram he had sketched. "You see he has used my system of reflectors about as I designed it. The focus of one curve coincides with the focus of the next, and the result is a thin beam containing nearly all the radiations of the arc."

"Very simple," remarked the admiral, dryly. "Very simple indeed. But, admitting this strong beam of light that, as you say, could set fire to that sealer, and be invisible in sunshine, how about the beam that is invisible by night? That is what I am wondering about."

"Here, sir," removing the thick disk from around the light. "This contains the prisms, which refract the beam entirely around the lamp; and disperse it into the seven colors of the spectrum. All the visible light is cut out, leaving only the ultraviolet rays, and these travel as fast and as far, and return by reflection, as though accompanied by the visible rays."

"But how can you see it?" asked an officer. "How is the ship it is directed at made visible?"

"By fluorescence," answered Metcalf. "The observer is the periscope itself. Any of the various fluorescing substances placed in the focus of the object-glass, or at the optical image in front of the eyepiece, will show the picture in the color peculiar to the fluorescing material. The color does not matter."

"More simple still," laughed the admiral. "But how about the colored lights they saw?"

"Simply the discarded light of the spectrum. By removing this cover on the disk, the different colored rays shoot up. That was to attract attention. I used only white light through the periscope."

"And it was this invisible light that blinded so many men, which in your hands blinded the crews of the Japanese?" asked the admiral.

"Yes, sir. The ultraviolet rays are beneficial as a germicide, but are deadly if too strong."

"Lieutenant Metcalf," said the admiral, seriously, "your future in the service is secure. I apologize for laughing at you; but now that it's over and you've won, tell us about the spectacles."

"Why, admiral," responded Metcalf, "that was the simplest proposition of all. The whole apparatus—prisms, periscope, lenses, and the fluorescing screen—are made of rock crystal, which is permeable to the ultraviolet light. But common glass, of which spectacles are made, is opaque to it. That is why near-sighted men escaped the blindness."

"Then, unless the Japs are near-sighted, I expect an easy time when I go out."

But the admiral did not need to go out and fight. Those nine big battleships that Japan had struggled for years to obtain, and the auxiliary fleet of supply and repair ships to keep them in life and health away from home, caught on a lee shore in a hurricane against which the mighty *Delaware* could not steam to sea, piled up one by one on the sands below Fort Point; and, each with a white flag replacing the reversed ensign, surrendered to the transport or collier sent out to take off the survivors.

IN THE VALLEY OF THE SHADOW

There are few facilities for cooking aboard submarine torpedo-boats, and that is why Lieutenant Ross ran his little submarine up alongside the flag-ship at noon, and made fast to the boat-boom—the horizontal spar extending from warships, to which the boats ride when in the water. And, as familiarity breeds contempt, after the first, tentative, trial, he had been content to let her hang by one of the small, fixed painters depending from the boom; for his boat was small, and the tide weak, bringing little strain on painter or boom. Besides, this plan was good, for it kept the submarine from bumping the side of the ship—and paint below the water-line is as valuable to a warship as paint above.

Thus moored, the little craft, with only her deck and conning-tower showing, rode lightly at the end of her tether, while Ross and his men—all but one, to watch—climbed aboard and ate their dinner.

Ross finished quickly, and sought the deck; for, on going down to the wardroom, he had seen among the visitors from shore the one girl in the world to him—the girl he had met at Newport, Washington, and New York, whom he wanted as he wanted life, but whom he had not asked for yet, because he had felt so sure of her.

And now this surety was jolted out of his consciousness; for she was there escorted by a man she had often described, and whom Ross recognized from the description—a tall, dark, "captainish"-looking fellow, with a large mustache; but who, far from being a captain or other kind of superman, was merely a photographer—yet a wealthy and successful photographer, whose work was unusual and artistic.

Ross, though an efficient naval officer, was anything but "captainish"; he was simply a clean-shaven, clean-cut young fellow, with a face that mirrored every emotion of his soul. Knowing this infirmity—if such it is—he resolutely put down the jealous thoughts that surged through his brain; and when the visitors, guests of the captain, reached the deck, he met them, and was introduced to Mr. Foster with as pleasant a face as the girl had ever seen.

Then, with the captain's permission, he invited them down to inspect his submarine. A plank from the lower grating of the gangway to the deck of the smaller craft was all that was needed, and along this they went, the girl ahead, supported by Mr. Foster, and Ross following, with a messenger boy from the bridge following him.

At the hatch, the girl paused and shrank back, for the wide-open eyes of the caretaker were looking up at her. Ross surmised this, and called to the man to come up and get his dinner; then, as the man passed him and stepped onto the plank, the messenger got his attention. The officer of the deck desired to speak with him, he said.

Ross explained the manner of descent, admonished his guests to touch nothing until he returned, and followed the messenger back to the officer of the deck. It was nothing of importance, simply a matter pertaining to the afternoon drill; and, somewhat annoyed, Ross returned. But he paused at the end of the plank; a loud voice from below halted him, and he did not care to interrupt. Nor did he care to go back, leaving them alone in a submarine.

"I mean it," Foster was saying vehemently. "I hope this boat does go to the bottom."

"Why, Mr. Foster!" cried the girl. "What a sentiment!"

"I tell you I mean it. You have made life unbearable."

"I make your life unbearable?"

"Yes, you, Irene. You know I have loved you from the beginning. And you have coquetted with me, played with me—as a cat plays with a mouse. When I have endeavored to escape, you have drawn me back by smiles and favor, and given me hope. Then it is coldness and disdain. I am tired of it."

"I am sorry, Mr. Foster, if anything in my attitude has caused such an impression. I have given you no special smiles or favors, no special coldness or disdain."

"But I love you. I want you. I cannot live without you."

"You lived a long time without me, before we met."

"Yes, before we met. Before I fell under the spell of your personality. You have hypnotized me, made yourself necessary to me. I am heartsick all the time, thinking of you."

"Then you must get over it, Mr. Foster. I must think of myself."

"Then you do not care for me, at all?"

"I do, but only as an acquaintance."

"Not even as a friend?"

"I do not like to answer such pointed questions, sir; but, since you ask, I will tell you. I do not like you, even as a friend. You demand so much. You are very selfish, never considering my feelings at all, and you often annoy me with your moods. Frankly, I am happier away from you."

"My moods!" Foster repeated, bitterly. "You cause my moods. But I know what the real trouble is. I was all right until Ross came along."

"You have no right, Mr. Foster," said the girl, angrily, "to bring Lieutenant Ross' name into this discussion."

"Oh, I understand. Do you think he can marry you on his pay?"

"Mr. Ross' pay would not influence him, nor me."

"Well, I'll tell you this"—and Foster's voice became a snarl—"you two won't be married. I'll see to it. I want you; and if I can't have you, no one else shall."

"Whew!" whistled Ross, softly, while he smiled sweetly, and danced a mental jig in the air. Then he danced a few steps of a real jig, to apprise them of his coming. "Time to end this," he said; then called out, cheerily: "Look out below," and entered the hatch.

"Got a bad habit," he said, as he descended, "of coming down this ladder by the run. Must break myself, before I break my neck. Well, how are you making out? Been looking around?"

The girl's face, pale but for two red spots in her cheeks, was turned away from him as he stepped off the ladder, and she trembled visibly. Foster, though flushed and scowling, made a better effort at self-control.

"Why, no, lieutenant," he said, with a sickly smile. "It is all strange and new to us. We were waiting for you. But I have become slightly interested in this—" He indicated a circular window, fixed in the steel side of the boat. "Isn't it a new feature in submarines?"

"Yes, it is," answered Ross. "But it has long been known that glass will stand a stress equal to that of steel, so they've given us deadlights. See the side of the ship out there? We can see objects about twenty feet away near the surface. Deeper down it is darker."

"And I suppose you see some interesting sights under water," pursued Foster, now recovered in poise.

"Yes, very interesting—and some very harrowing. I saw a man drowning not long ago. We were powerless to help him."

"Heavens, what a sight!" exclaimed Foster. "The expression on his face must have been tragic."

"Pitiful—the most pitiful I ever looked at. He seemed to be calling to us. Such agony and despair; but it did not last long."

"But while it *did* last—did you have a camera? What a chance for a photographer! That is my line, you know. Did ever a photographer get a chance to photograph the expression on the face of a drowning man? What a picture it would be?"

"Don't," said the girl, with a shudder. "For mercy's sake, do not speak of such things."

"I beg your pardon, Miss Fleming," said Ross, gently. "It was very tactless in me."

"And I, Miss Fleming," said Foster, with a bow, "was led away by professional enthusiasm. Please accept *my* apology, too. Still, lieutenant, I must say that I would like the chance."

"Sorry, Mr. Foster," answered Ross, coldly. "We do all sorts of things to men in the navy, but we don't drown them for the sake of their pictures. Suppose I show you around, for at two bells the men will be back from their dinner. Now, aft here, is the gasoline engine, which we use to propel the boat on the surface. We can't use it submerged, however, on account of the exhaust; so, for under-water work, we use a strong storage battery to work a motor. You see the motor back there, and under this deck is the storage battery—large jars of sulphuric acid and lead. It is a bad combination if salt water floods it."

"How? What happens?" asked Foster.

"Battery gas, or, in chemical terms, chlorine gas is formed. It is one of the most poisonous and suffocating of all gases. That is the real danger in submarine boats—suffocation from chlorine. It will remain so until we get a better form of motive power, liquid or compressed air, perhaps. And here"—Ross led them to a valve wheel amidships—"as though to invite such disaster, they've given us a sea cock."

"What's it for?" asked Foster.

"To sink the boat in case of fire. It's an inheritance from steamboats—pure precedent—and useless, for a submarine cannot catch fire. Why, a few turns of that wheel when in the awash trim would admit enough water in two minutes to sink the boat. I've applied for permission to abolish it."

"Two minutes, you say. Does it turn easy? Would it be possible to accidentally turn it?"

"Very easy, and very possible. I caution my men every day."

"And in case you do sink, and do not immediately suffocate, how do you rise?"

"By pumping out the water. There's a strong pump connected with that motor aft there, that will force out water against the pressure of the sea at fifty fathoms down. That is ten atmospheres—pretty hard pressure. But, if the motor gets wet, it is useless to work the pump; so, we can be satisfied that, if we sink by means of the sea cock, we stay sunk. There is a hand pump, to use on the surface with dead batteries, but it is useless at any great depth."

"What do you mean by the awash trim, lieutenant?" asked Foster, who was now looking out through the deadlight.

"The diving trim—that is, submerged all but the conning-tower. I'll show you, so that you can say that you have really been under water."

Ross turned a number of valves similar to the sea cock, and the girl's face took on a look of doubt and sudden apprehension.

"You are not going to sink the boat, are you, Mr. Ross?" she asked.

"Oh, no, just filling the tanks. When full, we still have three hundred pounds reserve buoyancy, and would have to go ahead and steer down. But we won't go ahead. Come forward, and I'll show you the torpedo-tube."

Foster remained, moodily staring through the deadlight, while the other two went forward. Ross noticed his abstraction, and, ascribing it to weariness of technical detail, did not press him to follow, and continued his lecture to Miss Fleming in a lower tone and in evident embarrassment.

"Now, here is the tube," he said. "See this rear door. It is water-tight. When a torpedo is in the tube, as it is now, we admit water, as well; and, to expel the torpedo, we only have to open the forward door, apply compressed air, and out it goes. Then it propels and steers itself. We have a theory—no, not a theory now, for it has been proved—that, in case of accident, a submarine's crew can all be ejected through the tube except the last man. He must remain to die, for he cannot eject himself. That man"—Ross smiled and bowed low to the girl—"must be the commander."

"How terrible!" she answered, interested, but looking back abstractedly at Foster. "Why do you remain at this work? Your life is always in danger."

"And on that account promotion is more probable. I want promotion, and more pay"—he lowered his voice and took her hand—"so that I may ask for the love and the life companionship of the dearest and best girl in the world."

She took her gaze off Foster, cast one fleeting glance into the young lieutenant's pleading face, then dropped her eyes to the deck, while her face flushed rosily. But she did not withdraw her hand.

"Must you wait for promotion?" she said, at length.

"No, Irene, no," exclaimed Ross, excitedly, squeezing the small hand in his own. "Not if you say so; but I have nothing but my pay."

"I have always been poor," she said, looking him frankly in the face. "But, John, that is not it. I am afraid. He—Mr. Foster, threatened us—vowed we would never— Oh, and he turned something back there after you started. He did it so quickly—I just barely saw him as I turned to follow you. I do not know what it was. I did not understand what you were describing."

"He turned something! What?"

"It was a wheel of some kind."

Ross looked at Foster. He was now on the conning-tower ladder, half-way up, looking at his opened watch, with a lurid, malevolent twist to his features.

"Say your prayers!" yelled Foster, insanely. "You two are going to die, I say. Die, both of you."

He sprang up the ladder, and Ross bounded aft, somewhat bewildered by the sudden turn of events. He was temporarily at his wits' end. But when Foster floundered down to the deck in a deluge of water from above, and the conning-tower hatch closed with a ringing clang, he understood. One look at the depth indicator was enough. The boat was sinking. He sprang to the sea-cock valve. It was wide open.

"Blast your wretched, black heart and soul," he growled, as he hove the wheel around. "Did you open this valve? Hey, answer me. You did, didn't you? And thought to escape yourself—you coward!"

"Oh, God!" cried Foster, running about distractedly. "We're sinking, and I can't get out."

Ross tightened the valve, and sprang toward him, the murder impulse strong in his soul. In imagination, he felt his fingers on the throat of the other, and every strong muscle of his arms closing more tightly his grip. Then their plight dominated his thoughts; he merely struck out silently, and knocked the photographer down.

"Get up," he commanded, as the prostrate man rolled heavily over on his hands and knees. "Get up, I may need you."

Foster arose, and seated himself on a torpedo amidships, where he sank his head in his hands. With a glance at him, and a reassuring look at the girl, who still remained forward, Ross went aft to connect up the pump. But as he went, he noticed that the deck inclined more and more with each passing moment.

He found the depressed engine room full of water, and the motor flooded. It was useless to start it; it would short-circuit at the first contact; and he halted, wondering at the boat's being down by the stern so much, until a snapping sound from forward apprised him of the reason.

The painter at the boom had held her nose up until the weight was too much for it, and, with its parting, the little craft assumed nearly an even keel, while the water rushed forward among the battery jars beneath the deck. Then a strong, astringent odor arose through the seams in the deck, and Ross became alive.

"Battery gas!" he exclaimed, as he ran amidships, tumbling Foster off the torpedo with a kick—for he was in his way. He reached up and turned valve after valve, admitting compressed air from the flasks to the filled tanks, to blow out the water. This done, he looked at the depth indicator; it registered seventy feet; but, before he could determine the speed of descent, there came a shock that permeated the whole boat. They were on the bottom.

"And Lord only knows," groaned Ross, "how much we've taken in! But it's only three atmospheres, thank God. Here, you," he commanded to the nerveless Foster, who had again found a seat. "Lend a hand on this pump. I'll deal with your case when we get up."

"What must I do?" asked Foster, plaintively, as he turned his face, an ashy green now, toward Ross.

"Pump," yelled Ross, in his ear. "Pump till you break your back if necessary. Ship that brake."

He handed Foster his pump-brake, and they shipped them in the hand-pump. But, heave as they might, they could not move it, except in jerks of about an inch. With an old-fashioned force-pump, rusty from disuse, a three-inch outlet, and three atmospheres of pressure, pumping was useless, and they gave it up, even though the girl added her little weight and strength to the task.

Ross had plenty of compressed air in the numerous air flasks scattered about, and, as he could blow out no more tanks, he expended a jet into the choking atmosphere of the boat. It sweetened the air a little, but there was enough of the powerful, poisonous gas generated to keep them all coughing continually. However, he seated the girl close to the air jet, so that she need not suffer more than was necessary.

"Are we in danger, John?" she asked. "Real danger, I mean?"

"Yes, dear, we are," he answered, tenderly. "And it is best that you should know. I have driven out all the water possible, and we cannot pump at this depth. Higher up we could. But I can eject the torpedo from the tube, and perhaps the others. That will lighten us a good deal."

He went forward, driving Foster before him—for he did not care to leave him too close to the girl—and pushed him bodily into the cramped space between the tube and the trimming tanks.

"Stay there," he said, incisively, "until I want you."

"What can I do?" whimpered the photographer, a brave bully before the girl, when safe; a stricken poltroon now. "I'll do anything you say, to get to the surface."

"You'll get to the surface in time," answered Ross, significantly. "How much do you weigh?"

"Two hundred pounds."

"Two hundred more than we want. However, I'll get rid of this torpedo."

Ross drove the water out of the tube, opened the breech-door; and, reaching in with a long, heavy wire, lifted the starting lever and water tripper that gave motion to the torpedo's engine. The exhaust of air into the tube was driven out into the boat by the rapidly moving screws, and in a few moments the engine ran down.

Then Ross closed the door, flooded the tube, opened the forward door, or port, and sent out the torpedo, confident that, with a dead engine, it would float harmlessly to the surface, and perhaps locate their position to the fleet; for there could be little doubt that the harbor above was dotted with boats, dragging for the sunken submarine.

As the torpedo went out, Ross noticed that the nose of the boat lifted a little, then settled as the tube filled with water. This was encouraging, and he expelled the water. The nose again lifted, but the stern still held to the bottom. There were two other torpedoes, one each side, amidships, and though the dragging to the tube of these heavy weights was a job for all hands, Ross essayed it.

They were mounted on trucks, and with what mechanical aids and purchases he could bring to bear, he and the subdued Foster labored at the task, and in an hour had the starboard torpedo in the tube.

As he was expending weights, he did not take into the ‘midship tank an equal weight of water, as was usual to keep the boat in trim, and when the torpedo, robbed of motive power and detonator, went out, the bow lifted still higher, though the stern held, as was evidenced by the grating sound from aft. The tide was drifting the boat along the bottom.

Another hour of hard, perspiring work rid them of the other torpedo, and the boat now inclined at an angle of thirty degrees, down by the stern because of the water in the engine room, but not yet at the critical angle that caused the flooding of the after battery jars as the boat sank.

Ross looked at the depth indicator, but found small comfort. It read off a depth of about sixty feet, but this only meant the lift of the bow. However, the propeller guard only occasionally struck the bottom now, proving to Ross that, could he expend a very little more weight, the boat would rise to the surface, where, even though he might not pump, his periscope and conning-tower could be seen. He panted after his labors until he had regained breath, then said to Foster:

“You next.”

“I next? What do you mean?”

“You want to get to the surface, don’t you?” said Ross, grimly. “You expressed yourself as willing to do anything I might say, in order to get to the surface. Well, strip off your coat, vest, and shoes, and crawl into that tube.”

“What? To drown? No, I will not.”

“Yes, you will. Can you swim?”

“I can swim, but not when I am shot out of a gun.”

"Then you'll drown. Peel off."

"I cannot. I cannot. Would you kill me?"

"Don't care much," answered Ross, quietly, "if I do. Only I don't want your dead body in the boat. Come, now," he added, his voice rising. "I'm giving you a chance for your life. I can swim, too, and would not hesitate at going out that tube, if I were sure that the boat, deprived of my weight, would rise. But I am not sure, so I send you, not only because you are heavier than I, but because, as Miss Fleming must remain, I prefer to remain, too, to live or die with her. Understand?"

"But, Miss Fleming," cackled Foster. "She can swim. I've heard her say so."

"You cowardly scoundrel," said Ross, his eyes ablaze with scorn and rage. He had already shed his coat and vest. Now he rolled up his shirt-sleeves. "Will you go into that tube of your own volition, conscious, so that you may take a long breath before I flood the tube, or unconscious, and pushed in like a bag of meal, to drown before you know what ails you—which?"

"No," shrieked Foster, as the menacing face and fists of Ross drew close to him. "I will not. Do something else. You are a sailor. You know what to do. Do something else."

Ross' reply was a crashing blow in the face, that sent Foster reeling toward the tube. But he arose, and returned, the animal fear in him changed to courage. He was a powerfully built man, taller, broader, and heavier than Ross, and what he lacked in skill with his fists, he possessed in the momentum of his lunges, and his utter indifference to pain.

Ross was a trained boxer, strong, and agile, and where he struck the larger man he left his mark; but in the contracted floor space of the submarine he was at a disadvantage. But he fought on, striking, ducking, and dodging—striving not only for his own life, but that of the girl whom he loved, who, seated on the 'midship trimming tank, was watching the fight with pale face and wide-open, frightened eyes.

Once, Ross managed to trip him as he lunged, and Foster fell headlong; but before Ross could secure a weapon or implement to aid him in the unequal combat, he was up and coming back, with nose bleeding and swollen, eyes blackened and half closed, and contusions plentifully sprinkled over his whole face.

He growled incoherently; he was reduced by fear and pain to the level of a beast, and, beast-like, he fought for his life—with hands and feet, only the possession of the prehensile thumb, perhaps, preventing him from using his teeth; for Ross, unable to avoid his next blind lunge, went down, with the whole two hundred pounds of Foster on top of him, and felt the stricture of his clutch on his throat.

A man being choked quickly loses power of volition, entirely distinct from the inhibition coming of suppressed breathing; after a few moments, his movements are involuntary.

Ross, with flashes of light before his eyes, soon took his hands from the iron fingers at his throat, and, with the darkening of his faculties, his arms and legs went through flail-like motions, rising and falling, thumping the deck with rhythmic regularity.

Something in this exhibition must have affected the girl at the air jet; for Ross soon began to breathe convulsively, then to see more or less distinctly—while his limbs ceased their flapping—and the first thing he saw was the girl standing over him, her face white as the whites of her distended eyes, her lips pressed tightly together, and poised aloft in her hands one of the pump-brakes, ready for another descent upon the head of Foster, who, still and inert, lay by the side of Ross.

As Ross moved and endeavored to rise, she dropped the club, and sank down, crying his name and kissing him. Then she incontinently fainted.

Ross struggled to his feet, and, though still weak and nerveless, found some spun yarn in a locker, with which he tied the unconscious victim's hands behind his back, and lashed his ankles together. Thus secured, he was harmless when he came to his senses, which happened before Ross had revived the girl. But there were no growling threats coming from him now; conquered and bound, his courage changed to fear again, and he complained and prayed for release.

"Not much," said Ross, busy with the girl. "When I get my wind, I'm going to jam you into that tube, like a dead man. I'll release you inside."

When Miss Fleming was again seated on the tank, breathing fresh air from the jet, Ross went to work with the practical methods of a sailor. He first, by a mighty exercise of all his strength, loaded the frightened Foster on to one of the torpedo trucks, face downward; then he wheeled him to the tube, so that his uplifted face could look squarely into it; then he passed a strap of rope around under his shoulders, to which he applied the big end of a ship's handspike, that happened to be aboard; and to the other end of this, as it lay along the back of Foster, he secured the single block of a small tackle—one of the purchases he had used in handling the torpedoes—and when he had secured the double block to an eyebolt in the bow, he steadied the handspike between his knees, hauled on the fall, with no word to the screaming wretch, and launched him, head and shoulders, into the tube.

As his hands, tied behind him, went in, Ross carefully cut one turn of the spun yarn, hauled away, and as his feet disappeared, he cut the bonds on his ankles; then he advised him to shake his hands and feet clear, pulled out the handspike, slammed the breech-door to, and waited.

The protest from within had never ceased; but at last Ross got from the information, interlarded with pleadings for life, that his hands and feet were free.

"All right. Take a good breath, and I'll flood you," called Ross. "When you're outside, swim up." The voice from within ceased.

Ross threw over the lever that admitted water to the tube, opened the forward door, and applied the compressed air. There was a slight jump to the boat's nose, but with the inrush of water as Foster went out, it sank.

However, when Ross closed the forward door, and had expelled this water, it rose again, and he anxiously inspected the depth indicator.

At first, he hardly dared believe it, but in a few moments he was sure. The indicator was moving, hardly faster than the minute hand of a clock. The boat, released of the last few pounds necessary, was seeking the surface.

"Irene," he shouted, joyously, "we're rising. We'll be afloat before long, and they'll rescue us. Even though we can't pump, they'll see our periscope, and tow us somewhere where they can lift the hatch out of water. It's all over, girl—all over but the shouting. Stand up, and look at the indicator. Only fifty-five feet now."

She stood beside him, supported by his arm, and together they watched the slowly moving indicator. Then Ross casually glanced at the deadlight, and violently forced the girl to her seat.

"Sit still," he commanded, almost harshly. "Sit still, and rest."

For, looking in through the deadlight, was the white face of Foster, washed clean of blood, but filled with the terror and agony of the dying. His hands clutched weakly at the glass, his eyes closed, his mouth opened, and he drifted out of sight.